Helix Dreams

by

Michael Davies

Helix Dreams

For information address mickiedaltonbooks@lycos.com

First Printing 2016

ISBN: 978-0-9942171-3-4

Published by The Mickie Dalton Foundation
NSW
Australia

To Greg and Penny

For all the support, the good ideas, the reviews and the friendship

Other Books by Michael Davies

The Nightmares of God
The Janus Conspiracy
A Friendly Killing
Accounts of a Killing
Dreamkill
Ready, Steady, KILL!

For the Young Adults (12-18)

The Many Worlds of Mickie Dalton
The Many Galaxies of Mickie Dalton
The Many Universes of Mickie Dalton
The Strange World of Mark and Anna

For the 8-12 age group

The Julie Malloy Gang and the Smugglers
The Quest for the Locket
The Secret of Yuri Kirilenko
The United Nations and the Extra-Terrestrial
The Secret of Charlotte's Cello
The Star of the Yshan Kings
The War of the Yshan Empire
The Star of the New Yshan Empire
The Red Fog of Time
The Mysterious Recorder and the Door to Elsewhere
Prisoners of the Picture
A Step Into the Past

For the Little Ones (3-5)

Mary's World

And in non-fiction

The Business School Approach to Writing Your Novel

Prologue

You can't travel back in time.

Einstein said so. Hawking said so. Any number of physicists, mathematicians, cosmologists and assorted geniuses all say so. Quantum theory suggests that it might, under some circumstances and with deeper understanding of the forces that created the Universe, be possible to travel back in time, but there are no signs of how that might come about.

So you can't travel back in time.

You can go forward. Just sit still and you travel forward. Fly at massive speed around the world like a satellite and time travels at a different rate than on the ground, which is something the satellite navigation systems have to take into account. Fly out to the edge of the solar system at a significant fraction of the speed of light, turn round and come back and you'll find the people you knew are years older while you have aged much less. But you can't travel back in time.

However, there may be a perfectly satisfactory alternative.

Chapter 1 - 2015

The call that Gareth Lawson got from the laboratory at five o'clock one morning was the starting gun to finding that alternative.

"Garry," said Bill Askins. "You need to come and see this."

The world was about to face the greatest upheaval since the comet that wiped out the dinosaurs.

Garry stood in front of the huge video monitor in the lab. The picture was not the best quality, it was grainy, a little jumpy and the colours weak. There was no sound. The scene looked like it was shot from a hand-held camera held by somebody walking along a city street. Many others were walking in the same direction though a few walked towards the camera and passed behind. The picture changed a little as the camera reached a small park on the left, at the far side of which was a building built of a reddish-brown brick encrusted with years of industrial grime. Garry counted nine storeys and the building extended at least a full city block to the left.

"Where is it?" he asked. His voice was calm but he was working hard to control the excitement because he knew the implications of what he was seeing.

"No idea," replied Bill Askins. He was staring at the screen with rapt attention, his heavy, broad face that resembled that of a low-intellect farm boy but hid an IQ around 180 revealing no expression.

"Those styles," said Garry. "They look pretty ancient. Maybe soon after World War II and I think they all look British, somehow. I reckon the fifties."

"And it's a kid," said Bill. "Note how everybody else seems quite a bit taller, so perhaps he's only about ten or eleven."

"He?"

Bill looked down at his notes. "David Peter Jackson," he said. "It's a sample we took five years ago, he was 65."

On the monitor, the picture blurred and vanished.

"That's all you have?" asked Garry.

"That's it," agreed Bill. "Three minutes, twenty seven seconds of somebody's amazingly ordinary, mundane memories."

"When did you get it?"

"At three this morning. I'd been playing with some settings, did some fine tunings at random and suddenly *that* appeared. I've been replaying it quite a few times and again, I managed to get some improved picture quality but no sound."

"What the hell were you doing at three in the morning?"

Bill looked briefly at his boss with a pained expression. Bill was a law unto himself at Blueprints. Nobody *ever* questioned what he was doing or why or when. He just did things and left others to gasp at the genius he displayed and the results he got.

Garry grinned cheerfully and walked to a computer terminal. "What was that name?"

"David Peter Jackson," replied Bill. "File Number PE5467."

Garry tapped the details in, waited a few seconds then read from the screen.

"David Peter Jackson, born in August, 1942 in Manchester, England. Went to a junior school in Flixton, outside Manchester until aged eleven, did his eleven-plus exams successfully and went to Manchester Central Grammar School in Whitworth Street in central Manchester. Let's have a look at that school ...."

Another few moments passed while the search took place and Bill came to stand behind his boss. A picture appeared on the screen. It was taken from a different angle than they had seen, obviously from the far end of the small park, but the building was definitely the same as the one on the large monitor.

"Bloody hell!" said Garry. "Bill, I think we've been and gone and done it!"

A rare smile appeared on the big face above him.

"Bloody oath!" said Bill Askins.

"Can we try another one?" asked Garry.

"Let's," said Bill. He sat behind another terminal and began keying instructions. "This is Hannah Ross," he said after a few moments. "We took this sample five years ago when she was thirty, single, in great health, a games teacher at a school just down the road in Wokingham." He moved from behind the computer and sat down before a control panel that seemed crammed with dials, tuning devices and flashing lights.

On the screen, there was nothing but fuzz, like a television not connected to an aerial, but without the hiss.

"I'm just tuning to the same settings I had before," muttered Bill.

Garry sat back and watched as Bill's hands played on the controls with a delicacy that seemed out of key with his large hands.

"Ah!" said Bill. "Well, look at that!"

The fuzz had gone from the screen to be replaced by a hazy picture, badly out of focus but recognisable as a scene on a boat, quite a large boat. There were people in the scene, leaning up against the railing, all looking in a single direction, all looking cheerful and excited.

It must be summertime Garry decided, people were dressed lightly, the atmosphere was celebratory. For a second or two, the screen was filled with the face of a young woman in profile. She looked in her twenties, pretty, windblown and was saying something, then she turned full on and smiled, still talking.

"Can we get a lip reader in?" asked Bill.

"As soon as the secretary gets here," replied Garry, thoroughly entranced by what he was seeing.

The picture swung around and more people appeared and the sight of land quite close gave some perspective to the scene. This was a holiday or tourist cruise within a harbour of some sort.

Meanwhile, Bill was fine tuning his equipment and by tiny increments, the picture was becoming clearer and the colours more intense.

In front of the watchers, the people leaning against the rails began directing cameras at some point off to the right.

"What the hell are they...." muttered Garry and stopped as his unfinished question was answered.

Right in front of the watchers was the huge statue on the small island, the arm held high, holding the flame, the crown atop the white face of one of the most famous images in the world.

Garry let out the breath he had been holding since the image swung into view.

"New York," said Bill. "Well bugger me, it's the Statue of Liberty."

He moved back to the computer screen and tapped some instructions, stared at the screen and laughed.

"Hannah Ross," he said. "Her parents took her on a trip to the States to visit her mother's sister who lived in Connecticut. She was three."

"Why don't you give her a call, see if she still lives locally and can come in and validate what we're seeing?"

"I'll do that," said Bill. "Let's give her time to have breakfast, though."

"And I think I'd better call Madam," said Garry as exhilaration swept through him like the finest champagne.

* * *

The young woman sat quietly in the laboratory as Bill set up the monitor. She looked nervous and overwhelmed by the wealth of expensive, complex equipment all around the place.

"Let me explain exactly what this is about," said Garry. "About five years ago, you let us take a sample of your DNA for research purposes."

She nodded, looking anxious. "You never told me what the research was about, I remember, but I know I gave my consent. Have you found something wrong?"

"No, no, not at all," said Garry urgently. "You appear to be in perfect health. Our research was based on a theory that a person's DNA contains more than the blueprints of a person."

"I'd heard that scientists believe that a lot of our DNA is obsolete junk," she said. Anxiety had been replaced by interest.

"That's the conventional wisdom," agreed Garry. "But the driving force behind this company is not in the least conventional and she believed that Nature just doesn't work that way. So for six years we've been working on finding out just what that 'junk' is."

"All this to check out a wild theory?" She looked around the room. "This lot cost more than a few quid!"

Garry laughed and Bill turned round from his work to smile in appreciation, for Hannah was a most attractive woman. She was of middle height, slender and obviously athletic as befitted the games teacher at the high school. Dressed in a well-fitted, dark blue suit with a white blouse open at the neck, her long brown hair falling to her shoulders, she presented a highly pleasing image. Garry felt a small wave of loneliness and need and suppressed it quickly.

"Our owner is a wildly rich woman," said Garry. "The company she set up with her husband back in 1980, made billions from developing successful drugs for cholesterol control and others and she lets other pharma companies make them under licence, so now we're just a research organisation. My project team, 'Blueprints' is Karen's particular hobby."

"And that research is all about this junk in the DNA?" Hannah said. "And you've found something?"

Garry didn't answer but pulled a folder towards him and extracted a sheet of paper.

"Hannah, before we go any further, I need to get something settled."

"That sounds serious," she said with a small laugh, though she looked uncertain.

"It is," agreed Garry. "I'm going to reveal some information about a major current research project. We have long known that if this project is successful, the repercussions in society all over the world could be significant."

"Wow!" she said. She wasn't smiling.

"Wow indeed," he said. "This document is part of the Official Secrets Act. We have to ask this because the Government has been advised of what we are doing and they are concerned about international reactions should it come out before we are ready. I have to ask that you sign it before we go any further and after that you will be bound by it and face prosecution should you reveal anything about what you are about to see. I should tell you that very few of the Government's inner cabinet know about this and all in all, in the whole world, only twelve people know including the people here."

"Good grief!"

"It's critical Hannah. Word of this could cause immense global upheaval."

For a few seconds she stared hard at him then she drew the sheet to her and read it carefully. Finally she looked at the desk, saw a pen and signed the document.

Garry examined her signature with equal care and slid the paper back in the folder.

"You said you'd found something," she said quietly.

"Indeed we have. I want you to look at the monitor. Bill?"

They both turned to watch the monitor which displayed the fuzz for a second or two then cleared to show the scene on the harbour cruise boat in New York. Hannah watched in some puzzlement but emitted a scream of shock as the young woman's face appeared and filled the screen.

"Oh my god! That's my mother!" Both hands clasped to her face, her mouth wide open, she stared at the screen. Tears began to roll down her cheeks.

"Do you remember this episode?" asked Garry.

Hannah shook her head, struggling for control.

"No!" she gasped. "But I know we all went to the States to visit my aunt, I must have been about two or three."

She turned to stare at Garry. "Where did you *GET* that picture? It's a movie, nobody was taking a movie that I know of!"

"We got it from your DNA," replied Garry softly.

"From my DNA? You mean my DNA records my memories and you can play them back?"

"That's the theory."

She stared back at the screen but the scene had vanished to be replaced by the fuzz. "Do you have any other memories?"

Garry shook his head. 'No, but we think we'll be able to find it all one day."

"What, everything? Every single second from birth onwards?"

He nodded. "Quite possible."

"But how can that tiny molecule hold all that data? It would fill huge amounts of disk on a computer."

"Good question," said Garry. "But the images are stored in quantum format and that tiny molecule, well, when you lay out a DNA strand, it can be three metres long."

She stayed silent, absorbing the extraordinary experience of the last few minutes and the startling information she had received. Then she spoke, her voice reflecting anxiety.

"But that means you could see some things... things I don't want you to see, really, this is horrible..."

"Hannah!" Garry put his hand on her wrist. "Hannah, I promise you, we'll destroy your DNA sample immediately."

She calmed down rapidly. "Okay, thank you, but is there any way you can record that bit I just saw? Burn it to a CD or something?"

"Not a chance," Bill chimed in. "Not until the machine can sign the Act as well."

"Okay!" She smiled. "But could I see that scene again?"

Chapter 2

It was nearly noon before Garry watched from his office as the yellow Maserati entered the parking lot of Life Technology, the parent company of Blueprints and parked in the spot reserved for it by the front door. He flinched as she narrowly missed his own car, his forty-year old MGB and stopped at a horrible angle that overlapped the spot next to it. Garry worried every time he saw Karen Petrova climb into her beautiful car, half expecting to hear from the police that she'd had some awful accident caused by her appalling driving. He wondered how many outraged motorists she had left breathing hard and shaking with anger on the hour's drive from her luxurious apartment near Harrods store to the industrial park by the river in Reading.

He watched the diminutive figure ease herself from the low seat and slam the door shut. She was dressed in her normal fashion, an elegant flowing dress that had cost perhaps a year's salary for his secretary, shoes to match, no hat. She marched briskly in through the front door and Garry could almost feel the heightened electricity in the whole building that was the norm when Karen Petrova went anywhere.

The energy levels swirled and spun and it was just a few moments later in which Garry could almost have sworn that he felt the approaching winds, the vision appeared in the open office doorway. He was already on his feet and just for a second or two they stared at each other. For Garry, every meeting was a small shock, each time the extraordinary magnetism of the woman being greater than he could remember.

She was tiny, not much over five feet high, petite, couldn't weigh more than a slim ten-year old girl and black eyes sparkled in the pale, beautifully made up face. Jet black hair was tied in a ponytail and hung down to her neck. Scarlet lipstick completed the whole extraordinary image.

The moment of silent mutual appraisal over, she swept into the office where Garry was waiting in front of his desk. She put her hands up and cupped his face as he placed his on her minute waist and lightly kissed her cheek. She stared deep into his eyes as if trying to see if there was any chance he'd been telling her untruths during the short phone call early that morning then they released each other and sat down at the coffee table by the window.

"So, my strange little Welsh person, you and Village Idiot have succeeded? We will change world?"

Garry had learned how to hide his amusement with her. Despite an almost British sense of humour, she never cracked a smile except when it was to deliver a slicing destruction of anybody who had annoyed or offended her and those smiles could frighten the bravest man. She spoke with a slight Russian accent and mannerism, but Garry was absolutely certain that this was an affectation. She had lived in the west since 1964 and with an IQ a fair way above his own quite impressive level, probably not far short of Bill Askin's extra-genius quota, Garry would have given any odds that she spoke perfect English but had never heard her speak in any way other than the slightly Russian manner.

"Yes, Madam, we have. I'm almost frightened to think about what may come of this."

They were the best of friends, had known each other since he had been head-hunted over a decade ago to manage a strange new project being set up within the enormously rich and successful pharmaceutical research firm, Life Technology in the industrial park near Reading in Berkshire. It pleased them both that she should be called "Madam" during business matters.

They were interrupted by the door opening and a young man pushed in a trolley holding a full-scale silver samovar. It was an almost priceless antique that Karen had discovered on a trip back to Russia soon after the fall of the Soviet Union, a twin of the one she had in her apartment in London and one of the traditions of the company was that she was served Russian tea in this manner when she visited.

Silence ruled as the young man poured tea from the samovar into a glass held within a silver holder, used a silver claw to place a single sugar cube in the cup and placed it carefully in the glass before placing the glass on the coffee table before her. He repeated the performance for Garry and quietly left, not before winking at Garry from behind Karen's back.

She picked up her glass, took one delicate sip, replaced it and leaned back in her chair.

"Tell me," she demanded.

Much of it had been related to her that morning, but she had just returned from her daily run, was heading for the shower and said nothing other than that she would be in Reading as soon as she could.

"Your theory is absolutely proven," Garry began. "There is no doubt that a person's DNA is more than a blueprint for the person's physical characteristics, but it also serves as a recording device of that person's memories. Today we finally got to see a tiny fraction of the memories of two people. During the morning, we have called both those people and they confirm that what we saw was certainly what they had experienced. The first man said he walked that stretch of road to school after getting off the bus every school day between the ages of eleven and sixteen when his family moved to another part of the country. The woman lives locally and she came up to see the same images. It was quite a shattering experience because she does not actually remember the episode, she was two at the time, but the woman in the picture was her mother. We had a lip reader come in from the hospital and she said that woman's words were, *"I've always wanted to see this, Peter! I'm so glad I'm doing it with you and Hannah!"* Peter is her father's name."

"And that's all we have?" she said, picking up her glass again.

"For now. Bill is confident that he can get clearer images, but sound is so far unobtainable."

"But you cannot identify dates of what you see?"

"Not yet. Nor do we have any control of what we see. All we have done so far is get a couple of short scenes. They appeared quite at random."

"Could that be all there is? Just few minutes of occasional odd memories?"

He shook his head and finally picked up his own glass of tea. "I suppose that's possible. But I doubt it. If memories are being recorded, the mechanism obviously works. I imagine it's quite possible that some people's systems work better than others and there will be gaps, but I'm quite convinced your theory holds. It's highly probable that every second of one's life is recorded in the DNA."

She sipped her tea thoughtfully.

"Show me," she said.

"No problem," he replied and stood up.

A few minutes later, they entered the laboratory and Bill stood up as Karen walked in.

"Good morning, Madam!" he said with a wide grin. Garry knew that Bill Askins had very little respect for the majority of the world's seven billion people, but Karen Petrova was one of the exceptions. In fact, Garry suspected that Bill had a serious case of hero worship where she was concerned, for the work she had done that had helped so many millions of people, made so many billions for the company and for her vision in funding the research of the Blueprints team.

"Good morning, Village Idiot," she said with a calm stare. "I understand you have done something useful at last in your worthless life?"

It was their usual by-play and Garry knew they both enjoyed it. Karen's admiration for the extraordinary genius of Bill was unbounded and she had once told Garry that she thought Bill's abilities probably exceeded those of her father, Karl Michailovich Petrov, Russian winner of the Nobel prize in the early sixties for his development of artificial skin that had saved so many lives of soldiers and burn victims.

"Sit down, Madam," said Bill. "Be prepared to have your mind blown away."

"Not likely prospect," she murmured but took a seat before the monitor.

Twenty minutes later, she looked calmly at the other two.

"Yes," she said. "Now we change world."

Chapter 3 - Moscow, 1964

Karen Petrova looked suspiciously at her parents. They were clearly bursting with excitement and she wondered just what they were hiding. She stared alternately at them as they all sat in the lounge room of the spacious and well-furnished apartment. Privileges were not unknown to one of the greatest scientists of the Soviet Union, married to the daughter of a senior member of the Communist Party and war hero.

Her father caught the look and grinned cheerfully.

"How would you like to travel, daughter mine?" he said.

"Travel, Poppa? Are we going on another trip?" Karen felt delighted. The last trip, her very first outside Russia was to Oslo to watch the great events of the Nobel prize awards and her father walking onto the stage to receive his.

"More than a trip, little one. They are letting us go to England."

"England! Poppa...." For a moment, Karen was so overwhelmed with questions she couldn't pick which one to ask first. "Poppa, why are they letting us go to England?"

Karl Michailovich Petrov looked pained.

"Karen, your mother is the daughter of one of our greatest war heroes and a senior member of the Politburo.

Your father has a Nobel prize. When one of the greatest universities in the world invites me to lecture for two years, not even the Communist Party would refuse them. So we are going to Cambridge."

"I personally asked Nikita Krushchev," said her mother, Ekaterina. "He can refuse me nothing, I know!"

Karen laughed loudly. She had met the General Secretary of the Communist Party a few times and she had noted the way he looked at her mother with barely suppressed adoration. Krushchev and her grandfather had been friends for many years and Ekaterina had been regarded as a favourite daughter since she was a toddler. Now, as a startlingly beautiful, petite woman, she had been able to twist the supreme Soviet leader around her little finger for many years. Karen was quite certain that the recent thaw in relationships between the Soviet Union and the West was largely because of her mother's influence on Krushchev.

"But what about my studies?" she asked anxiously as the thought struck her. "Next year is my final year. What will I do? Will I have to start again? Will I even be able to get a place?"

Petrov held up his hand to stop the flow.

"Your transcripts were sent to Cambridge a month ago. Your place is reserved for you starting September. We have always ensured you studied English from the beginning, so you will have no difficulties. Little daughter, I have every faith you will graduate with the highest honours the following June and then do your doctorate, just as you have always dreamed. The Chancellor at Cambridge was naturally impressed by somebody who enters University at fifteen and gets top grades throughout the first two years."

Karen sat back with a sense of delight. England! Somewhere she had dreamed of seeing since early childhood, visions of green fields, lakes, rustic villages seeming so beautiful compared to the bleak miseries of Russian life.

Three weeks later, they flew to England and Karen was totally in love with the country from the first moment.

* * *

"The degree of Bachelor of Science in Pharmacology, with First Class Honours goes to Karen Petrova and with it, the Chancellor's prize for academic excellence...."

* * *

"The Degree of Doctor of Philosophy in Pharmacology is awarded to Karen Petrova. Congratulations, Doctor Petrova!..."

* * *

"Dear Doctor Petrova, the Faculty of Science welcomes you to your Post-Doctorate Fellowship at Harvard. All of us are very excited at the prospect of working with you...."

* * *

"Dear Doctor Petrova, all of us, Faculty and staff at Oxford University are delighted that you will join us for the new university year. We are aware of the number of offers you have received from Universities around the world and your decision to join us is most welcome...."

* * *

The party at the opening of the new academic year at the University of Oxford was a splendid affair. Karen knew that she was the centre of attention despite being so tiny or maybe because of it, but mainly because of her reputation resulting from the work she had done at Harvard. Her slender frame encased in her first ever little black dress, her pale, perfect face with the bright scarlet lipstick that had become her trademark fashion statement, all created an image that was the talk of the town. The evening became a whirl of introductions, new faces, sometimes faces that had famous names attached to them, people whose works she had studied, critiqued, who had critiqued her work, it was rapidly becoming some fantastic haze of colour. And then...

"Hector Forbes, genetics."

She looked up into the warm, smiling face of a middling height, slightly stocky young man and studied his eyes intently.

"Karen Petrova," she said.

"I do believe that every single person in the room knows that," he said, barely suppressing a laugh. His soft Scottish accent was the most charming thing she had ever heard, she thought.

She had no idea what was happening inside her. No man had ever sent such warm rushes through her body or given her such a tingle. She felt she could talk to him just by looking into his eyes, she *knew* him. Carefully, she reached out and touched his wrist, feeling a small shock run through both of them.

"You and I, we will change world," she said.

Chapter 4 - 2015

"Trouble is," said Bill, holding his coffee mug in both hands as if seeking comfort from the heat, "trouble is, I've got the scanner able to read that stuff that's called junk, but now that it's doing that, I think it needs a re-design. The current specs will never read anything finer than that."

"How long?" asked Garry.

"Six weeks to redesign, couple of months to build the thing."

Garry sat back. His project had no deadlines, he knew. All of this resulted from a deeply held conviction of Karen's late husband, Hector that the mass of so-called 'junk' in the DNA held something more critical. From the start, the project had no specific target, other than to find out what that was. It was Karen herself who had postulated her own belief that it was a record of a person's life, but she had nothing to support that theory. Stunning as the discovery was, Garry was equally startled that the tiny woman had somehow keyed in on the answer. He decided that such intuition was the mark of true genius.

"What's the objective?" he asked.

"Two parts," said Bill. "Right now, I can't focus fine enough, I think the data are stored in far smaller detail than we'd thought. But the main thing is the continuity. If the recording is continuous, if it's like a continual film strip, there has to be a start and a stop."

"What if it's random access?" asked Garry. "What if chunks of memory are stored all over the place?"

"Thought of that," replied Bill.

Why am I not surprised? Garry asked himself, hiding his smile.

"And that's why I can only find the one memory incident," continued Bill. "So that means there must be some sort of index stored somewhere and updated with each new memory recording."

"Just like a computer," said Garry. "Okay, get to it. We can keep the staff occupied going through more of our samples with the current equipment, see if they can find more than just one random memory."

Bill didn't reply. He was staring at some point on the far wall, completely oblivious to the outside world. Garry had seen this before. Bill was already at work, reviewing the circuits, the power settings, the structure of the equipment needed to go deeper and deeper into human DNA and identify every atom of what was in there. Garry knew that Bill would not come out of this near-catatonic state until he was ready and that could be hours. It could last overnight and on many occasions had done so.

Garry got up and left. Bill had taken over his office and there was damn-all Garry could do about it, nor did he want to.

He walked out into the general office area, found a spare computer and began mapping out a work schedule to occupy his staff. He knew they'd be excited by what they were doing, examining the DNA of several thousand people and seeing if they could extract the odd random visual memories that their owners had no idea existed.

* * *

Several weeks passed. The five researchers, all sworn to secrecy, developed a routine of examining the DNA samples and using the existing equipment to explore the unstructured parts of the material. Some samples provided nothing beyond the fuzzy screen and were returned to storage. On just two occasions, the researchers found more than one memory sample. With the DNA of a middle-aged female accountant, the researcher saw two completely different memories, one of the woman's childhood, playing with friends in a garden, one of watching a couple walk down the aisle of a church after being married. A teenage boy had a vivid memory of playing cricket and taking a difficult catch and another one of a teacher looking angry for some unknown reason.

But they persisted and within a couple of weeks, the number of memory episodes the team found began to increase. None of the episodes lasted less than fifteen seconds, none more than three minutes and thirty-two seconds.

Not all the memories were so mundane as the first two.

The squeal of shock from the general area caused Garry to lift his head from his own terminal. A short distance away, one of his staff was staring at her screen, her eyes wide, her hands held to her cheeks. Penny Barstow was young, blonde, pretty and had a doctorate in genetics, as did most of his team, though one was a graduate in pharmacology. Right now, she looked like a teenager. The occupant of the next desk, a Pakistani man leaned over to see what the fuss was about and let out a bellow of laughter which caused the rest of the room to get up and go and see what was going on, showing various reactions as they got there.

Curious, Garry joined them. The picture showed the upper torso of a very pretty and very naked woman, her generous breasts bouncing in unison as she stared up at the watchers, obviously engaged in an energetic sexual encounter.

"He must be up on his straight arms," commented one of the watchers. "Likes to get a good look!"

"With that view, who could blame him?" added another.

Garry couldn't help laughing. His team needed a few light moments and he let the display go on until the scene ended. There was no doubt it was very erotic and the deep red flush on Penny's face showed her own reaction.

"How long, Penny?" he asked, struggling to keep his voice controlled.

She coughed, swallowed, took a deep breath. "Three minutes, thirty seconds," she said faintly.

"Obviously made quite an impression," said one of the men and in general laughter, they went back to testing their own samples.

The other one caused problems.

The room was silent. After the first horrified yell, nobody could say a word. They all watched in appalled silence as the woman's face was smashed into a bloody pulp by several heavy blows with what looked like a poker. The body collapsed to the floor, a grey carpet of an ordinary looking house. Blood spread slowly from the wreckage.

The scene faded. One of the men rushed to the washroom, holding his mouth, the two women were sobbing into their hands, everybody else displayed varying degrees of shock and horror.

"Who is it?" asked Garry.

"Graham Allen Porter," said the researcher, a young man from Birmingham called Phil Nichols. His face under the shock of red hair was white, making his equally vivid moustache into a shocking red line that emphasised his horror. "The sample was taken three years ago in Lincoln when he was thirty six."

Garry addressed the room. "Okay, everybody, that was horrible and you must not under any circumstances talk about it. I'll talk to Madam and see how best we go about this without revealing what we're doing. But I suggest you all take the rest of the day off, get your minds off it, but do NOT get drunk, stoned, high, *anything* in company with anybody else and risk spilling the crap."

He watched quietly as his team closed down their systems and left, none of them saying a word. Garry picked up the telephone.

* * *

"Let me get this straight," the large man across from Garry's coffee table said. His tone indicated his belief he was dealing with a nutcase. "You want me to sign the Official Secrets Act and then you'll show me absolute proof of a murder committed somewhere, some time by a bloke whose name you'll give me when I sign it? Have I got that right?"

Detective Inspector Andrew Melling of the Thames Valley Police had the expression of somebody trying to offer him a packet of dog turds.

"That's about it," said Garry.

"I've heard some bullshit in my time, Mr Lawson, but I think this beats 'em all." The detective's Berkshire accent was strong. "I've had people confessing to murders they didn't do, hell we *always* get some fuckwits coming to the station and confessing to murders that either never happened or happened somewhere far away. But nobody has ever asked me to sign the bloody Official Secrets Act before they did."

"Inspector, do you know what this place is?" asked Garry. "And do you know who's behind it and what we do?"

The large man stared at him. "You're a medical research lab," he said. "And you're owned by some stinking rich Russian woman who has a farm up near Hungerford and a place in the snottiest area of London somewhere. So what?"

Garry suppressed his irritation, understanding that his demands of the officer certainly sounded extreme.

"Professor Karen Petrova is considered possibly the most brilliant pharmacologist in the world," he said. "Her father was a Nobel Prize winner when she was a girl, she entered university at fifteen, graduated from Cambridge with a first class honours degree, got her doctorate there, did some brilliant work at Harvard and was the most sought-after scientist in the world when she went to Oxford as a lecturer. Her products are among the widest-selling drugs in the world, they're licenced by other manufacturers and this organisation now does only research. Some of our work is top secret, but my specific project is known to only about ten people. Not even the Managing Director of Life Technology knows what my team does and I am completely independent of everybody but Karen Petrova."

The detective went as still as a lizard on a rock. He stared hard at Garry then held out his hand. "Give me the form," he said.

The signing done, Garry stood up.

"What I'm going to show you will prove to you that a particularly brutal murder was committed by a man called Graham Allen Porter at least three years ago, possibly in Lincoln. I will not be able to tell you anything about the technology that provided the material and you will not be able to use it as evidence in any subsequent trial."

Melling almost exploded. "Then what the hell am I doing, signing that shit?" he said loudly, his temper about to boil over.

Garry held up his hands to try and placate the man.

"Like I said, you will see incontrovertible proof of a murder. Knowing that it happened and knowing who did it will let you focus sharply on finding the evidence and the proof for a trial. It's a hell of a lot better than you have now."

Melling calmed down. "Okay, I suppose. Who else has seen this evidence?"

"Only my five researchers and all of them are sworn to secrecy."

Melling was beginning to look interested. "Let's see this," he said.

Garry nodded and led the way down to the lab. It was empty, the staff having taken the day off as Garry had requested. He went to the main screen, switched it on and sat down at the control panel. The screen came alive with the fuzzy silence that they now knew to expect and the appalling scene unfolded.

"Holy SHIT!" exploded Melling. "What the hell was that? How did you get that film?"

"It's not a film," said Garry. "Here's the bit you cannot reveal or use. We have developed a technology that allows us to see some memories of events recorded in a person's DNA. We have the DNA of some thousands of people, all taken with their consent for research purposes. Finding the ability to read these memories was expected, but we're as stunned as you are finding this episode."

Melling was shaking his head. "This is too weird," he said. "How do I believe that gory scene is real, that you haven't just bodged it up using computer graphics?"

"Here's how we'll prove it to you. I'm going to take a sample of your DNA if okay by you. Meanwhile, you go back to the station and start looking into this Porter bloke and find out where he is now. Tomorrow afternoon, come back here and we'll see if we can find something in your DNA that you will remember. If that's enough to prove the truth of this, you take it from there."

Melling paused, considering this. "Sounds fair enough. You've got the equipment here?"

Garry walked over to the cabinet at one wall, took out a collection jar and a swab, came back and rubbed the swab a few strokes on the inside of Melling's cheek.

The detective grinned as Garry slid the swab back into the jar. "I've seen that done a few hundred times, never had it done to me!"

"Okay, we'll be ready after lunch tomorrow," said Garry.

"See you about three."

"I'll show you out," said Garry.

Twenty four hours later, a rather nervous-looking Detective Inspector Melling sat next to Garry as one of the staff set up the system.

"We found two episodes from your life," said Garry. "I'm pretty sure this is one you'll remember."

The picture finally appeared and Melling gasped, clutching the arms of his chair as if afraid he might fall off. The screen showed a thin, dark man, his face convulsed with fury, staring straight at the viewers. Garry had little trouble reading his lips, the man was saying, "What do you mean by it? What do you mean by it?" The words were almost audible, so furious was the speaker. The picture rocked as the man landed a heavy blow on the head of a much smaller Andrew Melling with one hand and then with the other and then became just a view of the man's shoes as obviously Andrew dropped his head in terror. Mercifully, the scene ended.

Garry looked sideways at the man. Tears were rolling down his cheeks and his hands were clenched in helpless rage.

"Your father?" Garry asked.

Melling could only nod and wipe his eyes.

"Let's get back to my office," Garry said.

It took half an hour before Melling had regained control, the trembles that had shaken his body had calmed and the tension had died down. He had gulped down half a glass of the very fine Islay Scotch that Garry kept in his office for the occasional visits by Madam who drank nothing else other than the tea from her Russian samovar. Garry almost flinched as the sizeable portion of the £300 bottle of twenty-four year old liquid vanished like water into dry sand and thought about Madam's reaction had she seen it.

"I think I was about ten," Melling finally croaked and cleared his throat. "But that could have happened at any time until I turned fifteen. It was a fairly common event."

"And then what?"

"And then I beat the living shit out of the bastard." Melling finally grinned. "I've never enjoyed anything so much until I discovered girls!"

Garry laughed and poured another, much smaller helping of the single-malt scotch into the policeman's glass. The odour of peat wafted through the office and Garry poured himself a small helping. *Just to be sociable*, he told himself.

"God, that was dreadful," sighed Melling. "But it sure as hell proved your point. How in God's name do you do that?"

"Can't tell you," said Garry. "But will you take the case?"

"Up to a point," said the detective. "It probably didn't happen on my patch, so I'll have to send it to the local boys in Lincoln, once we discover where and when it happened."

"Any progress on that?"

"Some." Melling took out his notepad. "I found a bloke of that name and the right age still living in Lincoln. Not a nice one, he's had a couple of assault charges against him, served three years for one of them about ten years ago. Lots of drunk and disorderlies, driving under the influence, all the usual signs of your common or garden thug."

"And the woman he killed?"

"More complex. I've got a call in for a Missing Persons search for a woman of that description, but it could have happened at any time in the last twenty years, assuming he didn't kill her when he was about fifteen or younger. Once I have those details, I'll give it to the Lincoln people, assuming that's where it happened. Christ knows how I'll explain this to them or to my guv'ner, but I suppose I'll tell them it was just one of my informants."

"Please keep me up to date," said Garry.

"I will." Melling looked at his glass as if seeing it for the first time. "Bugger me!" he said. "This is great stuff!"

"It certainly is," agreed Garry. "Karen charters a small jet every year and flies up there to buy some selected bottles of the very finest malts at each of the distilleries on Islay. This bottle here cost about three hundred quid."

"How the rich live, eh?" said Melling. "Tell her thanks from me."

"Getting that Porter bloke will be more than enough thanks," said Garry.

Chapter 5 – Garry Lawson

Garry drove his MGB slowly out of the industrial estate and headed for his small house in the pleasant suburb of Earley. His evening would be quiet and peaceful, as all his evenings were, as he rarely socialised. He prepared a meal of lamb chops, mint sauce, mashed potatoes and green beans, working carefully and precisely as the strains of the Brahms' First Symphony filled the house. He went down to his wine cellar, a specialised work that had cost him some thousands to have built and selected an Australian Merlot from the Hunter Valley and brought it back to settle down for a thoroughly enjoyable meal. The meal cleared away, plates in the dishwasher and Brahms replaced by Vivaldi, he lay back in his recliner with the rest of the bottle and thought about events.

His father, a draughtsman in Monmouth had been pleased by Garry's obvious intelligence and they had come to his graduation from Cardiff University with a Bachelor's degree in chemistry. The Master's degree, three years later had caused some strain, though.

"Are you going to get a proper job, now?" his father asked. "You don't seem clear on what you want to do."

Garry knew his father was right, he really had no drive in any direction. Getting the degrees was intellectually satisfying but emotionally blank. Nothing got him excited. But the interviews by the corporate head-hunters in the final weeks at University resulted in an offer from a pharmaceutical company in the midlands and he found himself engaged in the manufacture of pills and caplets and pouches for powders. It paid well, he bought the MGB, a small house, dated a few women and told himself he was happy and successful.

Promoted to manager, he found himself. He was good at controlling the many facets of his operation, the people, the resources, the processes and when he took over the job of another manager as well as his own during the other man's illness, he found it even easier to manage double the complexity.

The head-hunter's call after two years resulted in a move to Chester as boss of a small company making the equipment that made pills and caplets and pouches for powders that had been his first job. The money was excellent, he married, he kept the MGB despite his wife's complaints... and he was miserable. None of this satisfied him. Angela moved out and he sort of missed her, but not that much. The car remained his primary joy and his weekends spent motoring with the roof folded away as he roared through the Pennines or the hills of North Wales, lunching in small country pubs, these were the things that sustained him.

The call came one morning in the office.

"I have something that might really interest you," said the head-hunter.

"That would be a change," said Garry. He and Peter Clare talked almost every month. It was Peter who had found him the job in Chester and he had a permanent commission from Garry to find the job that would finally get Garry's blood running with excitement.

"You know Life Technology, of course," said Peter.

"Of course. My previous company made the blood pressure pills they licenced to us. A real cash cow, very effective."

"Like many other pharma companies," agreed Peter. "They stopped all manufacturing themselves a couple of years ago, they just do research now, not all in the pharma business."

"So I heard."

"Do you know anything about the founders and owners, Hector Forbes and Karen Petrova?"

"Not a lot. I gather Forbes' family is rich and he funded the company while she did the research. People say she's probably the most brilliant pharmacologist in the world."

"They're probably right," agreed Peter. "And now she's worth billions. Forbes died last year and she wants to do something in his memory. They were very close."

Garry said nothing. A small tingle of excitement ran around his gut.

"She's setting up a specific project within Life Technology," the head-hunter continued. "It's called 'Blueprints' and she wants somebody to run it."

"I'm not a research scientist," protested Garry, feeling the tingle fade.

"Garry, she can buy all the research scientists in the UK if she wants. She told me to look for somebody who can control complexity, see through the fuzz and manage what may well be a team of lunatics looking for something without knowing what it is."

The tingle returned.

"So just what *are* they looking for?" Garry asked.

"Garry, all I know is that it's something to do with DNA and it's all about a theory her husband had. She seems to believe in it and she wants to follow up on it. Money is obviously no object."

"You're right, Peter. It interests me."

"I thought it would."

Two days later, Garry took the train to London and met Karen Petrova, shown into her presence in her London apartment by a tall, muscular young woman who didn't speak a word. The luxury of the place astounded him. As soon as he sat down, the young woman vanished, to be replaced by a similar woman, wheeling in a beautiful silver samovar on a trolley. Tea was poured into tall glasses held in filigreed silver holders, a cube of sugar dropped in and the glass handed him with a long silver spoon. He sipped the tea cautiously, deciding this was the weirdest job interview he had ever had.

Across from him, Karen Petrova sat on an expensive-looking sofa. She was dressed in a long, flowing silk creation in deep yellow with shoes to match. Garry knew nothing of fashion, but he had no doubt that the dress and shoes came from the finest designer and boutique in London, if not the world. Her face was pale, clear and had the smoothness of a child's. The lipstick was the startling element. It was bright scarlet and forced itself on the vision of the watcher as the absolute centrepiece of the whole astonishing creation.

After fifteen minutes, he also decided that she was the most extraordinary person, man or woman he had ever met by a huge margin. Her eyes penetrated his inner self, her intellect left him shaken and though the brilliant red lips never smiled, Garry heard the sharp British humour peeking out on occasions though her speech mannerisms were curious. She retained just a trace of a Russian accent but more obviously spoke in the Russian manner, without any use of "a" or "the." The project took his breath away.

"Just what will we look for?" he asked. Somehow the agreement that he was taking the job had been made without a word being said on the subject.

"Hector heard scientists say DNA was mostly junk," she said. "Hector said nature doesn't work that way. Junk must contain something. You will find it."

"What do you think it is, Madam?" The title came naturally to him. A small gleam in the eyes of an otherwise expressionless face told him she liked it.

"Records," she said. "Records of person's life. Maybe other stuff, but mainly records. You will have all equipment you want, hire your own staff, just tell me what you find."

"And when we find it?"

"Then we change world, you and I."

The interview was over, but she had one more surprise. She touched a button on the small table next to her.

"Peter tells me you drink fine scotch," she said as one of the women appeared, carrying a leather briefcase.

He laughed. "Peter knows me well."

"Good. These you will take home. One goes to your office and you and I, we share drink when I come to office."

He opened the briefcase and found two bottles. He pulled one out and almost gasped as he saw the label. It was thirty-year-old single malt scotch from Islay, the source of his favourite brands. He realised she was studying him.

"You approve?" she asked.

"Oh, Madam, do I approve!"

"That was question. I'll assume answer. Good. You and I, we will get on," she said.

A month later, after interviewing candidates for his job that Peter sent him, getting the new woman settled and fully briefed, Garry moved to Reading. His life had changed completely and he had finally found the work that engrossed and fulfilled him. He was hunting the Snark and after ten years he thought he had found the tracks of the beast. No more than ten other people even know the Snark existed. It gave him a good feeling.

* * *

The first few weeks of the new job were frantic, ordering computers and furniture and calling several headhunters in the scientific field. That last was tricky, because he had no real profile of what he wanted. He did a lot of research on his own into the nature of DNA, but found much was over his head, so he set up a meeting with Ray Gallard, a Professor of Genetics at Cambridge University, trading on the name of Karen Petrova to get the man's scarce time.

"You're working for Karen Petrova?" the professor said, his awe, admiration and possibly some envy evident in his tones.

"I am indeed," said Garry. "And she's given me a major challenge. What I need is something along an *'Idiot's Guide to Genetics!'* I'm a pharmacist by trade, a manager by preference, but I need to know what I'm managing and what sort of people I need to do the real work."

Professor Gallard smiled. "I think I can help," he said.

An hour later, Garry felt a lot more confident in his understanding of the DNA molecule and its structure.

"And I can suggest a couple of people to you, if you're hiring," the professor said at the end.

"That would be wonderful," replied Garry.

"Penny Barstow is young, brilliant and massively frustrated," said Gallard. "She's working for a medical company in Bristol, suffering all the issues that young, brilliant and pretty women have always suffered in the commercial world and she needs open skies to fly in. She's also my niece!"

"Sounds interesting," said Garry. "Of course, I can't promise anything."

"No need to. One meeting and you'll be begging her to join!"

Garry laughed and stood up. "Sounds like what I need. Get her to call me."

"I will," said Gallard, also standing. "The second one is a young Israeli man, Avram Fischer. He's a medical doctor but also has a Ph.D. from Harvard Medical School. I'll have him call you, too."

"It's been a great meeting," said Garry. "I owe you a lot."

Gallard shook his head. "I cannot work out how much I owe Karen for the help she and her husband, Hector have given me. Consider this just a tiny part repayment."

Feeling delighted with the results and seeing another glimpse into the effect Karen Petrova had on people, Garry returned to Reading and a few days later, received a phone call from one of the people recommended to him by Ray Gallard and hearing that Avram was in England, asked him to come and visit.

* * *

Avram Fischer was a rebel from the start. Even from the first day when he turned five and his orthodox Jewish father took him down to the kindergarten near Haifa Bay, things were not peaceful.

"I don't want to wear those things," he said firmly when he was given a yamulka to put on his head and his first silk prayer shawl. "They look silly."

His teachers hid their surprise and left him to read the books that were in the library, the usual books for children, lots of colour pictures and very little text. But after half an hour, the teacher sitting in the room with him, writing her essay for her external degree course was distracted when Avram came and stood next to her.

"These stories are stupid," he said. "Don't you have anything more interesting?"

Startled, she stared at him. His dark eyes looked firmly back at her and she realised that this little boy had a face of much greater personality and expressiveness than any other child of five.

"Come with me," she said and led him out of the kindergarten library and down the corridor to the junior school and its library.

"Why don't you look through these?" she asked, sitting down at the desk and watching him. He worked his way along the shelves of fiction and moved to the non-fiction section where he selected a book about the planets in the solar system. He sat on the floor and was engrossed for the next hour until the bell rang for lunch.

A few years later, when his father took him to the local barber to have his hair set in the traditional ringlets, Avram rebelled loudly.

"That looks stupid," he shouted, tears running down his cheeks and pulling hard at the ringlets, hurting his scalp badly. On the way home, he tried to pull his jacket over his head and rushed to his room as soon as he got in. The parents didn't hear him gently sneak into the bathroom, pull a pair of scissors from the medicine cabinet and cut off the offending ringlets, leaving a head like a hayrick after a storm had passed through.

Both parents were deeply upset by their son's misbehaviour and attitude and consulted Rabbi Morris.

"The boy clearly is hostile to ritual and tradition," said the Rabbi gently. "I've talked to him at some length and it's clear he's exceptionally intelligent with a probing mind. He's probably going to grow up to be an atheist and abandon Judaism. I'm sorry, Aaron, but he's not going to be a Rabbi like you had dreamed. These things you cannot force on a rebellious mind."

"Will he do his bar-Mitzvah and join the community?" asked the mother with her hands clenched tightly on her dress.

"Unlikely," said Rabbi Morris. "His training should start now if he is to play his full part. But we could not force him to learn, nor to come to Schule and go through the ceremony."

"So what should we do?" asked Aaron Fischer.

The Rabbi shook his head, sadly. "You can't force a child down a path he doesn't want to follow, not without causing serious damage. Let him find his own way. I suggest you send him to school in America, I'm sure he'll do well enough to get to University and maybe he'll fulfil the other promise that all Jewish Families want for their children."

"What is that?"

The Rabbi released a full and cheerful grin. "We know that in Jewish tradition, a foetus is not considered viable until it has its medical degree in its briefcase."

The tension broke and all three laughed as the parents accepted that they had a remarkable son and he could not be forced into any traditional mould.

The Rabbi was right about the bar-Mitzvah.

"I'm not doing it," said Avram. "And you can't make me. It's all silly."

Aaron shrugged. "It's what Reverend Morris said you would say. So tell me, Avram, what do you want to do?"

"Play baseball."

"What?" Of all the answers Aaron might have expected, this was furthest from any of them.

His son smiled. "You never come to sports days at school. You've never bothered to find out that we have a baseball team. You don't know that I can hit a ball more often and further than anyone, even the senior boys at the High School."

"But what good will that do in Israel?" Aaron was in deep distress.

"Israel? Nothing, Father. But in America? Now we start to talk serious benefits. Big, big money."

Despite himself, this caught Aaron's interest. "You think you could play in those big leagues? Some players make millions, I know."

Avram shook his head. "I think I could, yes, but that's not the object. If I can go to a high school in America, I bet I can get a baseball scholarship and get through Medical School that way."

"You want to go to Medical School?"

"Well, you know the old joke, father. To a Jewish mother, a foetus...."

"Is not viable until it has a medical degree in its briefcase, yes, I've heard that one."

*   *   *

"And that's how it worked out?" asked Garry, chuckling softly.

"A good high school in Boston, played for the team, voted Most Valuable Player all three years, batting average of .343..."

"What does that mean? I don't know baseball."

"Like a cricket batsman averaging over ninety every year. Big bucks."

"Wow! Okay, then what?"

"Scouts from the big leagues offering contracts, Universities offering scholarships."

"Just as you had planned."

"And one of those was from Harvard. I took it. And the rest, as they say, is history."

"And the doctorate?"

"Almost automatic, I never really planned to be a general practitioner but I didn't know what specialty to go for. But I didn't play baseball anymore. I accepted an offer from a big medical company in Chicago to lead a research group, but I've got bored. I need something that will just blow my mind when I find the answer to the meaning of life."

"I honestly don't know if what we're doing will give you that."

"You're set up by Karen Petrova?"

"Yes."

"Funding is not an issue?"

"None at all."

"What are you looking for?"

"The meaning of life in DNA."

"That comes from Hector Forbes?"

"Yes."

"Count me in," said Avram.

Chapter 6

Garry hardly saw Bill over the next three months. He knew that the Village Idiot as Karen loved to call him preferred to work at night, free from the noise and interruptions of the normal work environment, even though the small group knew to leave him strictly alone and he had his own private work area. Occasionally there was a Bill sighting, usually because he had worked all night and just kept going into the day.

A couple of times, Garry passed him in the corridor, but despite Garry's greeting, Bill's gaze remained fixed on the floor as he went by and Garry was quite certain that Bill simply hadn't noticed him.

On a similar occasion, they met in the washroom and stood at adjacent urinals, but Bill simply stared at the wall, washed his hands when he had finished and walked out, all without a sign of acknowledgement.

There was a more public moment when Bill ambled into the cafeteria area. Garry had from the start arranged for a catering company to provide several hot meals in a buffet. The caterers came in at eleven, ensured everything was hot and ready and then departed without seeing any of the staff. At three, they returned and cleared away, leaving snacks, pastries, a large urn of coffee and one of tea. Garry wanted no chance of accidental leaks of information from his staff but he also wanted his people well nourished and healthy.

All the research team members were in the cafeteria enjoying the various dishes as Bill entered. Silently, they watched him go to the serving area, take a helping of roast chicken, vegetables and rice, carry his tray to a solitary table and sit down, ignoring everybody. Nobody was offended, they all knew this man and his working methods and the genius behind it.

Bill filled a fork and raised it to his mouth, stopped and put it down, staring at the far wall. After two or three minutes, he stood up and walked out.

There was a ripple of soft laughter, some shaking of heads in admiration and the team resumed their own meals. Garry wondered just what inspiration had struck Bill at that moment.

*   *   *

That afternoon, Garry had a visitor.

"I thought it would be better to talk privately than risk a phone call, given the secrecy involved," said Detective Inspector Andrew Melling.

"Good," said Garry. "What's happened?"

"We got the bastard," said the detective. "The guys in Lincoln have kept me in the loop all the way, though I don't think they believe a bloody word about an informant. Anyway, they found this Porter bloke and had a private chat with him and they said he was obviously scared shitless about something. That gave them the reason to look through the Missing Persons file and unsolved cases and they finally found the victim, a young woman who'd been dumped in a field near Sleaford with injuries that matched what I saw. That was about six years ago. So they got a court order, searched his house, lifted the carpets and checked the floor underneath. They found traces of blood, even though he'd thrown out the original carpets. Some had seeped through. They even tracked down the car he'd owned at the time of the murder and they found tiny blood traces in the trunk and the DNA matched that of the victim. They hauled him in and they invited me up for the interview."

Melling watched the screen in the observation room next to the interview room. Two detectives sat on one side of a conference table, a uniformed officer stood by the door. Across from the detectives, a thin, wiry man in his forties sat looking down at his lap. His face was pale and he shook with occasional tremors. Next to him sat a middle-aged woman that Melling assumed was the court-appointed lawyer.

"The date is Friday, September the twenty-fifth, 2015," said one of the detectives. "The time is two-fifteen pm and we are in the Lincoln City Police Station, West Parade, Lincoln. Present in the room are Detective Inspector Paul Harding, Detective Sergeant Arthur James, public defender Mrs Charlotte Hayward and Graham Allen Porter. Graham, you have been formally charged with the murder of Anne Jennifer Murdoch on or about July 13th, 2009 in Sleaford, Lincolnshire. Do you understand the charge?"

Porter's face remained directed at his hands, but he nodded.

"For the record, Mr Porter has nodded his understanding of the charge. Graham, we found traces of blood matching the blood type of the victim in the floor boards of your house. Public records show that you were the tenant of that house at the time of the murder. Do you have anything to say about that?"

"No." Porter's reply was barely audible.

"Records also show that at the time of the murder, you owned a green Toyota Corolla, licence number TIL 8331. Examination of that car revealed more blood traces matching the blood type of the victim in the trunk. Anything to say about that, Graham?"

Porter finally lifted his head and glared at the detective.

"How the bloody hell did you find out?" he grated. "It was six years ago, nobody saw me, nobody has ever asked me about it and now all of a sudden this is happening. How?"

The interrogator was unmoved. "We received information leading us to consider you a suspect," he said. "Your statement and question indicate that you are acknowledging responsibility for the murder of Anne Murdoch. Do you wish to confirm it?"

"Yeah, I did it," said Porter.

In the next room, Melling stood up and prepared to return to Reading.

"It's got me thinking," Melling said to Garry as he reached the door. "Do you think what you did will ever become common technology?"

"I can't be sure, but I think so," Garry replied. "And yes, I realise the implications for the criminal justice system. We could well have a time when a suspect provides a DNA sample, the machine sees him or her committing the crime, game set and match. A trial is simply the presentation of that evidence to a judge who hands down the sentence, maybe after considering any mitigating circumstances."

"That's about what I was thinking," agreed Melling. "Hell, maybe you could take the *post mortem* DNA of the victim and possibly see the perpetrator. It could sure as hell make our jobs easier and save a fortune in trials."

"And avoid any chance of wrongful convictions or letting the guilty go free," said Garry. "But we have a long way to go before we get to that stage."

Melling stood up and extended his hand. "I may come and see you again," he said.

Garry took the hand. "Always happy to help," he said.

Chapter 7 – July, 1972

"I don't think I have ever tasted anything so astonishing!"

Karen Petrova slowly put the tiny glass down on the bar in the tasting room of the distillery and took a deep breath. "It's still wonderful as it goes down!"

"It could even make you believe there is a God!" said Hector Forbes as he held his own glass up to his nose and took a long, appreciative sniff with each nostril in turn before sipping carefully, holding the eighteen-year-old scotch on his tongue and then letting it slide down his throat.

"Oh my!" he whispered. "Every time I drink this stuff, it astounds me again."

The young man behind the bar smiled with genuine pleasure. He had clearly been captivated by the tiny woman tasting her first single-malt scotch and the delight she had shown in the experience, while her husband was possibly the most knowledgeable expert in scotch he had met.

"That was eighteen years old," he said. "Would you like to try the twenty-four year old?"

There was a small chuckle from Hector. "I'm not sure my wife can handle it," he said. "But I certainly will!"

Karen turned her glowing eyes on him. "You will not drink alone," she said. "I will certainly try twenty-four year old. This is drink of gods!"

They both waited while the barman picked up the other bottle and painstakingly poured a small amount into fresh glasses. Around them, the gentle hum of other visitors to the distillery provided a pleasant background while the aroma of the peat-flavoured liquor filled the air.

Karen carefully watched her husband and followed him as he went through the ritual of sniffing the scotch and then taking a small sip, letting it roll round his tongue before swallowing.

"Hector!" she exclaimed. "How could I have lived this long before tasting this?"

"It's all been a waste," he said and kissed her on the forehead. "Marrying me has produced amazing experiences!"

"Quite correct," she said and touched his cheek.

On finishing the second glass, she was clearly affected by the alcohol in her tiny frame.

"We must have bottle of this," she said, struggling to focus on the bottle from which the last sample had been poured.

"A bottle? My lovely wife, we Forbes' do not do things by the *Bottle!* A case is required! Here, young man, my credit card, please arrange for a case to be sent to the address I am about to give you."

A little while later, they left the tasting room with Karen clinging firmly to Hector's arm and walking uncertainly.

"I just don't think I have ever felt so happy!"

Karen lay back against Hector's chest, his left arm around her waist as they looked across the beach at the deep blue of an unusually calm ocean.

"Coming to Islay was a good idea, then?" said Hector.

"Almost as good as being married to you!"

"Ah, well there I agree with you, tiny pharmacologist! And we have only done Bowmore, Laphroaig and Ardbeg distilleries. A few more still to try!"

She chuckled and nuzzled her face into the side of his neck. "And you have bought case of their oldest scotch at each of them! Is this to be routine for the rest of our honeymoon?"

"During the day, yes. At night, well, there are other things to do."

"I am very glad about both, dear husband. I'm not sure I ever want to go back to Oxford. Why don't we spend rest of our lives drinking nectar of gods, eating incredible seafood and then those night-time activities you mention?"

"We could, I suppose, but we have a couple of doctorates that we should be putting to good use and students to teach, concerts to go to and a whole lot of world still to see."

"I suppose so. Actually, if we have to get serious again, I was thinking about that. I have idea for couple of new formulations for pills that I'd like to make up. How do you think I should go about it?"

"Interesting. Will you want to market them?"

"I really would. But I can't do that as University professor."

"No, you can't. You need to have your own company, have the licences to make new drugs and then you have to get them approved by the authorities and you know what a complicated process *that* is."

"Which all takes money," she said into his neck.

"Money we have," he replied. "The Forbes tribe is obscenely rich. I think I have an idea."

"Tell me," she murmured, feeling drowsy in the warmth of the sun, her closeness to her new husband and the wonderful air of Islay.

"A friend of mine has a tiny little company called Life Technology. He ran out of money a few years ago, so there's nothing there now but the name and the licences, but he used to make aspirin and a couple of over-the-counter sleeping pills. Why don't we buy the company and its licences, equip it with the stuff you need and see how your new pills work. Knowing you, they'll be brilliantly successful, we can build up manufacturing and you can become as rich as your amazing husband!"

She tightened her arms round his neck.

"Would you really do that for me? What if it failed and you lost couple of million pounds?"

"Do you know what the academic world is saying about you, sweetie? They reckon you're the best pharmacologist in the world. You won't fail, you'll become as disgustingly rich as my family already is and then you'll do what you promised when we first met."

"What's that?"

"As you put it, 'we will change world' and I've always known we would do it."

She chuckled.

"Hector?"

"Yes, love?"

"I think I'd like to start those night time activities early today."

"You do have the most brilliant ideas, my love. Let's go."

Chapter 8 - 2015

Bill was waiting at the front door as Garry walked in at eight in the morning.

"Got it," the big man said succinctly.

"Let's see it," replied Garry and walked behind Bill to the highly personalised workshop that nobody but Bill entered alone.

It looked like an electronics scrap yard at first sight. Workbenches on two walls were covered with electronic units of various sizes and a soldering kit stood against one end of a third wall. The fourth had a device on it. Part of it had been taken from the existing scanning unit, but the entire bench was taken up with what looked like a mess of wires and hardware. Above the bench, on a wall-mounted frame was another monitor, not as large as the one in the main work area, but still sizeable. Garry had seen the first version of the original scanner and it had looked like this, what the engineers called the breadboard version and it had been condensed into the compact unit that now existed. The untidy mess spread out in front of him would be rebuilt the same way once the testing had been validated, he knew. Once again, Garry felt overwhelmed at the extent of Bill's genius. Not only a brilliant geneticist, but a self-taught electronics engineer who created the boundary-breaking equipment in the laboratory.

"So what's it all about?" Garry asked.

Bill went to the whiteboard above one of the benches and picked up a marker pen.

"It works almost exactly like a random-access computer file," he said, drawing a rough circle about a metre wide. "Memories are plugged into the recording medium, the so-called 'junk' DNA in variable blocks of time and it looks like the maximum is what we've already found, three minutes and thirty-two seconds. The blocks are recorded anywhere there is space." He drew a few smaller circles within the big one, scattered at random throughout the area. "The problem was to find out how these smaller blocks are connected in some sort of sequence."

"So have you found multiple memories now in a single DNA sample?"

Bill looked smug. "Damn right!" he said and touched a switch on the bench. The monitor lit up with a view that Garry realised was the interior of a pub.

"I'm using Porter's DNA sample," Bill said. "It looks like he can't complain and nobody's going to tell him."

Little was happening on the monitor. Garry worked out that Porter was sitting at a small table against one wall, the bar directly in front of him. A man appeared from the observers' right, he was dressed in jeans and a grey flannel shirt. He walked up to the bar and leaned against it. A few seconds later, a young woman appeared on the other side of the bar, the two exchanged a few words and she poured a pint of beer, received payment and the man drank the beer slowly.

"No sound, then," Garry said, a comment, not a question.

"Nothing I can find yet," replied Bill.

Garry smiled inside at the "yet." It represented Bill's utter conviction that he would at some point be able to read a person's life from the moment of birth up to the point at which the DNA sample was taken.

The scene on the monitor continued in its dull, uneventful way, remarkable only for the astonishing technological breakthrough that it represented.

With a small flicker, it changed. Porter now appeared to be sitting in a school room with several children around him. Garry estimated they were about ten.

"A childhood memory," Bill said. "Looks like Junior School."

"Not sequential, then?" Garry was watching the screen as one of the girls in the row ahead of Porter turned round and grinned at him. At the front, a young man, presumably the teacher, said something unheard and the girl resumed her position.

"No, like I said, random access," replied Bill. "But that means there must be an index recorded somewhere and updated each time a new block of three minutes or so of memory is written to the DNA."

"This reminds me of nothing else but a standard computer system," Garry said. "It's weird, this logical structure could be a standard warehouse management system with the inventory file being updated as new items are brought into the warehouse and stored in a randomly selected location that can be found by automatic fork-lift trucks."

Bill looked thoughtful. "Yes, that's a definite parallel."

"But you think you can see every block of memory now?"

"Obviously I haven't fully tested that," said Bill. "I have no desire to sit here through forty years of the memories of a low-grade thug, as that would take... ooh... what?.... forty years! But yes, I think it's all here."

Garry chuckled.

"Okay, well done, Bill, that's quite astounding. Now we need to get this mess tidied up from the breadboard stage to a functioning machine."

"I'll call the company that did the last one. It drove them crazy, building something they couldn't understand, had no idea what it did or how it did it! This one will send them completely insane!"

"But you do trust them to keep quiet about this and build the new unit in secret?"

"No problems," replied Bill. "I told them there'll be several stages to develop and I'll go to somebody else if anyone lets out a peep. They've worked out it's some form of scanning device, but they can't work out any more."

"Great! I'll call Madam," said Gary and walked up to his office, his thoughts a mixture of delight at what Bill had achieved, fear about how any of this might have been developed without his extraordinary genius and some nagging worries about where all this was taking them.

Chapter 8 – Bill Askins

William Hawker Askins was a complete mystery, even though a source of pride to his parents. Jerry Askins had run his tobacconist business since he had taken it over from his father after working as an assistant with his parents since leaving school at fifteen. He had married a suspiciously up-market girl, which caused some difficulties with friends and families for a few years. She'd actually completed high school, even gone to teacher's training college and taught at the local junior school, but at least she was a Yorkshire lass and gradually Jerry's social circles grew to accept her.

Bill was their only child, a large kid at birth, which had caused his mother a lot of difficulties and in many ways was a disappointment. He was clumsy, looked dull and often seemed unable to comprehend what was going on around him. But he started infant school with the other kids at the age of five after some apprehension about whether he was retarded. The conversation with the head mistress when they went to pick him up after the first day was startling and completely unexpected.

"I must say, you have done a wonderful job getting Bill to read so well," said Mrs Pickford, the headmistress with a beaming smile. "I've never seen any child with that skill at this age, he's right off the scale!"

Jerry and Maureen gaped at her.

"You what?" said Jerry and turned to stare at his wife who looked equally dumbfounded.

"You must have been reading to him from the very beginning," continued Mrs Pickford, not seeming to notice the incomprehension before her. "I wish all parents would do that! Some academics think that you should read to the child even before birth, they're certain the embryo hears things."

"But... I didn't know Bill could read!" Maureen finally managed to say. "Frankly, we've always thought he might be a bit retarded, he doesn't say much and he doesn't play with the other kids in our street."

It was the turn of the headmistress to be astonished.

"You haven't been teaching him to read?"

"Well... no," said Jerry. "Like Maureen said, we've always thought he was a bit simple, I mean, he *looks* simple."

The teacher sat back in her seat, her face alive with interest.

"When school started this morning," she said, "we had the usual screaming hysterics from several kids who had been left by their parents for the first time in their little lives, but we got that sorted out and we had the kiddies playing with toys quite happily. But William had no problems at all. As soon as he entered the main room with all the others, he went straight to the bookshelf and took out a book, settled down in the corner and stayed there quietly. The book was one for the oldest kids here, the seven-year olds."

She paused and looked at the two stunned faces across her desk.

"So I went over and sat down with him and asked if he could read some of the book aloud and he did so, completely fluently, no problems at all. He was better than any ten-year old, to be honest."

The parents seemed incapable of speech.

"Maureen, I know you've taken time off teaching until William could come here," said the teacher. "What do you do during the day?"

Maureen looked a little embarrassed. "Well, keeping the house tidy takes quite a lot of work, as well as looking after the boy, of course. And I've been doing a bit of dressmaking, something I was keen on as a girl."

"Do you have the television on during the day?"

"Yes, I do. I like to keep up with current affairs, so I leave it on the news channel all day."

"And you have the text running with it?"

"Yes, 'cos sometimes I'm running the sewing machine or the vacuum cleaner and I don't like to miss anything."

"There's your answer," said the teacher. "He's learned to read that way. I've heard of such cases, I never thought I'd meet one!"

Both parents were staring at her.

"You mean he's not simple?" stammered Jerry.

"Simple! Let me tell you something else. One of my teachers gave William an introduction to arithmetic. She showed him how to do some addition and subtraction problems, just simple things. He had it beaten within an hour."

The parents looked like they'd been through a washing machine, utterly dazed and baffled.

"But what are we going to do?" pleaded Maureen. "That sounds like he needs special schools, or maybe I should stay at home and teach him, I'm a qualified teacher after all, but I have to get back to work, we need the money…"

Mrs Pickford held up her hand and stopped the slightly hysterical flow.

"He needs to go to school and learn how to cooperate with other children. So keep him coming here. The County has a program for gifted and talented children, we'll get visiting teachers on a schedule and we'll be given a written program of what to. Frankly, I'm very excited by all this."

On the short walk home, William strolled along between his parents, hands in pockets, lost in thought. Attempts by his parents to get him to talk about his first day at school got very few results. Finally, in some desperation, Maureen asked, "William, why didn't you tell us you could read so well?"

William looked up. "You never asked me," he said. "You need to have more books in the house."

At the weekend, Maureen took William shopping around the Thrift Shops, Salvation Army shops and similar and eventually found a complete five-year old set of *Encyclopaedia Britannica*. William absorbed every page like a vacuum cleaner picking up dust.

At Leeds Grammar School, William sailed through all the courses, invariably coming top in every subject, though his favourites were biology and physics. Despite his general physical clumsiness, he also showed a high aptitude for snooker, though no other sports. He explained it as a realisation that the game was all about velocities, calculation of angles and anticipation of the opponent's moves, rather like celestial mechanics.

At sixteen, having jumped his second and fourth years, William graduated with all the requisite certificates and was offered scholarships by almost every university in the UK.

He went to Cambridge because Stephen Hawking was there and because his idol, Karen Petrova had studied there.

His parents were still baffled by their son.

His first class honours degree in Pharmacology hardly raised a furrow on his brow, so he sat in on many lectures in electronic engineering and selected Genetics for his Doctorate, continuing his casual studies of electronics to fill up his time.

His most profound moment was seeing Stephen Hawking sitting in his office, having deliberately found out where it was and walked around the faculty. Another similar moment of power came when he looked up the records of Karen Petrova, having been fascinated by the woman after reading about her academic prowess and seeing her speak at a conference at the University.

He was flooded with offers of post-doctoral fellowships from all over the world and in confusion and indecision about what he wanted to do, he went to Australia for a year, taking any job he could find.

The small paragraph in *"The Sydney Morning Herald"* caught his eye one morning.

"Internationally renowned scientist, Professor Karen Petrova, whose company, Life Technology has developed many of the most successful pharmacological products in the world has

announced that she is setting up a subsidiary research organisation to be called Blueprints. The new organisation is in memory of her late husband, Hector Forbes, the equally renowned geneticist who died of cancer two years ago. Details of the role and objectives of Blueprints are not revealed, except to say it will concentrate on the structure of DNA. Blueprints will be controlled by Garry Lawson, a successful executive in the pharmacology industry with a reputation for management of large complex, un-structured operations."

Not bothering to write or telephone, Bill booked the first flight back to the UK that he could. Taking a day to recover from the jet lag, he arrived in Reading at eight in the morning and waited by the doors of Life Technology until people began showing up.

He was shattered when he was told that Blueprints had not yet started operations.

"Next week," said the middle-aged man dressed in casual clothes. "Right now, I think Garry is still settling in his replacement in Chester."

"Can I see Doctor Petrova?" asked Bill. "I really want to talk about joining this operation."

"And who are you?" asked the other man in some amusement, studying the broad farmer's face, untidy hair and exhausted eyes still showing the effects of twenty-seven hours of travelling from Australia. The suit looked like he'd worn it for the flight.

"Bill Askins. Who are you?"

"I'm Doctor Greg Mullaney. I'm the Chief Executive Officer of Life Technology. So, Bill, are you qualified to work for Blueprints?"

The fatigue made Bill a little irritable. "I went to Cambridge when I was sixteen," he said. "I have a first in pharmacology and a doctorate in genetics. I have more post-doc offers than you can shake a stick at and I'm a better electronics engineer than any of those ratbags at Apple or Microsoft."

Bill had picked up quite a few Australian figures of speech in his months in Sydney.

Mullaney looked hard at him. "You'd better come in," he said. "I may have a surprise for you."

Bill followed him into the spacious, light-filled building.

"Had breakfast?" asked Mullaney.

"No."

"Let's eat. We have an excellent canteen and you look knackered. Where have you come from?"

"I left Sydney the day before yesterday."

"That's home?" Mullaney opened the door to the canteen and the delicious odours of coffee and bacon filled the air. He led Bill to the counter where three or four other people were collecting meals. Exchanging morning pleasantries, he ordered a bacon and egg roll and coffee. "Same for you?" he asked.

Bill nodded, a little unbalanced at the speed of events.

Mullaney led the way to a table and sat down, Bill took the seat across from him.

"No," said Bill.

Mullaney grinned. "No, Sydney is not your home?"

"Leeds."

"Good. So no work permit issues. In about thirty minutes, Doctor Petrova will arrive. She's been spending the weekend at her property up the road in Hungerford. You can talk to her."

Bill said nothing. Few things left him wordless, but the thought of meeting somebody who had so influenced his thinking and his life certainly had that effect.

The food arrived and Bill attacked his with energy, to the amusement of Mullaney.

Twenty minutes later, they were sitting in Mullaney's office overlooking the car park and the River Thames beyond it.

"When I was a kid," Mullaney said, "all this was cow pasture. I went to school not far from here in a place called Winnersh and we used to row here. See that boathouse?" He pointed to a structure about a hundred metres away. "That wasn't there then, but behind it is the original building and the boats we rowed then are still there."

He turned back to Bill and smiled. "That was the conversational stuff to put you at your ease. Now, any moment, Karen will arrive, assuming she hasn't been arrested on the drive down, caused massive pile-ups and can miss the other cars in the car park. Any or all of those are possible, if not probable. She is without a doubt, the worst driver I have ever seen on the roads. But she somehow makes it down here every week to check out the formulations my people are developing. She looks at the data, makes a couple of suggestions and these always improve the product."

Bill grinned nervously. "What's she like?"

"Unique."

Bill got no time to respond as he saw a bright yellow Ferrari enter the car park, make a slightly uneven approach to the building and stop, half over the lines that marked out the space.

"So far, so good," murmured Mullaney. "She buys a new car of that sort of insane nature every two years, god knows what her insurance premiums are and I'm sure the insurance company only covers her because we insure all the company vehicles and the building with them. Somehow, she's never had an accident but every time I see her drive away, I worry about what I'll hear in the next hour or two. And I'll lay odds that she has caused massive rage and fear in large numbers of drivers."

Bill watched as the woman climbed out. She wore a bright red, flowing dress, red shoes and carried a yellow handbag. Energy seemed to radiate from her, even at this distance. Five minutes later she arrived at the open doorway. Both men rose to their feet.

"Young Gregory!" she said. "What catastrophic calamities have you caused this week?"

Bill was a bit shaken, but realised Mullaney was not in the least offended.

The executive looked at his watch. "Well, let's see. An outbreak of plague in West Africa which your crappy products don't seem to be handling, Denghi Fever breaking out in New York and all people under five feet high in Australia are suffering from legs rotting and dropping off. And it's only nine o'clock."

Her face was expressionless. "So not bad day then?"
"Fair."

She turned to Bill. "Who is this?"

"This is Bill Askins. He seems to have some worthless degree from some tinpot college in Cambridge, much like yours and he must be quite insane because he wants to work for you."

For a few seconds, her pale, perfect face with its huge eyes stared deep into Bill's soul. The brilliant scarlet of her lipstick seemed to draw all attention and he stared helplessly. Finally she sat down and the men followed suit.

"You look like village idiot," she said calmly.

By now, Bill had caught on. "I use it as camouflage," he said. "If people knew just how brilliant I am, I'd spend all my days turning away job offers."

She looked hard at him. Bill saw Mullaney hide a smile and turn to stare out of the window.

"You got doctorate at Cambridge?"

"I did. And my first in pharmacology, like yours."

"You look too young, even for village idiot."

"I went to Cambridge when I was sixteen."

"Almost as young as you were, Karen," said Mullaney.

"Indeed. And subject of doctorate?"

"The same as your husband, Doctor Forbes. Genetics. And I got the Chancellor's prize, like you did."

"And he says he knows more about electronics than those ratbags at Microsoft and Apple," added Mullaney, obviously enjoying the whole occasion.

"So you are modest village idiot as well as insane?" said Karen. Her face was expressionless, but Bill was certain there was a spark of laughter in her dark eyes.

"I am uniquely qualified," Bill replied.

Karen turned back to Mullaney.

"When does our strange little Welsh person arrive?"

"In ten days," Mullaney replied.

"Can you use modest, insane village idiot until then?"

"No doubt, Karen. I have toilets that need cleaning, floors to sweep and some electronics that don't work."

Bill held his breath, but Karen seemed done with him. Mullaney turned to him.

"Bill, go home, get some sleep, come back tomorrow. And don't wear a suit. Nobody wears a suit here."

Bill let out his breath. "Thank you, Doctor Petrova," he said. "I'll give you my best."

She nodded, but said nothing.

Greg held out his hand and Bill took it.

"Thanks," said Bill and walked out. He knew in his heart that even if he had been asked to sweep floors and clean toilets, he'd have taken the job in order to work for Karen Petrova.

Chapter 9 – 1982

"We can't keep up with demand!"

Karen Petrova was dressed in a white laboratory coat, a net over her hair and plastic shoes over her feet. She stood outside the manufacturing room where three machines were tended by two workers each.

"I did tell you, little genius that you'd succeed," said Hector.

"Yes, but like this! Sales reached ten million pounds for year and it's only August. And that's just for three pills we make. I've got lots of ideas for other drugs, we could make cholesterol drug, antacid, blood pressure..."

"STOP!" Hector Forbes held up a commanding hand. "Take a deep breath."

Instead, Karen laughed in sheer exhilaration. "Hector, I never believed it could happen like this!"

"Well, I did. Now it's time to reach for the stars and grab the universe. You need to expand. MASSIVELY!"

"Hector, I know you. You have plan already made?"

"Outline only. There's an industrial park in Reading, by the River Thames. It's a perfect location for distribution, close to London airport for international connections, on the M4 and connecting to all the other motorway routes.

Why don't we buy a patch there, build a custom-design building for you and set up facilities for just about any expansion?"

"You know me, husband mine, I am dutiful, obedient wife, I shall do as you ask."

"I should bloody well hope so! Now, get out of that silly clothing, I have something for you outside."

"Ooh! How exciting! Give me ten minutes."

"Not a second more."

She turned and ran into the changing room and emerged well within the allotted time in stylish jeans and a white sweater.

"Now," she said, "what is surprise for your dutiful, obedient wife?"

"This way." Hector led the way out of the side of the building to the car park which held just five spaces for the Life Technology staff. Only two of them had cars and the third space was taken up by Karen's little Honda sedan. Beside it was parked a Ferrari coloured a bright, dramatic red.

"Where's my surprise?" she asked.

"There," he said, pointing at the Ferrari.

Karen was immobile, her mouth open in shock.

"That's mine?"

"Happy birthday," Hector said.

"It's not my birthday," she said, staring at the Ferrari.

"Let's pretend."

"Hector, I can't believe... How did you know I have always wanted Ferrari?"

"You mentioned it once. And this one matches your lipstick."

"As it should, of course! Can I get in?"

"It's your car," he said and handed her the keys.

She took them and slowly walked to the car, opened the door and slid into the driver's seat. For several minutes she sat there, studying the instrument panel, trying the driving position and adjusting the seat to suit her.

"Hector, it's gorgeous."

"Yes, it is. Now, I have to get back to work, I have a class in an hour and then I can call the industrial park and make an offer on that patch. You probably need to get back to work, and then you can drive home when you're ready, Please drive carefully and I'll see you at the house."

"Have I ever told you how much wisdom and genius I displayed by marrying you?" she said.

"Never," he said. "You can do it tonight over dinner."

"It's deal," she said and carefully extracted herself from the car. She stood up, stood on her tiptoes and kissed him.

"Now we change world," she said and ran back into the building.

* * *

"We are now the new owners of a bare patch of ground by the Thames in the industrial park," announced Hector. "I want you to meet with the architects as soon as you can and design the building you need."

"I know exactly what I want," she said. "I've had design in mind since we bought company."

"Why am I not surprised?"

"Because you know you married incredible genius wife, that is why."

"I've always known that. So tell me, what do you plan?"

"You know I have received many requests from other companies to licence my pills for them to manufacture?"

"I do. Given the enormous demand for your products, that's probably the best way to go unless you want to own some gigantic factory."

She shook her head. "Too complicated. I think I will just design new drug, make enough to test and get through government trials, then licence. So just small manufacturing area, one machine for each type of drug, then licence it to another manufacturing company."

"This sounds an excellent plan, my tiny genius."

"Hector, you are making my dreams come true. You have never told me what your dreams are."

"I have had two," he said. "One was to marry an incredibly beautiful Russian scientist and change the world with her."

"Silly man!" she said with a wide, glowing smile.

"The other is to find out what is really going on with DNA."

"Explain," she said.

"Too many scientists have claimed that our DNA contains a lot of useless rubbish, left-over junk from millions of years of evolution."

"And you don't think so." It was a statement, not a question.

"I don't think so. Mother Nature doesn't work that way. I'm certain there are things within the helix strand that we haven't found yet and could change the very nature of what it means to be human."

"Can you look for them?"

"Not currently. I have budgets for research of course, but nothing that could handle something of that scope, nor do I have the time. I would need to develop scanning machines far better than anything known now and have several people simply searching for *something*, anything that might give a pointer to something deeper. But with the teaching load and supervising the research of several doctoral students, I just can't get to it."

"We must think of ways to do this."

"We must. Pour me some more wine and tell me about this building you want."

Chapter 10 - 2015

The phone call that Garry received about eight that evening was a pleasant surprise.

"Is that Garry?" said the woman's voice, sounding hesitant and a little anxious.

"It is," he replied, echoes of familiarity sending warm ripples through him.

"This is Hannah Ross. I came to your offices some time ago and you showed me some scenes you had taken from my DNA."

The ripple became a surge of pleasure.

"Oh, hello! Hannah, how nice to hear from you!"

"Oh, I do hope so!"

Garry could hear the relief in her voice and realised she must have been nervous about calling him. It was an unusual thought.

"I'm not that frightening," he said with a laugh. "I only seem to scare off waiters, flight attendants and barmen who seem unable to see me!"

She chuckled. Garry decided it was a nice laugh and that he'd like to hear it again.

"Did you want to talk about the scenes we showed you or more generally about the work we do?" he asked.

"Both, really," she replied, her voice sounding more relaxed.

"I'd be happy to do both, though you realise that a lot of this is top secret as we told you last time."

"Yes, I remember that, but I'd really like to see you again."

The warmth in her voice was doing strange things to Garry and he remembered the effect she'd had on him when they met at the office.

"Would you like to have dinner one night?" he asked, his mouth feeling dry.

"That would be lovely!" she said.

"How about Friday?"

"Friday is perfect. Do you know the King's Head in Wokingham?"

"I do. They serve a great dinner there. Shall I meet you there at seven?"

"I'll really look forward to that," she said. "And whatever you can tell me about yourself and your work, I want to hear it."

Another few simple but warm exchanges and they said their goodbyes. Garry replaced the phone, feeling like a teenager again.

"Wow!" he said loudly, got to his feet and went to the cabinet where he kept his best bottles of scotch and poured himself a large one. He found it difficult to think of anything but Hannah Ross for the rest of the evening and later fell asleep with memories of her trim body and intelligent face filling his mind.

He was in the lounge bar of the pub before seven, nerves churning his insides. The last date with a woman had been some years ago, since before joining Blueprints and the long, intense but exciting days since then had generally kept his mind away from regrets. He was well aware of the effect Hannah had had on him when she visited the office and he decided his main worry now was that he'd somehow mess up the evening.

When she appeared at the doorway to the lounge, the reaction in him was strong. She was wearing a close-fitting blue dress with a simple neckline and a hem that stopped an inch or two above the knees. The lines of her body held his eyes until he looked up to her face with large eyes and a wide, generous mouth in a beautiful complexion *She's lovely*, he thought. He took a deep breath and rose to his feet as she walked up to him, her gaze direct and searching. She stopped just two or three paces from him.

"Hi!" she said softly.

"Are you as nervous as I am?" he asked, struggling to keep his voice under control.

"Petrified!"

For a few seconds they stared at each other then broke out laughing. Again, he decided that hearing her laugh was worth a great deal of effort on his part.

"Well, we seem to have got over that," he said, feeling his throat relax and warmth race through his body. "Let's sit down and have a drink before we have dinner."

"You are clearly a man of great ideas," she said gravely and sat down in the seat next to his in one graceful motion.

"It's why they hired me," he replied and watched her face as she smiled, feeling like the sun was shining on him. For a few moments they looked at each other.

"I've been thinking about that time in your office," she said. "I'll never forget how it felt seeing a scene from my own memories that I can't remember directly, how young my parents looked."

"It's a shock," he said. "I haven't tried it myself, though obviously I could at any time. But I've seen how it affects so many people and I don't think I want to try that."

"I understand. You only had that one scene, though. Have you been able to get any more from anybody?"

"Hannah, I hate to have to do this, but I must remind you about that Official Secrets thing you signed. I'm going to tell you more, but you must remember, you really can't tell anyone else about this."

She nodded. "I do understand. I think it scares me a bit wondering what will happen when it all does get out."

"It's scaring all of us," he said. "But that's the thing about science. It doesn't care about repercussions. What we're finding is so immense, I have no doubts the world's going to change in ways we can't imagine yet."

"How did all this start?" She leaned forward, her face alive with interest.

"Ah! Let me tell you about the remarkable Doctor Karen Petrova!"

For fifteen minutes, he told her about the tiny multi-billionaire, her fit, perfect body and pale face with the red gash of a mouth, her style of dressing and her appalling driving while buying a new Ferrari or Maserati every year or so, her love of fine scotch, her antique samovars and her persistence in clinging to a Russian mode of speech, even though she had lived in England for over fifty years.

She followed his every word, clearly fascinated by the subject until they were interrupted by the waiter calling them to their table.

"I was going to tell you where we were with our research," he said after they had ordered their meals and the waiter had brought a bottle of Australian Merlot. Garry waved away the ritual of tasting and poured a glass for each of them.

She sipped hers appreciatively and put the glass down. "Yes, you were."

"We recently discovered how to find more scenes from a person's DNA," he said. "In fact, we can see the entire life, as far as I can tell. But what we can't do yet is find the sequence. It's a bit like a computer with random access files, we can find lots of scenes but they're in no particular order. So we can't start at the beginning and read the whole life until the point at which the sample was taken and we can't home in on any specific time or date."

"But you will," she said confidently.

He smiled at her. "We will. That group I have there, they must be the most amazing bunch of dedicated scientists you could find anywhere and Bill, the resident genius just keeps breaking down barriers. Karen calls him the Village Idiot and she thinks the world of him."

She returned the smile, making Garry feel a bit dizzy. "I wonder why this ability exists?" she said, picking up her glass and taking another sip.

"That's an extraordinary question," he said. "Almost everything in nature is a survival mechanism, so there must be a reason and yet here we are, thousands of years along in the history of mankind and only just learning about it."

"So do you think you'll one day be able to see every second from the moment of birth and also find a specific date to examine?"

"I'm sure of it."

"That's a bit scary."

"It is," he agreed. "And I'm not sure we humans are ready for that knowledge. But it's there to be discovered and we can't stop learning. But we've spent too long on this. Tell me more about Hannah Ross."

She laughed. "Why don't you read my DNA and tell me? You'll probably find more than I know myself!"

He shook his head. "We destroyed the sample we took from you as you asked. I couldn't and I wouldn't do that."

She reached over and touched his hand. "I was only joking," she said. "I trust you absolutely."

He folded her fingers in his own. "So tell me," he murmured.

The rest of the evening passed in a haze of warmth and happiness and by the time Garry got home he was feeling happier than he could ever remember.

Over the following weeks, Hannah provided exactly the break from the constant pressures of work at Blueprints that Garry needed. The relationship became warmer and warmer until the inevitable happened and she stayed over at his house in Earley one Friday night.

"That was really lovely," she said, sitting across from him at the kitchen table as he served scrambled eggs, toast and coffee. Her smile was warm.

"What, breakfast, or last night?" he asked as he poured the coffee from the plunger pot.

"Silly man!" she replied. "Breakfast is just the very nice extra!"

"Glad you think so," he said with a smug grin. "I hope we can do it more often!"

"Count on it!" she said and took a mouthful of eggs. He did the same and for a few moments, there was a comfortable, intimate silence.

"Of course, Wokingham is not too far from here," he said.

She smiled. "Several of our girls live around here," she said. "They take the bus in to school every day. I think our Head Girl actually lives just round the corner from here. And quite a few of the staff, too."

It didn't seem to need any more to be said and the following week, Hannah moved into the house.

Chapter 11

The next few weeks were frustrating for all the team as they waited for the new equipment to be designed and built. Bill's huge, untidy breadboard design was rebuilt under his direction by the electronics company that had made the previous machine and they produced three working models that resembled nothing more than a plain grey filing cabinet about the height of a desk. A standard computer monitor and keyboard completed the ensemble and the researchers took a week to learn how to use it. The several thousand DNA samples from people around the world were all stored in a secure unit and could be selected by an instruction from the new box's keyboard and scanned. Once sure of their skills, the team began reviewing memory blocks and searched for some indication of how to place them in a chronological sequence.

The work could have been intensely dull. But all the team knew that what they doing was going to have an explosive effect on the world and its society at some stage, so they persisted. Most of the subjects' lives consisted of hours and hours of basic routine, going to work, sitting at home, talking to friends and relatives and the team found themselves going through these hundreds of hours without the benefit of sound to identify the sequence of events.

Initially there were episodes of shock, embarrassment, disgust, but eventually they all adjusted to the standard scientific detachment in which they were all trained and merely saw data, not personal events. Sexual contacts no longer amused or titillated, occasional violence no longer shocked and bizarre practices no longer disgusted.

There were still moments of astonishment, however. One of the team suddenly let out a small cry of shock as she saw herself in the monitor. She was being greeted by somebody whose name she didn't recognise at all, but when she was able to recall the event, she remembered it was the friend of a fellow student at University who had come to Convocation Day for the giving of degrees.

A similar memorable moment when the Queen appeared on the monitor, apparently walking down a line of people at some formal occasion at which the DNA's owner had been present. The consensus of the group was the event had been at least thirty years ago, judging by Her Majesty's appearance.

And there was another killing, this time during a robbery at a store. The view of the man whose DNA sample was being tested showed three men carrying shotguns leaving a car, running into a store that looked like a jewellery shop. When all were in, they waved their guns at the three female assistants who started filling bags with items on display. One appeared to offer resistance and one of the men shot her at close range. Her head dissolved in an explosion of blood and matter that splattered against display cabinets and at that moment the scene ended.

In dead silence, the group watched the episode again and Garry picked up the phone and called Detective Inspector Mellings.

Another scene that caused great excitement was a man's face, very close, looking down. His face was filled with pride and the group could all see that the man said, "Well, hello, young man!"

"It's the memory of a new-born baby," whispered one of the team. "He can't be more than a day or two old!" She keyed in a query on her keyboard. "Declan James Head," she read aloud. "Born September 15th, 1972. Well at least that's one block of memory we can place pretty accurately!"

"And it also shows that memories start being recorded pretty well from the beginning," added Garry. "I'd say Hector Forbes' theory was just about spot on."

And so the team continued the disciplined, grinding work of research, running the same tests with infinitesimally different settings again and again as they slowly and professionally plotted how blocks of memory were recorded in the massively elongated strands of DNA. Bill kept hitting the same walls, scanner technology, processor speed and the great mystery of just how the astonishing computer that was the human body functioned and those walls kept tumbling under the relentless, non-stop attacks of Garry's team of researchers. The team had grown to thirty by 2017.

Garry's life remained happy and stable as Hannah provided warmth, love and excitement to what had been an empty home world for him for so many years. They talked a lot about the project and Garry learned to trust her with more details of what they were doing and what developments were occurring.

Chapter 12 – 2017

From his office, Garry heard the scream of exhilaration from the researcher's desk. He stood up and walked to the area where the entire group, now fourteen strong was gathered round the desk of Penny Barstow, the woman who had first seen the erotic images of the bouncing breasts of the girl having energetic sex. Her face was again flushed, but not with embarrassment as then but with utter delight.

"I've found the index!" she shouted as Garry appeared.

Garry felt a surge of excitement and he struggled to remain calm. There had been false discoveries in the past. "You'd better show us," he said. "Put it on the main screen."

Penny sat down again at her keyboard and clicked a few buttons and on the massive three-metre wide screen at the back of the room, the image came alive with the grey mass of the DNA helix at high magnification.

Five minutes later, Garry broke the silence of absolute fascination that had followed Penny's quiet demonstration of her discovery.

"I want you to show Madam as soon as she gets here," he said. "I'll call her right now."

*　*　*

"It's in a completely different area from where we've been looking," said Penny Barstow. She spoke with quiet confidence to the entire staff of the company seated in the conference room, listening with silent intensity.

"There's a tiny, thin thread starting way back at the base of the molecule and it's spiral shaped, taking very little space indeed," Penny continued. "What I first saw was just a dot and I didn't examine it until last week because there seemed bits of more potential elsewhere. But when I put maximum magnification onto it, I saw the spiral thread and I was able to pull that out and start tracking along it. It's really long when extended, almost as long as the DNA molecule itself, about two metres. This acts as the index to the file and shows the location of each memory spot which itself is placed anywhere there's a convenient-sized location. It behaves exactly like a random-access file in a modern computer."

There was a tiny exhalation of breath in the room.

"So now you can read each memory recording in sequence?" asked Garry softly.

Penny nodded. "I've spent three days trying to read the index and I still can't work out how the memory location is recorded, but so far, I've tried reading a whole day at a time in a person and it seems to work perfectly well," she said.

A burst of applause ran through the room and Penny looked astonished as if she hadn't noticed anyone else present.

"So you can now read whole life of person from start to finish?" Karen Petrova spoke softly but everybody heard what she said.

Penny nodded. "Yes, Madam, I do believe we can, but of course, we can only read up to the point where the sample was taken."

At that point, Bill got to his feet, looking a little embarrassed.

"Penny, that's quite brilliant," he said. "I've been looking at that for the last hour. We can read the entire life from the birth of the subject right up to where we take the sample. But the problem is that I still can't home in on a specified time and date. And I have no idea what the indexing method is. It isn't like a computer giving a cylinder-track address, it's a quite different reference system and I can't read it yet."

"So you cannot start at moment of birth or find particular day in person's memory?" asked Karen as Penny took a seat at the side, looking ecstatically happy.

Bill shook his head. "We can start at the very beginning, yes. But finding a specific date without going through the entire history day by day, not yet, no. That's my next target. But I think that will be easier than finding this index."

"Bill, what about sound?" A young woman at the back of the room looked embarrassed as if she had asked a deeply personal question. "Is there any sign at all of getting that?"

Bill looked irritated. "Not so far," he said, barely audible to the room.

His embarrassment was saved when another researcher asked the question that Garry had been wondering about and was about to ask also.

"Penny, you haven't said how you track along the thread," said a man on the front row. "How do you do that?"

At that point, Penny looked concerned. "Look," she said, her hands moving in an agitated manner. "There's something very strange about that and I've been feeling nervous about raising it."

The room went silent.

"Fact is," said Penny, "I don't know! I laid the thread out after extracting it with the electro-magnetic device that Bill designed, but as soon as I started looking at it in close detail, the images began appearing. As I moved along, the images kept coming and if I moved forward or backward by bigger increments, the appropriate images appeared. It's almost as if the thread was reading my mind."

Murmurs of astonishment ran round the room.

"Any ideas, anyone?" asked Garry.

After a second or two of silence, a woman spoke up. She was tall, solidly built with strong features that were normally immobile but could break into joyous laughter at any time. Garry had hired her after she had been working for one of the big pharmaceutical companies but had been bored by the monotony. Peter Clare had referred her to him and he had hired her on the spot. "There could be several possibilities," she said, "each wilder than the other!"

"Go on, Deborah," said Garry.

"One is that we're into relativity issues," said Deborah. "As Heisenberg suggested, the observer is influencing the experiment in some way. The other is one that sci-fi writers have played with for decades, that perhaps there's some telepathic ability in humans. I know that there have been decades of experiments looking for this, but nothing has ever been proved."

"So who's the telepath?" asked Penny, looking fascinated. "Me or the DNA strand?"

"Either or both," replied Deborah.

"Good grief!" whispered Penny.

Garry stood up and moved to Bill's side. "This has been another astounding breakthrough," he said, smiling at Penny. "I'm going to recommend that we all start by learning how we find this index and then working on detecting just how it works so that we can find a specific date and time and get back to the very first few seconds of a person's life. Each of you, please follow up on this very weird way of reading up and down the index, see if we all get the same results as Penny did. If you do, then we have something very strange and wonderful in our findings. I have no doubts also, that the study of the very beginnings will be fantastic value for psychologists, the medical world and education specialists. Any questions?"

A moment of silence hung in the air, then Avram Fischer raised a hand.

"Yes, Avram?" he said.

"Garry, I was thinking about the possibilities that one day, this technology will be used in crime detection, particularly as proof of a crime. But what about false memories? We know that some hypnotists and therapists have had their patients report things like being raped as a child when it has turned out not to be true. Is it possible that such memories might show up in these records even though they never happened?"

Garry felt some disturbance that he hadn't thought about that one before.

"Avram, that's a hell of a good point. I don't know, we haven't encountered such a phenomenon as yet. I think we'll need to address this when we can key in on a specific time and date. When we're sure of that, I will contact a few psychologists, therapists and suchlike and find some cases of false memory. Then we can take a DNA sample and see what shows. Thanks, Avram, you've hit a key point there. It will certainly be critical if this ever becomes a part of the legal system."

He looked round the room. "Anything else? No? Okay, let Penny run a training session on how to identify that spiral and unwind it and see if anyone can work out how the indexing works. Madam?"

"My congratulations," said Karen. "Soon we will change world more than I ever thought." She looked at her watch and pointed at Garry's office.

Garry grinned. He knew exactly what was next on the schedule.

As they left the room, he heard just one comment from Bill.

"We're going to need a better scanner," the big man said.

Garry sighed and then smiled as he recalled his first meeting with Penny.

* * *

"Penny, please sit down."

Only three days had passed since Garry's trip to Cambridge and Penny had called him the day after his meeting with her Uncle, Ray Gallard. Garry invited her to come and talk, intrigued by the energy she seemed to exude over the telephone, as well as the reference from her Uncle.

She is certainly nice-looking, he thought to himself, appreciating the slender lines and graceful way in which she moved and took her seat across from him at the coffee table. *Now to see if Gallard was right about her intellect.*

"Why are you looking to change jobs?" he asked.

"I'm bored!" she said firmly.

"Explain."

"I have a first class honours degree in Genetics and a doctorate in the same subject. I did that in just three years and I was ready to go out and shake up the world! I didn't want an academic job, I thought I do more good in a practical environment. But at this company, they give me stuff that a junior lab assistant could handle, nothing to test me at all. The usual thing, I imagine. How could a pretty girl actually have a brain?"

"I can understand why that's frustrating. What do think you could give us?"

"Ray said you're funded by Karen Petrova. You're looking at DNA. One thing I've seen is that anything around Karen Petrova is exciting, brilliant, visionary and has a huge impact on the world. I want to be part of that and I know I have the talents to be useful."

"Do you know what we do?"

"Other than you're looking at DNA? No."

"Good. That's all I know at the moment."

Penny laughed in surprise. "That was unexpected!" she said.

"It's true. Karen's brief to me is simply to find out what else there is in DNA beyond the current knowledge. She knows there's something there, her husband..."

"Hector Forbes. I met him a couple of times at conferences."

"Yes, Hector Forbes, he said there is more."

"And if Hector Forbes said that, we can be damn sure there is. Please can I come and work for you?"

"I've got nothing set up yet, Penny. Furniture is being delivered now, computers are in place, but I still don't know what else I need."

"How many people have you got?"

"I'm it. There's a young man working in our other company next door who's supposed to be a geneticist like you, but reckons he's a hell of an electronics engineer. He'll move over when the offices are ready."

"I can help with all of that."

"I've no doubt. When can you start?"

"I'm supposed to give two weeks notice, but I'm doing nothing of value. I'm sure I can talk them into letting me go right away."

"If you can, start Monday. If not, call me."

The delight in her face lit up his office.

She could cause problems for the male staff, thought Garry in amusement. *Including me!*

"Do you have a place to live?" he asked.

"I'll spend the weekend here," she said. "I should find something."

"If not, book into a hotel, bill the company. I may be short of staff, equipment, business plan or anything else, but we're not short of money."

"This is wonderful! I'll see you Monday morning, count on it!"

He couldn't help laughing. *The company has made a great start,* he decided.

* * *

Carefully, he poured a portion of the twenty-year old scotch into the flute glasses that he had learned were the preferred option for such fine liquor and handed one to Karen. They sat opposite each other in armchairs across from the circular coffee table in his office. The aroma of peat mixed with roses, honeysuckle and liquorice wafted through the air and Garry knew he could take all the time he wanted to savour it before taking his first sip.

"My taste in scotch remains good, Garry?" she asked, completing the same ritual.

"Immaculate as ever, Madam," he replied.

She took another sip, her eyes closed. "My husband taught me about scotch," she finally said. "We went to Islay for our honeymoon and spent two weeks touring all the distilleries."

"I wish I'd met him," said Garry. "Everything I have ever heard about Hector says he was a wonderful man."

She kept her eyes closed as she breathed in more of the aroma, but Garry could see the sadness in her face.

"I miss him," she said finally.

Garry couldn't think of anything to say and stayed silent while she took a sip and obviously experienced the flavour going down.

"What are we going to do when you have finally found it all?" she asked.

"That's bothered me a lot," he replied. "But there are some major hurdles. Now that we've solve the indexing problem we'll be able to read a person's life from the moment of birth to the time of taking the DNA sample and identify the specific date as well. Getting sound is proving difficult, I know it's frustrating Bill no end."

"But you will," Karen said and there was no query in the words, it was a statement of fact.

Garry smiled. "We will. You've seen these people, they may be the best team of researchers in the world."

"Are you worried by what we will be able to do?"

He nodded. "Somewhat. As we've already seen, the most intimate and private moments will be available for view. We won't be able to keep this technology secret for long if it's going to be used for anything. I believe the criminal justice system will be the biggest users. We've already demonstrated how."

"And what happens when this technology gets out into common use?" she asked, her eyes fixed firmly on his.

He looked calmly back. "Then the world changes, just as you have always said."

She finished her drink and put the glass back on the table.

"I think I may be worried about that." She stood up, opened her handbag and extracted the car keys. "We must now talk to authorities. You will come with me."

"Of course," said Garry.

"Time for me to get home."

"Please drive carefully, Madam," said Garry.

"Don't be silly, funny Welsh person," she said and left in a whirl of colour and perfume, leaving Garry feeling like Alice in Wonderland, Karen's bright red mouth being the most vivid memory, like the Cheshire Cat's grin.

Chapter 13 – 2004

The Guardian, July 4th, 2004

The death is reported of Professor Hector Forbes, one of the most highly regarded geneticists in the world, Professor of Genetics at Oxford University. Diagnosed just seven weeks ago with a particularly aggressive form of brain cancer, Hector Forbes died in hospital where he had been for the last three weeks, mostly in a coma and under intense pain relief that gave him very few minutes a day of awareness. His wife, the renowned pharmacologist, Doctor Karen Petrova was with him the whole time until he died.

Professor Forbes was cremated yesterday in Oxford and his ashes scattered over the small rural property that the couple had bought just two years ago near Hungerford. Doctor Petrova has refused all interviews and has apparently retreated to the Hungerford property.

"I promise you this, Hector my love," said Karen aloud, sitting in the lounge room of the farm house. "You made my dreams come true. Now your dream is my dream and we will make that come true as well. But how will I live without you?"

Chapter 14 - 2018

The Prime Minister and the Home Secretary look uncomfortable, thought Garry in amusement, feeling his own nervousness at being in the company of the two most powerful men in the country dissolve at the sight. They had risen to their feet as he and Karen had been shown into the Prime Minister's office by a calm, middle-aged woman who had closed the door as she left. The four of them sat in armchairs around a large coffee table. A tray with a coffee pot and four cups, a plate of biscuits, milk and sugar sat on the table, but when Karen declined any, none of the rest helped themselves.

"Doctor Petrova, it is good of you to come and see us," said the Prime Minister. Garry thought he seemed unsettled at the presence of the tiny woman in a flowing blue dress and understood completely. Karen's presence could unsettle anyone.

"It was time," replied Karen. "My group is finding astonishing things and I must confess, we are concerned at implications."

"Would you explain?" said the Home Secretary. He was a tall, thin man, almost completely bald, clean-shaven and immaculately dressed in a grey suit with a blue tie and a black waistcoat.

Karen gave Garry a brief glance and he understood the instruction without needing more.

"Our brief was to find what else was in human DNA, as you already know," he began. "Doctor Petrova had always believed that it contained a record of our lives, every second of them, in fact and this we found. We are now able to see every moment of a person's life from birth to the moment at which we take the DNA sample, we can show it on a screen and if we take a sample from a corpse, we can see every moment until the person dies."

"God almighty!" exclaimed the Home Secretary. "Dare I ask, what do you see as a person dies?"

"Nothing but a fading of light," replied Garry. "We see no tunnel of light to Heaven, no angels, none of the stories told by people who have had near-death experiences."

"Good grief!" muttered the Prime Minister. "I can see the problems in all this immediately."

"Problems and benefits," replied Garry. "We have so far found two murderers by seeing the actual scene of the killings and both are now in prison for life, even though the evidence from the DNA could not be presented. But knowing with utter certainty who committed the crime allowed the police to search for and find all essential and conventional evidence."

"And can you hear conversations as well?" asked the Prime Minister. "That would make the whole thing even worse, I imagine."

"Not as yet," replied Garry. "It may well be that a sound record is not created, but we are looking for it. I have to say, that the brilliance of the team we have tells me that if it's there, we'll find it."

The Home Secretary looked thoughtful. "I'd be very uncomfortable at the thought that somebody could look through my entire life. It's not just any wrongdoings that could be uncovered, but the most intimate moments.... Doctor Petrova, this is very dangerous indeed. If this technology gets out... Mr Lawson, can that happen?"

Garry shrugged. "The genius of the technology was in the design, like all new technology. The technology itself is not difficult to reproduce, if one has the plans. Once the secret that this is possible gets out, other geniuses will develop it. Even if they don't, some way or another, the designs will leak. Nobody has ever been able to keep things secret for long."

The Prime Minister glared at him. "You could hardly be less positive, Mr Lawson. Do you understand how dangerous this is?"

"I'm a realist, Prime Minister and I've already seen the sort of details that can be revealed. But if America couldn't keep the Manhattan Project a secret, what chance of anything else?"

"That's what scares me," said the Prime Minister. "And the repercussions of such a technology becoming widely available may be more destructive to society than the nuclear bomb. What if somebody gained the DNA of some global figure, good grief, maybe our Queen and started publicly broadcasting personal scenes of her life? The idea is too horrible for words."

"We have considered that," said Garry. "And we agree, it's an appalling idea and to be honest, I don't know how to prevent it, other than severe punishment for anyone doing that to deter it from happening again."

"Maybe, Doctor Petrova, we should enact state security laws and have you shut down," said the Home Secretary in sudden determination. "This could certainly lead to enormous social unrest and probably violence. There is plenty of justification to close down your operation."

Finally, Garry was witness to one of Karen's cold smiles, something of which he had heard but never seen. She directed it at the Home Secretary and he visibly sat back in his chair.

"So you think I am fool?" she said softly. "Do you think I would not have considered possibility? Everything we do, every sample we have, every discovery we have made, every plan of our equipment is backed up to another location outside of Britain. If you try something as silly as that, I will simply move operation elsewhere. Within three days, we would be back at work and out of your reach."

Both the Prime Minister and his colleague seemed frozen in their chairs. Garry was highly amused and struggled not to show it. He knew that there was a constant backup to another site, that was standard disaster recovery procedure, but outside Britain? This was news to him and he wondered what else Karen had kept from him.

"Prime Minister," said Garry, trying to ease the situation. "Great discoveries have always caused problems and I think it's likely that this is one of the greatest ever. Yes, it can and probably will result in some upheavals, but scientific truth just cannot be suppressed, however hard we try. And to be honest, I think there's more to come from our operation. As Doctor Petrova has said from the beginning, she always knew that she and her husband, Doctor Hector Forbes would change the world."

"I just don't see how this can improve things," said the Prime Minister. Stress was making his throat tight and his words came out as a croak.

"I've given you one example of how," replied Garry. "We can streamline the criminal justice system once we can use DNA images as evidence. No need for complex courts, no need for long trials, absolute proof of guilt or innocence and no longer the injustices of jailing the innocent or letting the guilty go free."

"We would need water-tight procedures to ensure fairness," said the Home Secretary. He seemed interested in what Garry had told them. "Some form of security to ensure the correct sample has been taken and that independent experts have verified the procedure. Yes, I can see how that would be a great advance."

"It will be a long time before we can do that," said the Prime Minister. "This has to come out into public awareness and be established as true science first. I think we'll have problems before then."

"The thing I might fear most is how some governments will use this as a weapon against their own people," said the Home Secretary. "Imagine some governments, say in Iran, Saudi Arabia or some of the old Soviet satellite countries, how they would take DNA from every citizen and have people going through them looking for incidents of something that could be used against them. Meetings where the leaders have been criticised for example, and then that person is arrested and killed."

"It is probable," said Karen. "Certainly my old country would have done that and today's Russia is probably no different. It worries me, too."

"But then look at the other side of that," said the Home Secretary. His face showed considerable excitement.

"Imagine how easy it would be to check out people applying for positions of high security, such as atomic research or within our security services. It would absolutely guarantee an accurate check and do it simply and quickly."

The Prime Minister looked at him. His hostility seemed to fade somewhat. "This is true," he said and looked into the distance for a few moments, obviously in deep thought before coming to a decision.

"Doctor Petrova, while my reservations remain very strong, it's clear that some advantages could result from the use of this extraordinary technology. The more I think of it, the more value I can see, particularly in the criminal justice system, as you have already pointed out. I believe that I must set up a detailed enquiry into this to devise secure procedures and this will need us to brief several people, all of whom will be very high-ranking personnel in the government and specialists in law, civil liberties and criminal justice."

Karen nodded. "That would seem highly appropriate, Prime Minister. I will look forward to seeing how this develops."

"Doctor Petrova, Mr Lawson, our thanks for the meeting," said the Prime Minister, clearly bringing procedures to an end. "Please continue to keep us informed of developments. I'm not a religious man, but I have to say this – I will pray that no great harm results from the work you have done."

Somehow, Karen was excluded from the male ritual of handshakes and the meeting broke up.

Chapter 15

With the discovery of the primary tracking system and the ability to read a person's life sequentially from the very first second, the pace of work and the excitement level increased. The two major focal points of the team's efforts were to find just what was the mechanism between the tiny thread that recorded the index of the memory section location and the accessing of that memory. The great mystery remained in the way in which the researchers could move up and down with only the mental impulse. All the researchers found that they could do it, though with some samples it took intense concentration.

"Could that mean that some people have more or less telepathic abilities?" suggested Garry in one of his regular review sessions with the team.

"We think so," replied Penny. "We took samples of those where one of us had experienced difficulties and asked all the others to try reading up and down the thread. All of us had difficulties, but the reverse was also true – with the threads that were easy to read, all of us could read them with equal ease."

"That's not necessarily proving telepathic abilities," said Bill. "We could still be in the realm of relativity and the observer is affecting the process in some other way, more along quantum theories."

That caused several moments of general noise as individuals discussed the possibilities with each other. Garry made no move to stop that. He had long ago realised that this team functioned best when left alone to work things out for themselves.

When the buzz subsided, Garry took over.

"I'm not sure it matters for now how this is working. We'll probably stumble on it one day as we continue digging. But the key is that it does work and we need to keep looking at just what else we have in this extraordinary thing called DNA."

Gradually, that question faded into the realms of just another mystery while the team concentrated on becoming accustomed to reading sections of a person's history sequentially.

While the team focused on that, Bill retreated further and further into his cocoon as he looked for the sound recording that he was certain must be present somewhere.

Garry knew that of all the astonishing moments in his life since meeting Karen Petrova and the beginning of his hunt for the Snark, the moment when they found the audio track was quite probably the most momentous.

It began quietly enough.

Garry was working through the severely boring task of reviewing the costs of the previous month when Bill appeared at his doorway. It was the first time he had seen the large man in three weeks as Bill had locked himself away in his private workshop and worked mostly nights. He would not have been certain that the "Village Idiot" as Karen liked to call him was even around, but for a few reported sightings in the washroom and that the lights were on when Garry occasionally drove around the industrial park out of curiosity.

"Can I have everybody in the place come and see something?" asked Bill.

Garry looked suspiciously at what looked like a grin on Bill's lips and tried to suppress the excitement. Bill had never requested public gatherings before, preferring normally to show his new developments privately to Garry and to Karen.

Garry stared hard, trying to see signs of what was happening, but Bill merely stared back.

"Okay," said Garry. "I think everybody's there, anyway. Let's go."

He rose and led the way to the main research area. He scanned the room and saw two empty work areas.

"Good morning, everybody," said Garry. "Can I have your attention?"

It took a few moments for heads to be lifted from papers and screen monitors.

"Who's missing?" asked Garry.

"Avram and Penny," replied one of the team. "They're in the canteen getting a snack."

"Would you go and get them? Bill has something he wants to show us."

That phrase was enough to cause a murmur of excitement round the room. Bill's occasional announcements were invariably astonishing and represented major break-throughs in the work of the company. The man who had spoken walked rapidly out of the room and returned a few moments later with the other two, carrying mugs of coffee.

"All yours, Bill," said Garry.

Bill walked to the computer station at the back of the room, under the three-metre main monitor, entered some data and the monitor came alive. It showed a still picture of two men in what looked like a pub.

"I took this from the sample of that murderer, Graham Porter," said Bill and touched a button. The two men flickered into movement.

"Hey, Graham, what's happening?" asked one.

"Not a lot," replied the other and took a deep draught of his mug of beer.

Bill touched the button again and the picture went immobile.

There was dead silence in the room for several seconds.

"Ho-lee SHIT!" said Avram.

"Exactly," said Bill. "We've got sound!"

Wild applause broke out in the room and Garry made his way up to Bill and shook his hand, grinning widely.

"The triumph of the village idiot!" he said. "Well done! Oh man, this is simply fantastic! Now you have to tell us how you did it."

Bill finally relaxed his self-control and broke into a laugh, deep and intense.

"Just half an hour ago!" he said, hardly audible above the noise of celebration in the room. "Can you get these peasants quiet so I can tell you about it?"

"I think so," replied Garry and turned to the room, his arms up for silence. It took just a few seconds as all the team was eager to hear how this new breakthrough had occurred.

Bell bent over the keyboard and the image of the DNA molecule appeared. Bill slowly increased the magnification and focused on the tiny dot that had been revealed to be a spiral thread containing the index to the memory segments.

He took a laser pointer and the red dot on the screen moved along the strand between the two threads of the helix to another minuscule dot. He expanded the image and showed another spiral thread.

"That's it," he said. "It's almost identical to the spiral that Penny found and what it contains is a similar index, but this points to audio segments that match the visual segments precisely. And like the other, records are stored in binary form at the quantum level, each particle representing a bit, exactly as in computer structure. The two spirals are obviously updated simultaneously and they are read in the same sequence, but for now I have absolutely no idea how this is done."

"You've tested this with other samples?" asked Penny.

Bill nodded. "The locations of the index spirals are the same in the ten samples I tested."

Each person in the room seemed to exhale their breath at that moment, as if waiting and anticipating the culmination of the intense searches of recent months.

Every single researcher turned their attentions to their monitors as they pulled up DNA samples and tested Bill's new discovery. Within a few minutes, the noise level rose sharply as sounds were emitted by the computers.

"OYE!!!" shouted Garry. "Hit the mute!"

The sound died and a roomful of grinning faces looked at Garry. "Get earphones!" he said, exhilarated by the events. "Time to tell Madam," he said and returned to his office.

Chapter 16

Garry had some difficulties now, recalling the slight sense of loneliness he used to experience on returning home from work each day. Although he had valued the solitude and freedom from tension, the emptiness sometimes had got to him, but Hannah's arrival had changed all that.

While sometimes she was late home when she had school functions or games training sessions, most often she was home when he got in and it was always with a pleasurable sense of anticipation that he saw her yellow Honda parked in the driveway.

After a quiet meal of baked salmon and a bottle of Moselle, they settled down in their customary place on the settee, Hannah resting against his chest with his arm around her waist as the stereo system played something from the classical repertoire that they both loved. This evening, it was Mendelssohn's music for *"A Midsummer Night's Dream."*

"Massive breakthrough today," murmured Garry as he sipped his scotch.

"Ooh! Do tell!" she said, cradling her own glass of the last of the white wine from dinner.

"Bill finally found the audio records. We've been struggling with that for over two years."

"Oh my goodness! So you can now hear everything being said as well as watch the action?"

"And any other sounds happening as well."

She twisted around so that she could look at his face. "You know, that sounds a bit scary."

He stroked her cheek. "Damn right, it is scary. To be honest, the whole thing has been scaring me for a long time. I just have no idea where this will take us."

"What does Karen think?"

"She has the same concerns. We've talked about it, but she's the ultimate scientist. If it's there, it has to be discovered and she's always believed that this was there."

She turned back to her original position and stared down at her glass in her lap. "I'm not entirely certain that everything has to be discovered. Maybe some things would be best left hidden."

Garry sensed the small tension in her. "Something wrong, honey?"

"I'm just worried about how people are going to react when they know we can see every second of their lives. I think it will turn ugly. I don't think God intended this for us."

"God?" Garry was startled. Religion had never risen as a topic for them before. As far as Garry knew, Hannah's religious views were much like his own, agnostic and she'd never indicated anything different.

"It just seems wrong," she said softly. "Will there ever be any official release of this stuff?"

"I think so," said Garry, trying to stifle the unease he was feeling. "Karen talked to the Home Secretary this afternoon. He and the Prime Minister had been quite keen on the idea of using the technology in the criminal justice system because it can provide absolute certainty of a person's guilt or innocence. She thinks they're planning to use it that way."

She leaned forward and got to her feet.

"I think it's wrong and it's going to cause trouble," she said, tears in her eyes and walked into the kitchen. Sensing her need to be away from him, Garry stayed where he was, seriously worried by this first coldness between them.

He stayed that way all evening and when he finally made his way to bed, Hannah was already there, apparently asleep. He undressed and carefully slid between the sheets wondering just what had happened between them. But after a few moments, she turned to him and cuddled up against him and all seemed well again.

Chapter 17 - 2018

The scene was much the same as the last time they had met just a year ago, thought Garry. The Prime Minister and Home Secretary sat in armchairs on one side of the large square coffee table, he and Karen sat in similar chairs on the other. Coffee had been served and Garry had decided to ignore the example set by Karen and this time poured himself a cup and sat back to watch the show. As always, it amused him to see the effect the tiny woman in the elegant green silk dress had on the two most powerful men in the country. They seemed more like schoolboys before the principal, he thought. The power in the group sat with Karen.

"Doctor Petrova, as you know, we have spent the time since last we met examining the technology you have developed," began the Prime Minister. "And I have to say, it has been a difficult, sometimes shocking process for all of us."

"I warned you that such would be case," said Karen.

"And indeed it was," said the Home Secretary, a somewhat rueful expression on his face. "I was grateful that you left me alone at your offices to view my own sample. But it was the only way I would finally accept the validity of the process, seeing scenes from my own childhood and later years displayed on that screen!"

"I agree with that," said the Prime Minister. "Despite the reports of almost fifty of our people who looked at their own lives, it was not until I went through the experience before I truly believed it."

"And so now you have accepted it, how do you plan to use system?" asked Karen.

"We indicated at our last meeting that the criminal justice system was the best possible application," said the Prime Minister. "And this is where we will introduce it."

"Of course, the big problem is telling the world that such capabilities exist," said the Home Secretary. "Naturally, we will have to do this in order to announce its use in the courtroom and it will be essential that we thoroughly describe in detail just what safeguards we will put in place."

"And these are...?" asked Karen.

The Home Secretary took a leather-bound notebook from the table and opened it.

"Initially, we must amend the law so that a DNA sample is mandated from somebody reasonably suspected of a crime," he said. "To date, this has been voluntary but now we must enforce it, providing there is sufficient evidence to point to a suspect. We cannot just take mass samples from everybody in the area, much as that would make the task easier. But the civil libertarians would rightly kick up a major stink if we tried that. I'm probably going to mandate a court order if necessary, if a reasonable suspect refuses a sample."

"However, it would be legitimate to ask for a sample to be volunteered, knowing that it would prove absolute innocence," added the Prime Minister. "We can do that, already. But now we must go a step further. Every sample must be taken at a laboratory licenced by the government and by personnel suitably qualified. If a sample shows the donor to be guilty of the crime, we must go further still. A second sample will be taken by a qualified geneticist, also licenced by the government who will make absolutely certain that the sample he takes is the one which provides the images. And even further – the defence counsel must do the same and make their own independent validation of the images with a similarly qualified and licenced geneticist. There must be no question at all of secretly switching samples to prove guilt or innocence."

Garry thought carefully about this and decided that it made excellent sense.

"It makes the role of a defence counsel quite negligible," he said. "There is nothing at all such counsel can do, once the images have been shown and verified."

The Prime Minister nodded at him.

"That is quite true," he said. "But only for the obvious physical crimes of murder and assault. We don't believe that these procedures would necessarily prove a case say, in fraud, money laundering, insider trading or similar crimes. It may be difficult to be absolutely certain of what the images show, but they may still provide indicators. There would still be a need for skilled counsel here, but as you say, Mr Lawson, the legal profession will lose a major source of income!"

"I suppose it means a murder or assault trial would be completed in minutes," said Garry.

"Indeed," said the Home Secretary. "The Prosecution has nothing to do but prove the validity of the source and the Defence would be limited to pleas for the court to consider extenuating circumstances. The country will save many millions of pounds in the administration of justice."

"I am very impressed," said Karen, drawing all the attention in the room back to her. "And I will support these procedures completely. Of course, we have full patents on technology but we will naturally licence equipment to be built and sold to any legitimate government organisation, such as Attorney General's Department for purposes outlined here today."

"Thank you, Doctor," replied the Prime Minister. "We would also wish to use it as we indicated last year, for the vetting of applicants for high security jobs."

"That could be done by Attorney General, surely?" said Karen.

"It could and we will make that ruling," replied the Prime Minister.

"And outside of these functions, what will you wish to do? Do you wish to allow foreign sales of my systems?"

The Prime Minister paused for a moment. "Do you have any thoughts on the matter, Doctor Petrova?"

"I do," she said firmly. "I do not wish any foreign country to be permitted to use these systems, though I will consider exemptions for Australia and New Zealand, possibly Canada. I do not trust any other country to use system legitimately for purposes such as we will use them."

"How about the USA?" asked the Home Secretary. "Most of us consider their legal system to be a horror. This might well save a lot of innocent people from the death penalty."

"I agree," Karen replied. "Do you have suggestion that does not involve full licencing?"

"How about we offer the technology on request?" said the Home Secretary. "But the taking of samples and the generation of images must be done by British qualified personnel with the same safeguards against sample switching."

"I would like to see detailed rules for such use," replied Karen.

"Agreed," said the Prime Minister. "We will develop these and submit them for your approval."

"And there is one more condition before we release technology," said Karen.

The two leaders looked suspicious.

"When you announce use of it, there will be no mention of my name or company name," she said. "I have no doubt that there will be hostility and anger at some stage, possibly violence. I wish that delayed as long as possible."

The Prime nodded. "I agree to that condition, Doctor Petrova and believe it to be a correct one."

The meeting broke up with the same ritual of handshakes which excluded Karen Petrova to her obvious relief.

* * *

The announcement was made a week later on prime time television on the BBC channels and a few selected commercial channels. Garry and Hannah sat before the television set and watched silently as the Prime Minister outlined the new technology and the safeguards which would be implemented in the revised court procedures.

When it was over, Garry got up, switched off the television and put on the Brahms Fourth Symphony before returning to the couch and putting his arm back round Hannah.

"It seems safe enough," she said.

He nuzzled the back of her neck, making her squirm.

"We all think so," he said. "And if Karen's happy, you can bet your life there's not a loophole anywhere."

"But it will only be used for cases of murder and physical violence?"

"Not entirely. The police may ask for reviews of a person's activities in cases of child abuse or others where it may help confirm what happened. But that will need much more care and they won't always prove a crime with absolute certainty."

"I suppose. They didn't mention the company or Karen?"

"Karen thinks there will eventually be public hostility to this technology because of the privacy issues. She wants it to take as long as possible so that there can be public acceptance before we get known as the developers."

Hannah seemed not entirely at ease, leaving Garry concerned at what was disturbing her. She remained distant again for the rest of the evening, seemingly lost in her own thoughts, but at bedtime, she was back to normal and initiated an exceptionally active session of sex that left them both exhausted and happy.

Over the next few days, Garry carefully read every newspaper on his computer, both British and overseas media that discussed the new laws. Mostly, there was considerable interest expressed with support for the fact that in the case of crimes of violence at least, absolute guilt or innocence could now be established. A few editorials expressed concerns about the intrusion into privacy that was now fully enabled and other writers discussed their concerns about just how other countries with fewer concerns about personal freedom than the UK could misuse the technology if they could get hold of it. Garry was relieved that nobody seemed concerned about the source of the developments as everybody seemed to assume that a government laboratory had been the creator.

Blueprints' name never came up.

Chapter 15 - 2018

"That's odd," said a young woman sitting at her screen.

Garry was walking through the area and heard her comment,

"What is it, Kathie?" he asked.

"Come and have a look," she replied with a gesture, still staring at her screen. "Look, Garry, this is a scene that looks quite old. Look at those cars, look at the style of dress."

Garry watched as the scene played itself out for another thirty seconds. Kathie was right, the scene looked like it was set perhaps in the 1960s. The few cars and then a bus were driving on the left, so this was happening most likely in Britain, Australia, New Zealand or perhaps Ireland or South Africa.

"Stop it and start again from the beginning, Kathie," said Garry. She touched a button on the keyboard and the picture began again. There was nothing dramatic about it, just the period setting. People walked by, cars passed on the road, a pair of children walked by in the other direction, nobody seemed to pay any attention to the watcher.

"Who provided this sample?" asked Garry, still not seeing why Kathie had expressed her astonishment.

"Well, that's the thing," Kathie replied, looking at the corner of the screen where the individual's details were displayed. "This came from an Andrew Carter. We took it three years ago when he was just twenty-seven."

"Twenty seven?" Garry now understood. "But that scene, the clothes, the cars, looks more like the sixties. How could this happen?"

"That's the question," she replied. "It doesn't make sense. Andrew was born in 1990."

Garry straightened up and looked around the room. He spotted the man he wanted to see. "Declan!" he called. "Can you watch the main screen? Kathie's switching something there." He spoke more softly to Kathie. "Switch it up there, will you?"

The slender, youthful-looking man nodded and sat back in his seat, looking at the far wall where the enormous main screen hung. He was short, delicately built and looked about sixteen but was actually in his mid-twenties and been awarded his doctorate in genetics just a year ago and hired by Garry within days.

"Declan, you're the car freak!" said Garry. "Have a look at this scene. Can you identify any of those cars? Kathie, play it again."

"What is this, *The Maltese Falcon?*" said Kathie with a laugh, but reset the image.

Declan stared at the scene for a minute. "That's a Ford Anglia a model 105E," he said at last. "It was introduced with that odd styling and that vertical rear window in 1959, so this can't be earlier than that. And that other one is an Austin Healey Sprite, not the bug-eyed Mark I version, so it's a Mark II. That was introduced in about 1961 or 1962, I think. This is interesting! Let me see if there's anything else."

He stared at the screen for a few more moments then pointed. "Hey, wow!" he said. "There's a Ford Corsair! I always loved that space-age design!"

They looked at the image of a sedan driving by, a bright red model with a bonnet that sloped down to a sharply edged crease and rear fins that reminded Garry a little of an American Thunderbird. The way the image stayed in the view suggested that the watcher was following the car as it went by.

"What year is that?" Kathie asked.

"No earlier than 1963, I think," replied Declan.

Abruptly, a woman appeared in view, obviously addressing the watcher. She seemed annoyed and led the observer to the side of the road where another car was parked. A man was standing by the open passenger door, smiling broadly. The woman climbed into the passenger seat and the watcher's viewpoint indicated that he or she, for it was not yet clear which, climbed into the rear seat. But as the viewer's eyes looked down, the image of a yellow and white striped dress filled the view. The image dissolved into the familiar silent hiss.

"A Ford Cortina," said Declan firmly. "A Mark I, looking very new. I'd say this was 1965. Where do these scenes come from?"

"From a man born in 1990," Kathie said softly. "And the viewer is a female. And cars apart, those fashions are pure sixties. Look at those flared jeans, Mary Quant dresses and white go-go boots!"

The three of them looked at each other.

"No possibility of a mistake?" Garry asked.

Kathie shook her head. "I've had a couple of views from the same sample that definitely show a young man's memories."

"Where does Andrew Carter live?" Garry asked.

"Oxford," Kathie said, looking at her screen.

"Call him," said Garry. "If you reach him, ask him to visit us, we'll pay his expenses, of course."

She nodded and picked up the phone.

Three hours later, a youthful, muscular man sat before the screen in the laboratory. He was still showing signs of shock after seeing a view that he remembered as being his graduation ceremony from Birmingham University when he was twenty-two and having had explained to him the technology behind the recordings and the enforced secrecy of the proceedings.

"Now I want you to look at something else," said Garry. "It's another scene we've taken from your DNA, but it's got us seriously puzzled. We're hoping you can explain."

"Okay," said Andrew Carter. "I'll try."

Kathie pushed the button and the screen again displayed the sight of a pavement, cars passing in both directions, the red Ford Corsair that seemed to hold the watcher's attention for a while and then the woman appeared, looking angry.

Garry stole a look at Andrew's face and he was staring raptly at the screen, but the expression also showed puzzlement as Andrew slowly shook his head. And then...

"Good God!" Andrew shouted. Several heads turned to look at the group.

"Stop it there," said Garry and the scene froze at the moment when the man appeared, holding open the car door.

Andrew was staring rigidly at the screen.

"That's my grandfather!" he said, his voice cracking with tension.

"How can you be sure?" asked Garry. "Is he still alive?"

"No," croaked Andrew. "He died when I was a kid, about eleven. But that car! My parents have a framed picture of him standing by that car, it was his first ever new car, a Cortina, a 1965 model. My mother said he was like a dog with two tails for weeks after!"

Garry felt the tension build in him as he recognised something quite incredible was happening.

"So those two are your mother's parents?"

"Yeah, I never knew my grandfather from dad's side, he died when I was still a baby. And now I recognise the woman, that was my grandmother... but they're both so *young!*"

The entire group fell silent. Around the room, everybody slowly became motionless as they sensed something monumental was occurring.

"But I thought you said the DNA recorded *my* life," Andrew said, seeming to breath hard as if he had just run some distance. "I wasn't born then! How could you have this scene?"

He looked around the room, almost as if seeking escape, then turned back to Garry.

"That brief flash of a dress at the end, was that my mother's viewpoint as she got in the car?"

Garry nodded. "We think it must be. Is there any chance you could talk to her and verify that?" Garry was struggling to control his breathing also as he tried to come to terms with what he had seen and the implications of it all.

"She lives quite near here," Andrew replied. "I'm pretty sure she's at home today. Can I use your phone?"

Garry nodded and Andrew reached for the phone by the computer monitor, dialled a number and waited a few seconds.

"Hi, Mum!" he said. "How are you doing?"

A female voice carried to Garry's ears but too soft for him to make out the words.

"Mum, something strange has happened and I need to ask you a couple of questions."

Even though the words were indecipherable, Garry heard the rising pitch of curiosity in the other woman's voice.

"No, not now," said Andrew. "I'll try and explain later. But that picture of granddad's new car you keep in the lounge, can you remember when he got that?"

Garry heard the laugh and a few words. Andrew put his hand over the speaker and said, "She does! She was twelve years old."

He took his hand away. "Mum, can you remember a dress you had then? It was a yellow and white striped thing."

More squeaks from the phone. These were so loud that Andrew moved the phone away from his ear and Garry heard the woman say quite clearly, "Andy, how could you possibly know about that dress? This is crazy!"

"Yes, mum, I know, this is very weird indeed, but I'll call you later and try and explain. But did you have such a dress?"

A second or two later and Andrew looked at Garry. "She did. She gave it to the Salvation Army a year later as she grew out of it." He turned back to the phone. "Thanks, Mum, I'll call you this evening."

Softly, in deep thought, he replaced the telephone. "What the hell's going on?" he asked.

"Something absolutely crazy," said Garry. "And not anything we ever expected. But it looks like you have at least one parent's memories as well as your own."

Andrew stared at him. "Holy shit!" he whispered.

"Exactly," said Garry. "Andrew, we've already had you sign an Official Secrets form. But this new discovery makes it even more essential that you do not reveal anything about what you have just seen. Somehow, you must avoid revealing to your mother what you just saw. I suggest you tell her that a historical society had stumbled across some photographs of the era and was looking for confirmation of what they had discovered."

Andrew looked worried. "I'm not sure I can do that. You don't know my mother."

"Andrew, you have to. Believe me, this development scares the hell out of me when I think of what it may lead to and it may even put lives at risk. Promise me you'll keep this away from anyone else."

Andrew seemed to come to a decision. "I promise," he said firmly, looking Garry straight in the eye.

There was little Garry could do but release Andrew to return home, pay his expenses for the travel and pray for Andrew's commitment to hold firm.

He had other questions on his mind.

* * *

"How did you find yourself on that track?"

He sat next to Kathie at her workstation, sipping at a cup of coffee. The whole office was buzzing with excitement at the new development and everybody was watching the conversation with intense interest.

"I was going through Andrew's sample," she said. "I'm not sure what happened... Ah! Yes, I think I decided to go back to his early childhood, see how far I could go and I was looking at his baby days, about six months old. And then it just happened! Up came this weird view from his mother's life we've been looking at."

"Show me," said Garry. "Put it up on the main display. Everybody, watch the main screen, please."

Attention turned to the huge monitor at the back of the room. It showed the section of the DNA molecule containing the thread that was now known to be the index to the life history of a person and a small inset showed the thin line of that thread.

"I enlarged the view of the thread," said Kathie, doing the same with the display and the thin line became a slightly thicker line showing bumps and indentations. As she did, the rest of the monitor was filled with an image of a young couple talking. The viewpoint was that of a child resting in the woman's lap.

"Did you get the sound?" asked Garry.

"I didn't have this scene," said Kathie. "This is a bit later than what I was looking at, but yes, I had the sound..."

She moved the cursor and a moment later the sounds of the young couple's conversation came through the speakers. Garry listened for a few moments, but the conversation was simply a chat about the mother telling her husband about her day at home.

"Anyway, I went back a bit...." said Kathie.

She concentrated on the thread of the index and slowly the focal point of the image moved to the left until the absolute beginning of the thread could be seen near the edge of the inset image.

"And then it jumped!" Kathie said. "I don't remember...."

"Hey, Garry, look!" shouted Avram in some excitement. "Look! Right on the edge of the index thread! Two dots! What are they?"

"Good grief! Now I remember, Avram! I just saw those dots and that's when it happened!"

"Concentrate on one of those dots," said Garry, almost breathless as he sensed incredible developments.

A second later, the image on the screen changed. It showed a group of schoolgirls, perhaps twelve or thirteen years old, dressed in old-fashioned blue gymslips. The sound was a meld of young girls shouting and talking and the viewer seemed to be one of them, in the middle of the group. A bell rang in the distance and the group fell quiet. Another woman's voice was heard, saying, "All right girls, file quietly into the classroom."

The viewer switched to this voice source and showed a young woman in a neat, conservative skirt and blouse. As if taken from a shoulder-held camera, the view showed the group walking through a large doorway into a dark, wide corridor and into a room lined with desks. The images faded.

"That's Andrew's mother, I'll bet," said one of the team.

"Those dots – they must point to a thread of the parents," said Avram. "Kathie, can you go back to the main sample again?"

"And see if the other dot shows anything different," said Kathie with a nod and a smile of excitement on her lips.

A few moments passed as the silent group watched the process. The index thread reappeared and then the centre of the image moved to left under Kathie's so-far not understood control. As it reached the beginning, the two dots reappeared.

"I used the upper one before," murmured Kathie, more to herself. "Let's see what happens...."

The image on the screen changed. At first, the watchers had difficulty in understanding what they were seeing. The screen was filled with blue, a bright, clear light blue and then the person looking at the scene lowered his eyes a little and mountains appeared in the distance, further down and a beautiful lake filled the screen. The viewer was obviously high up, because the lake stretched far to the right into the distance, but ended quite nearby on the left. Lines of yellow at various places showed beaches and almost vertically below, a half-moon of land curved into the lake, dotted round the water's edge with little coloured shapes, looking like a child's cartoon of a horseshoe.

"That's a camping ground," said Avram. "Those are tents. Whoever this is, it's from quite high up."

"It's Coniston Water in the Lake District!" exclaimed Penny. "My parents used to take me there for our summer holidays. They're up on Old Man Mountain! I've stood right where they're standing now!"

The view suddenly changed as the watcher jumped up and began running. As he did, his legs became visible, wearing shorts and running shoes and he ran towards a couple sitting on the grass looking out at the spectacular view. They laughed at him.

"Where do you get the energy, Jonno?" said the male.

"Isn't this fantastic?" came the reply, a young boy's voice.

"Incredible," said the woman.

The screen went blank and there was a collective sigh from the room.

"Good grief!" exclaimed Kathie. "We've got the parents' memories also. How on earth could that happen?"

"I'll lay you any odds you want," said Declan, the man who had identified the cars in the first views from Andrew's mother's memories. "I'll bet that every scene taken from somebody's parent's memories will end the same way, with the parents having sex. If not that, then it could be with the father donating sperm for artificial insemination and the mother being treated with that sperm to become pregnant."

"Oh my!" said Kathie. "You mean a person's memories are transmitted at the moment of conception?"

That's my guess," said Declan.

"And a pretty good one," added Garry.

"Both mother and father!" said Kathie in wonder. "This is incredible! But does that mean...? she said, almost jumping up and down with excitement. "Do the parents have the memories of THEIR parents as well?"

"Kathie, check that out," said Garry softly. He was having trouble breathing as the full implications of the day's discoveries were hitting him.

Kathie turned to her keyboard. The index track for Andrew's father was still on the screen and she concentrated on moving the timeline back to the beginning of the index. She stopped with a sigh, and Garry could see her hands trembling. The reason was obvious.

There were two dots at the very beginning of the track.

"Andrew's grandparents on his father's side," whispered Kathie.

The room was silent as everybody absorbed the implications of this discovery in their own way.

It was Avram who broke the silence with the question they were all asking.

"How far back does this go?" he asked.

Chapter 16

"Garry, this goes further than I ever dreamed possible," said Karen Petrova. She sat in the armchair of Garry's office, sipping carefully at the glass of tea that had been taken from the silver samovar kept especially for this purpose. She had driven from London as soon as Garry had told her of the momentous discovery.

"Nobody could have anticipated this," said Garry from the opposite side of the coffee table. "This is incredible, bizarre, wonderful..."

"And frightening," finished off Karen.

Garry was startled. Of all images he had ever had of the extraordinary woman before him, being frightened was never one of them.

"Why so?"

She sipped thoughtfully and Garry waited patiently, wondering just what was going on in the superb mind of the woman across from him.

"How far back have you gone?" she asked.

"Almost all just to great-grandparents. Declan's theory seems proven. At the time of procreation the memories of both mother and father are added to the DNA of the child or children. We've so far been doing a lot of pure historical research, listening to accents from a century or more before, seeing fashions and lifestyles, seeing how parents of those ages treated their children, and so on. This is a gold mine for historians, especially social historians. My researchers are having a wonderful time with this. Several have taken their own DNA and begun looking at their grandparents' lives, because they know so little about them."

"And are all your people pleased with what they found?"

Garry sat back. "No, not all of them, not all the time. One woman found that her grandparents had never married and that her grandmother had been raped by a thug from Manchester. One found that his grandfather had committed murder, killing a man and his son in a robbery attempt. And Declan found that his grandfather, a man he had always believed had been a World War II Battle of Britain pilot had been a clerk in an army depot in Birmingham. It upset him no end."

"And did you indicate that some people have gone further than great grandparents?"

"Only Declan. He's gone back several more generations. The problem came when he couldn't understand a word of what was being said in any of the scenes."

Karen placed her glass on the table and Garry stood up, refilled it at the samovar, added a single cube of sugar and returned the glass to her.

"History is so often different from what victors say," she said, slowly stirring the glass with the long silver spoon. "These are little examples but they still hurt people. Some may hurt far worse. What if research tore down major myths in country's history?"

"Are you suggesting we shouldn't follow this line of research?" Garry was astonished. He'd never see Karen so disturbed.

She shook her head, staring hard at her glass of tea. After a few moments, she spoke.

"I am scientist," she said. "All my life I have followed one rule of science that facts are all that matter, that truth is there to be discovered. Debate has always existed about atomic bomb, whether we should have developed it. But that led to atomic energy. Uranium was there, mankind would discover it."

Garry was uncertain where she was taking this argument, so he sat still and listened.

"Every new discovery can be used for good or bad," Karen continued, speaking softly. Garry was sure she was really thinking aloud, getting her ideas in order rather than explaining anything to him. He waited.

"This thing we have discovered, it will cause pain and distress. But never in my life will I prevent research into something for that reason, because what we have discovered will reveal difficult facts."

She looked up at Garry as if coming out of a private place and seeing him waiting.

"We will continue our work, Garry. But for now, we restrict it to trained professionals and we do not inform government."

"So how are we going to do it?"

"We will continue work of finding what else DNA holds. But we will now shift emphasis to being historical research unit."

Garry felt uncertain. "Our people are not historians, Karen."

"Historians I will find, Garry. But they will need all help possible to research data."

"I worry that some of the people may feel they have been superseded, no longer important. I'd hate to lose any of this remarkable group."

"Are there any fields of study that have come up that your people might want to work on?"

"Actually, yes," said Garry. "The whole issue of how we control the movement along the index track. Is this telepathy or is it some field of quantum theory?" As he spoke, he sensed the excitement of new fields to conquer.

Karen smiled her brilliant, crimson smile.

"My dear Garry, you have a completely free hand. Let your people do whatever they want. But they must be available to help new group we will establish here. Set up separate area for perhaps ten people, all equipment they need. And if anybody from company wishes to leave, they can have one million pounds as leaving payment."

"One million...? Karen, are you serious?"

"Garry, they have made come true dream that Hector and I had many years ago. There is no sum that could pay them what that is worth."

Garry took a deep breath. "Well, okay! Now who is this new group that you mentioned?"

She picked up her handbag and extracted the car keys. "I will call you when I have details and we will meet here again."

She stood up and Garry followed suit.

"Drive carefully, Madam."

She smiled her Cheshire Cat smile.

"Don't be silly, Garry. I am superb driver, as you know so well."

She walked out, leaving Garry stunned and shaken by the events of the day but still laughing at her parting words.

Chapter 17

Things happened quickly. Garry had no sooner set out a separate work area with ten desks, a complete scanning system at each and erected temporary walls to enclose the new area than Karen called him to prepare for a meeting in two days time.

Those days up till then hadn't been quiet. Garry called a mass meeting of all twenty of the staff and they gathered in the dining room with drinks and various foodstuffs to fill a battalion.

"You have all done astounding work," Garry began. "As Karen said, you have made an old dream of hers and her late husband's come true, in fact you have far exceeded her expectations because you have opened up astonishing capabilities for research into history and linguistics."

Kathie and several others exchanged worried looks.

"That sounds like the ending of a process," she said. "Garry, does this mean that we're closing down?"

"No, it does not," said Garry firmly. "But we are changing direction. However, we still need expert handling of DNA and there's no evidence that we have finished finding out what there is in the molecules. So here's what is happening."

He raised a hand to silence the wave of murmurs that ran round the room.

"First thing, a really nice bonus for everybody as a thank you from Karen. Every one of you will get a fifty thousand pound gift this month."

Stunned silence greeted his words and then it was broken by whistles and applause from everybody and happy smiling faces shone from all quarters.

"So now let me tell you how this group is changing," Garry continued when the noise had died. "As you've seen there's a new area off to one side and that's where some top level researchers are going to be placed. Karen said she'll be arranging for some historians to work and while they will be reviewing everything they can find, it will need you all to initially train them in how to find the different index threads and then assist them in any way they need. Meanwhile, you will have your own research projects, which as you know consist of pretty well anything at all you want to do."

He sat back to let them review this information as they wished and he looked around the room as several discussion groups worked on the subject. After ten minutes, he called for their attention again.

"One more thing, and this will certainly amaze you all. I'm sure that some of you may decide that this new structure is not for you. If so, here's the deal. If you choose to leave, you will get a farewell bonus of... wait for it... one million pounds."

If the reaction to the news of the earlier bonus had been profound, this one was almost cataclysmic. Garry looked around and saw silent faces, shocked into disbelief.

"A million pounds?" was the first spoken reaction, a whisper from Declan.

"A million pounds," said Garry with a smile. "Karen is a very generous woman and she knows how to treat people who have helped her."

There was another extended silence before Penny spoke.

"I don't know about anyone else, but I've had more fun since I came here than I ever thought possible. To have been part of these discoveries is the greatest thrill that I could have dreamed of in several centuries. So while it's possible we may not find anything this astounding in our own work, the thought of being part of what these new people will discover.. well, it's just impossible to miss. So bugger the million quid, I'm staying!"

The meeting lost all cohesion as people began to talk excitedly about the new direction that Blueprints was taking and Garry sensed that Penny's words had struck a chord with all of them.

Quietly, he rose and walked out, wondering if any of them would take up Karen's offer.

* * *

Two days later, he watched from his window as an elderly Mark II Jaguar parked in front of the building. A tall, black-haired man, Garry estimated in his forties climbed out of the left-hand rear door, opened the front passenger door and allowed Karen to exit with her usual graceful movement. She was dressed in her normal style, an elegant blue dress, matching shoes and handbag and her black hair was in a ponytail. From the driver's seat emerged a medium height woman in her fifties, looking very trim and fit, dressed in a smart trouser-suit with a white shirt.

Garry stood up and waited to greet them as they came into his office.

"Helene McCauley, professor of European and Middle East Studies," said the trim woman with a pleasant smile.

"And Gregory Ball, professor in Old English, Norse and Anglo-Saxon languages," said the black-haired man.

Garry felt a little over-whelmed.

"From Cambridge University, I assume?"

Both nodded. "Karen absolutely insisted we come and talk to you about working on some incredible discoveries you have made," said Helene McCauley. "She hasn't told us what they are yet, so I'm hoping you'll give us the details now."

"And how could we resist a request from Doctor Karen Petrova?" added Gregory Ball.

Garry felt some discomfort about the whole thing. He tried to work out why and put it down to the obvious reason that he was losing control of the entire operation. These two academics would be doing work that he could not control and would essentially be simply using his staff as assistants.

"And this is being funded by the University?" he asked. "I have to ask because this work is being kept a closely guarded secret, not even the government knows the full extent of what we do. We're worried about the anxiety and fears that might arise if people knew what we were doing."

Karen smiled. "Garry dear, I have just given University ten million pounds. And this project is separate, I am funding all salaries and costs for time to do this work."

"You can do this?" asked Garry. "You can simply hire senior University personnel for our project?"

"It's all above board," said Karen. "Work is continuation of what they already do, but with additional, technical resources that only we can provide."

Garry was unconvinced. "How many people do you plan on involving with the project? Because the more we have, the less likely is it to remain secret for long."

Helene seemed to sense his worry and discomfort.

"It will depend on just what areas we work in," she said. "But it's not a coincidence that my field includes Middle East Studies. That's where I shall be concentrating and I will probably need three or four researchers as we get further into the projects. And while Gregory specialises in Northern European languages, we will almost certainly need researchers in some Middle East languages."

"But you don't know what it is we are doing here?" asked Garry.

"We don't," agreed Helene. "Karen has implied that it's quite earth-shaking and will give us a massive boost to our work, but so far, she's said nothing. I'm assuming it's related to being able to read images in DNA since that has been the big development in your company, but beyond that, no, we're in the dark."

Garry looked at Karen.

"Madam?" he said, asking the obvious question.

She smiled. "Tell them everything, Garry."

Garry took a deep breath.

"As you know, as it's now public knowledge, we have found that a person's DNA contains a complete image record of every second of a person's life from birth up to the moment at which the sample is taken and we can now access that record and display it."

Helene nodded. "As soon will be the standard practice for court trials in some cases," she said.

"But what we discovered," continued Garry, "is that the DNA also contains the same memory records of every direct ancestor from their birth up to the moment at which they created their children."

"Good God!" exclaimed Gregory Ball.

"How far..." Helene's voice was a croak. She sipped at her coffee. "How far back?"

"We don't know," said Garry. "We've gone back three or four generations with a couple of people, but that's it so far."

"Now I know why Karen has called us in," said Helene, a little breathless from the shock. "We can go back and look at *everything!*"

"We would need to do some sophisticated statistical research," said Gregory, his face now alive with excitement. "We would need to know just how many samples we would need to take in specific areas to be able to look back to particular times and locations. But this is why you'll need my group so we can actually hear languages as they were spoken by contemporary people. Imagine hearing Latin or old Norse spoken as living languages!"

"And Aramaic," said Helene thoughtfully.

Garry looked at her. It seemed to him that she had something specific in mind, but he didn't feel he would get an answer if he asked her directly.

"So just what is it that you will need my team to do?" He was unable to hide his concerns and anxiety over the loss of control and the others seemed to sense it.

"Initially, show us how to use the scanners," said Helene. "And I have no doubts it will take a lot of work before we have the skills in reading back through ancestors' time lines, so I really do see your researchers as working closely with us."

"And will you keep us fully informed as to what you are finding?" asked Garry. "My people all have doctorates, they are highly trained researchers with inquisitive minds and while history is not their subject, they will want to play a full role in this work and see what you discover."

Helene smiled in sympathy. "I think we understand. I promise you that all your staff will be invited to every group review meeting and be fully briefed on everything we do."

Still not completely comfortable, Garry at least felt more confident that his work was not over.

Chapter 18

Garry need not have worried about the enthusiasm for the new work displayed by his researchers. Nor was there any need to worry about any of them leaving for the million pound bonus. Not one resignation was received. Although there was mostly silence in the main area as his people concentrated on their work, at breaks and lunchtime, the air was alive with chatter about the research being carried on in the new area.

Most of his staff put in several hours a day assisting the new history and language researchers become familiar with the scanning systems so there was general awareness of everything that was going on. But in their own work areas, some were concentrating on the cause of the apparent telepathic control of the time index and some devoted much time and thought to the question of just how so much data could be stored in small spaces. The more philosophically inclined spent time thinking about just why the human body had this capability.

After a while, Garry realised he could just leave them all to whatever they wanted to work on and he had no fears that any of them would just slack off. He had a perfect research team with perfect academic freedom and they needed no supervision.

Over a break in the restaurant one day, he was joined by Gregory Ball, the professor of languages.

"How's it going?" asked Garry as a conversation opener.

Gregory concentrated over swirling his spaghetti Bolognese into a spoon with a fork and carefully lifted it to his mouth. Garry waited patiently, knowing that many academics thought carefully before replying to some questions. At last, Gregory smiled.

"This is Research Heaven, Garry," he said. "I haven't gone back all that far yet, but I've already heard English, German and Russian spoken by people from a couple of centuries ago and I had absolutely no idea of how they sounded until now. Some of the changes have stunned me and I can't wait until we can come out into the open with this and show the world how dialects have changed in ways we had no concept of."

"Good grief, how many languages do you speak?" asked Garry in amusement and admiration.

Gregory speared a meatball and demolished it while he seemed to be counting. "Er.. Old English, Old Norse, Anglo-Saxon, well let's say I can *read* them, and I hope I get to be able to speak them fluently when we've finished, then Russian, German, Serbo-Croat and Italian."

"I'm impressed!" said Garry. "All learned at university?"

"Russian mother, Italian father, so I had those from childhood. Picked up the rest at school and university, I just seem to have this knack with languages."

"At Cambridge?"

"Yes, when I wasn't playing football!" Gregory laughed. "I even got a Blue for that!"

"You played for Cambridge? Now I am even more impressed! So what are you working on now?"

"So far, I've been grazing," said the professor. "Your brilliant people have been showing me how to find the ancestors' time lines and I've been leaping around to get some idea of what's out there."

"And what have you found?"

"Lots of evidence of population migration!" Gregory laughed out loud. "I've had samples from good, middle-class English people and found that four or five generations ago, their ancestors were in Germany, or Belgium or Russia or anywhere. The sample donors probably had no idea at all of any of this."

"So are you going to start digging into anything specific?"

"Still a matter of finding my way around. One problem is the expansion of samples. Take one person's DNA, there are two parents, four grandparents, eight great grandparents, sixteen of the next generation and it keeps on doubling. There's just no way of knowing where one can end up, not with the sort of population migrations of the last hundred years or so in Europe, anyway."

"Will it stabilise as you go back further?" asked Garry, intrigued by the problem.

"Almost certainly. The thing we're looking at is the number of samples we need to take from different areas before we can go back with any certainty of being in a particular region for a long period. This is assuming that the DNA does actually hold every preceding generation or just stops after maybe five hundred years or so. We've got the statisticians and operations research people working on that."

Gregory finished off his spaghetti and wiped his lips.

"Hey, I've got an idea!" he said. "I was planning a deep dive this afternoon, take a sample, follow it back for maybe ten or twelve generations and just see what I get. Why don't you come along and watch? I can guarantee it will be interesting!"

Garry felt excited by the idea. He hadn't as yet ventured into the new research area and this seemed like a good time.

"I'd really like that," he said. "Right now?"

"Right now," said Gregory and stood up.

"Okay, let's see... this sample is from a woman called Angela Jensen," said Gregory. "Born in Leicester, her parents were from Lincoln, she doesn't really know where her grandparents originated."

He flicked on the scanner and fine-tuned it to the familiar image of the tiny spiral coil that contained the images of Angela's life record.

"And so we go to the index....." Gregory seemed to be talking more to himself as he concentrated on the task. "And there we have it. So, by this process that we still cannot comprehend but has us guessing furiously, I can go to the base of the thread, see the two dots that represent her parents' lives..... select one... extract it and lay it out.... and again, go to the base." As he spoke, he also wrote down in a notepad exactly what he was doing, which thread he was taking and which dot he selected. He turned his head and saw Garry watching him.

"Standard research process!" he said. "Document everything! After all, I may want to get back to this timeline if something interesting shows up."

Garry watched, fascinated as always as he saw the astounding process of looking far back into people's lives.

Gregory selected another dot, straightened out the coil and again went to the base. Ten more times he did this and finally looked up at Garry.

"And so," he said. "We have a life in images and sound before us, I have no idea who, no idea where and no idea when, except that it will be a few hundred years ago. Shall we have a look?"

"Let's," said Garry, almost breathless with excitement.

"I'm focusing on a little way along the index," murmured Gregory. "I hope the person is maybe a teenager, a young adult..."

The screen flicked into a new image. The two men stared. The view was bleak, stony and mountains appeared near, just a few miles away. The subject of the image, not yet evident if male or female, was walking along rough ground with tufts of grass making the going difficult. Just ahead was an adult male, dressed in rough fabrics, a thick belt and a sword hanging from it. He was carrying a large object, but what it was was unclear.

The walkers reached a patch of ground in which a small pit had been dug. The man gently laid the burden down by the side of the pit and stood upright.

"I think you were right," said Garry. "Our subject seems a bit shorter than this individual, perhaps a teenager or even younger?"

Gregory didn't reply, he was clearly fascinated by the scene.

Sounds came from the speakers, a human, male voice, completely unintelligible to Garry, but the effect on Gregory was severe.

"Good God!" he exclaimed, his throat tight with shock. "That's Kven! This is Norway!"

Garry sat still, in some awe at the shock this had caused the other man. Carefully, Gregory wound the image back by the control of his thoughts and replayed the scene. The words came out again.

"Say goodbye to your mother, boy," said Gregory slowly. He took a deep breath. "Our subject is a young boy, that bundle is a dead woman."

He fell silent again as the boy approached the corpse and carefully removed the covering from her face. Her face seemed young, pale, but was disfigured by black swellings on her cheeks, ears and lips.

The man's voice came over the speakers again. Garry could now hear a Germanic tone to it, but with sounds that he couldn't place.

"The plague has taken her as it has taken almost all our people," translated Gregory, almost breathless. "That's the Black Death. Garry, this is Norway about 1350 when the disease took nearly sixty percent of Europe."

"What's Kven?" asked Garry softly.

"A dialect spoken mostly in north-east Norway, around the Tromso and Finnmark areas," replied Gregory. "It was more Finnish than Old Norse. Do you realise, Garry, we are the only people in the world who have heard that language spoken?"

Garry was still transfixed by the image on the screen. It appeared that the boy was covering up his mother's face then he moved to her feet and his father took her shoulders and carefully lowered her into the grave. The image flickered a second as the record moved from one section to the next then stabilised again. The man stood up and stared at his son.

"Oh Lord, he's got it," murmured Gregory. "Look at his face and neck."

He was right, the ugly pustules showed clearly. The man spoke again.

"Now you must go," translated Gregory. "I have it too. Leave me here to die with your mother."

The boy spoke, but Gregory shook his head. "I didn't get that," he whispered, clearly badly affected by the tragedy before them.

Garry was equally saddened. "What will you do now?" he asked.

"Follow this boy's life," replied Gregory. "I'll jump a week at a time, see where he ends up, if I can recognise the scene. It could be Iceland, maybe Scotland, the Faroes, or he may just stay in Norway. That will answer a few questions for me. But hearing spoken Kven! I can hardly believe it!"

"I see what you mean by this being Research Heaven," said Garry, feeling some envy at what the man had just experienced and the depth of emotion he was clearly feeling at the magnitude of the discovery.

He walked quietly from the room and returned to his own desk, quite shaken by the events and the realisation of the process he and his team had initiated.

For the next few weeks, life became routine for the team at Blueprints. Much of Garry's work became what he termed, "Management by Walking Around," making sure that he talked to all his staff and heard their ideas and any complaints and brewing problems. There seemed to be little in the way of problems. Being trained, disciplined researchers themselves, all his staff found themselves enthralled by what the historians and linguists were discovering and some of them took on the additional tasks of assisting the new team search through the histories of the DNA samples for anything that might be of value. So there were numerous occasions when they would call one of the linguists or historians over to their own monitors if they thought they had something interesting, and often they did.

The scene that Kathie stumbled on left Garry with a sick sense of dismay and a severe moral problem. She was white-faced when she walked into his office and sat in the seat by the coffee table without speaking for a few moments, her hands trembling slightly.

"This is dangerous," she said.

Gary waited and poured her a cup of coffee from the machine he kept in his office at all times.

"You know that the University people have been talking informally to their friends and colleagues around the world and obtaining samples of all sorts?" she said at last.

"Of course," he replied and placed the coffee before her. She stared at it intently as if looking for guidance.

"I've got a few from the Harvard people," she continued. "They're all blind studies, we don't know the identities except that they are all people from the Boston, Dallas and Chicago populations."

She sipped carefully from her coffee, looking thoughtful. "I've got two separate views of something and they scare the hell out of me and I don't know what to do."

"Want to show me?"

"Of course, I must, but can we do it here in your office rather than out there? I don't want to put anyone else at risk."

Garry's nose for danger began twitching. He moved another seat to behind his desk moved his own to one side, switching on the scanner he'd had installed in his own work space. Kathie left her cup on the table and took the seat, keying in the details of the sample, which like all of them were stored in the main file system.

"Both these scenes came from the grandparents of the donors," she said. "So I suspect both were very young when they saw these episodes."

The screen came to life with a huge crowd scene looking down a slight slope to a wide road about a hundred metres away. A motorcade was moving at walking pace toward the observer, a huge black open limousine, several police motorcycles and several other men on foot walking alongside the limo. It was a very familiar scene, Garry had seen videos of it many times.

"The Kennedy assassination in Dallas," he murmured. "Kathie, what have you got here?"

"Watch," she whispered. The viewpoint of the person who had supplied the DNA sample moved around the crowd and back to the green slopes behind. Garry heard the shots fired in the distance and just as the watcher turned his head, there was a glimpse of a man crouched behind the bushes on what Garry recognised as the infamous "grassy knoll." The noise level of the hysteria as the awful scene in the limousine was played out rose sharply, but the watcher was not focused on that but on the scene behind him. The man he had seen was busily packing something into a bag then he stood up and walked away, head down, his right arm carrying a weighty object. He disappeared as the watcher turned back to the assassination and the familiar chaos.

"I've got a second sample showing the same thing," said Kathie and keyed in another extraction command. The same scene started again but from the perspective of somebody a bit further away and to one side of the first watcher. The same man could be seen on the knoll, but this time the object he was carrying was clearer, looking like a trombone case, a sports bag... or a gun case.

"The second gunman," said Garry hoarsely. "The second gunman that the Warren Commission always denied existing but several people claimed to have seen."

"This denies all the official conclusions," said Kathie, her face still pale. "It looks like there really was a conspiracy, it wasn't just that one man in the book repository like all the people said could never have done it alone. Garry, what do we do with this?"

"Nothing yet. This technology isn't out in the open, if we tried showing that recording, they'd just say it was created with special effects and deny it completely. It could cause a nasty international incident for the British government and might set off some very ugly repercussions with the people who don't want it known."

"We'd better make sure nobody else sees it."

"You're right. Kathie, take those two samples out of storage and give them to me. I'll put them in a bank vault well away from here and we'll forget about it until circumstances change."

"It's covering up a crime," she whispered.

"A bloody dreadful crime, I agree. But until we get this technology fully accepted around the world, the evidence isn't worth anything. Maybe one day we can produce it. But right now, it's not conclusive, it's not legitimate and not acceptable in any court of law."

She nodded, stood up and walked out of the office, returning a few minutes later with the DNA samples in their secure plastic containers. Garry immediately left and headed into town where he placed the objects in the company's secure vaults. Only after he had left the bank did he feel he could breathe easily again, frightened by the implications of what he had seen. He wondered about telling Karen and decided not to extend the risk to anyone. He didn't tell Hannah, either.

Much excitement ensued when Declan found the monitor filled by a savage, bloody battle between men in armour with swords and axes. He switched it up to the main monitor and everybody stared in horrified fascination at the scene of carnage as men hacked at each other in close quarters amid the screams of pain and triumph.

Garry picked up the phone and called Helene's internal number.

"Who's your medieval historian?" he asked.

"Roger Betts. He's right here. You need him?"

"Right away," he said and replaced the phone. A few moments later, a middle-aged, stocky man wearing a bright yellow sweater and black jeans walked into the main area and stared at the monitor. He visibly flinched as the scene showed an armoured man strike a soldier in the middle of the helmet with a large, double-bladed axe, splitting the man's head in two, down to the neck. Blood and brains erupted, some of it into the face of the killer who rapidly wiped it away and continued hacking at the next man in front of him.

"Good God almighty!" said the man in the yellow sweater, looking ill.

"What is it?" asked Garry, struggling not to gag. Several of the researchers had put their heads on their desks, unable to watch the appalling sight.

"Hang on," said the other. "Let's see if I can see any banners. I'm Roger Betts," he added.

"Glad to see you," said Garry. "Is this what combat was like?"

"Pretty well," replied Betts, not taking his eyes off the monitor.

For a few moments, the only sound was the roar of battle from the screen, a horrible mix of screams from both men and horses and an overall background roar of what seemed like hundreds, possibly thousands of men shouting battle cries.

"It's Bosworth!" shouted Roger Betts. "My God, that's the battle of Bosworth! Can you stop the picture?"

Obediently, Declan put the image on pause and the scene froze. A short distance away, a small group of horsemen could be seen, one of them holding a long banner, an elongated triangle. Garry stared, but was uncertain what the details were in the riot of colour.

"See the red cross on a white background at the broad end of the banner?" said Roger, his face alive with excitement. "That's the Cross of England. Next to that is a red dragon, that's the Welsh Dragon. This is the banner of Henry Tudor who became Henry VII of England after this battle. This was the end of the Wars of the Roses, this is August 22nd, 1485!"

"So is that Henry holding the banner?" asked Declan.

"No, that's almost certainly Henry's standard-bearer, Sir William Brandon. If I'm right, we're going to see something astounding very soon."

"Who's the watcher? Can you tell?" asked Garry."

"One of Henry's knights, that's certain," Betts said. "The fact that he's close to Henry without being attacked says he must be on the Lancastrian side. And he's on a horse, which is why these scenes come from a slightly elevated position. Can you resume the picture?"

Immediately, there was violent movement off to the left and a group of knights on horseback rode furiously into view. One of them was carrying a banner, also triangular.

"Look at that!" shouted Betts in huge excitement. "That banner! The Cross of England again, but the boar! That's the banner of Richard III! He's leading an attack directly on Henry, hoping to end the battle there and then. And that's the King right next to the standard-bearer! This is *incredible!*"

Everybody was watching now, even those who had hidden their eyes from the bloody slaughter had raised them and were staring at one of the pivotal scenes in English history. The face of the man in armour next to the standard-bearer couldn't be seen under the visor but a thin band of gold circled his helmet. This was Richard III, King of England. He drove his horse directly into the group surrounding Henry Tudor and one massive blow from his sword drove through the head of the bearer of the standard and he fell from his horse.

"That man, that's Sir William Brandon, Henry's standard-bearer," said Betts.

The scene became nearly impossible to see from then on, as the watcher obviously lowered his own visor and moved in to protect Henry Tudor and the scene was utter confusion for a few moments.

"Richard got almost within sword-reach of Henry," said Roger. "But Henry's body-guards surrounded him and drove him away, back into the marsh lands close by. Watch – this is the end coming up."

From the right, another large force of soldiers led by knights on horseback appeared and joined in the attack on the King's force.

"Sir William Stanley," said Roger. "One of the worst opportunists of all time. He had kept his 6,000 men out of the battle until he could see what was the best side to take. Now that Richard has obviously failed to kill Henry, he's joined in on the Lancastrian side and that decides the battle and the war. Had he come in on Richard's side, English history and much of the world's would have been quite different without the Tudor dynasty."

The watcher's visor was lifted as he and several other knights began forcing King Richard further and further away from Henry. The King's guards were being slaughtered and the banner-bearer received an appalling blow with an axe that almost separated his left leg from his body. Murmurs of horror ran through the room and they doubled as another axe blow did the same to the other leg. The man fell from his horse, still holding the banner of the Cross of England and the symbol of the wild boar.

"Sir Percival Thirwell," said Roger. "A remarkable warrior."

But now, the King was surrounded and attacked like a wounded deer being mobbed by a flock of wolves. They could just see a raised arm holding a weapon that looked like a long-handled axe and it descended on the King's head with an audible crash.

"The King is dead," said Roger clearly. "Long live the first Tudor monarch, King Henry VII."

The attackers now stood silently around the body of Richard III. The gold circle round the king's helmet had come adrift and was lying in the muddy water of the marsh. One of the foot soldiers picked it up and handed it to the man whose vision had recorded this scene. He turned away and rode back to the group in the distance.

"Stop it there for now," said Garry. "I think we're all overwhelmed by what we've seen."

"You can record all that?" asked Roger.

"Of course," said Garry. "What happened next?"

"Henry Tudor is crowned King Henry VII within a few hours in a little village called Stoke Golding," said Roger. "That gold circle is used as the crown. I'm sure that if you return to this recording, you'll see that equally historic scene."

The room was silent. Everybody seemed quite drained of emotion at the horrors they had witnessed and the fact that this was a scene that had changed English history.

"Just imagine if Stanley had supported the King and defeated Henry," said Betts as he moved to the door. "With his six thousand men, that would have been certain. Then no Henry VIII, no split with the Catholic Church, no Queen Elizabeth I, everything would have been different. We have just witnessed a scene that changed world history. Garry, will you arrange to have that scene recorded for me?"

He waved and walked out.

The organisation fell into a routine, as much as the extraordinary findings almost every day could be called routine. One problem for the University researchers was that they had no way of searching for specific times and places. Population movements had been so extensive in the last two centuries that starting with the DNA of an English resident and going back through even three or four generations of ancestors could result in scenes from almost anywhere in the world with no certainty of the age of those scenes.

The linguists were fairly happy with that. Most of them deliberately went back many generations at random, just as Gregory Hall had done when Garry saw the tragic scene from Medieval Norway and the impact of the Black Death. The excitement of hearing Anglo-Saxon, Old Norse, old French and other languages from centuries before was overwhelming for them, just as the discovery of Kven as spoken in an isolated part of Norway had been for Gregory.

Much of what was seen was quite mundane, but for the fact that it was centuries old. But for historians, seeing everyday life in small towns around the world was exhilarating and hugely educational. Everything was recorded and the researchers were all excited and also frustrated at the prospects of publishing paper after paper once the technology was known and accepted, but for that they had to wait.

Garry's own team split their time between further examination of the properties of DNA molecules and some forays into more recent history and it was one of these that gave Garry the second scare and moral problem, one that was closely related to the first.

Declan walked into Garry's office one afternoon, his youthful face alive with anxiety and excitement.

"Can we talk about something?" he asked.

Glad to break the monotony of management reports for the accountant, Garry pushed his folder away and moved to the coffee table, taking a seat across from Declan.

"I was looking at some of the samples from Chicago," the young man said. "I had one from a young Mexican guy and I went to his grandparent's timelines more or less at random, hoping for some views of the Sixties, which is a period I've always found interesting as social changes went a bit crazy."

Garry sat quietly, waiting for Declan to get to the point.

"I was going through one of his grandfather's days, he was a kitchen hand in a hotel and I caught some bits saying it was the Ambassador Hotel in Los Angeles. He was really excited, because Robert Kennedy was giving a speech there the next day and he hoped he'd be able to see him. He said Kennedy had just won the Democratic presidential primary in California."

Garry felt a surge of worry as he realised where this was going, but said nothing.

"I tracked through his record and this man didn't get to hear the speech as he couldn't get away from the kitchen. I think you'd better see the rest. Can I use your system?"

Garry nodded and both men took seats behind's Garry's desk. Declan called up the images and the scene of a large kitchen area filled the screen. It was highly active, people moving everywhere and very well lit.

A flurry of movement occurred to one side and the watcher's head swung towards it and the scene was quite clear. The lean, handsome face of Robert Kennedy stood apart from the few men surrounding him as he smiled and waved to the people around, shaking hands with several of them.

The group moved to a narrow passage which was already partly obstructed by an ice machine and a small cabinet of some kind. Kennedy shook hands again with a man in kitchen clothing and then it happened. A man appeared from behind the cabinet and fired several times at Kennedy who fell to the floor. The gunman, that Garry knew from his reading of this event was Sirhan Sirhan was tackled by several of the men around and although he broke free for a moment, was finally pinned to the floor as the rest of the tragic event unfolded.

Declan stopped the images and took a deep breath.

"Amazing stuff," said Garry. "It will certainly provide more detail to the historians, but I'm not sure what your concerns are."

"Two of them," said Declan. "One is the issue of the number of shots fired. I've played that through a few times and I definitely count thirteen shots. Trouble is, the gun Sirhan used only held eight. There was quite certainly a second gunman. Talk about echoes of the first Kennedy assassination!"

Garry took a deep breath, wondering if he should tell Declan about Kathie's discovery and decided not to for now. "And the second concern?" he asked.

"I looked at some of the other samples we had and most of them had details of the donor's ancestors, just back to their grandparents. I was still looking for stuff about the Sixties so I had a look at all those donors' grandparents who had been noted as being ex-CIA. And that's when I hit the problem. Look at this."

He tapped the keyboard with a few instructions and another scene came up. Five men sat round a table, four of them could be seen by the watcher whose DNA this was. One of them was Sirhan Sirhan, clearly seen in full frontal clarity.

"The watcher is John Cartwright," said Declan. "He's the grandfather on the mother's side of the donor. He was CIA in the mid to late Sixties. Of course, we can see Sirhan Sirhan. No idea who the others are."

Garry watched in horrified fascination. The implications of a meeting between CIA agents and the killer of Robert Kennedy were appalling.

"He's fully prepared?" said one of the other men. He was a heavy set individual, almost bald with a fleshy face and thick jowls.

"He is," came from the speaker. It must have been the observer as nobody else appeared to have spoken. "We've had a year with this guy. He's had the full MKUltra treatment."

"That stuff hasn't always worked," said the first speaker. "You're sure of this?"

"We are. We gave him a full six hours in the sensory deprivation tank yesterday while the earphones kept repeating, "Must kill Kennedy, must kill Kennedy," several hundred times and another two hours this morning. Before we send him out this evening, he'll get the dose of that stuff our people developed and final instructions. Our guys will make sure he gets into the hotel and sticks close to Kennedy and give him the final trigger when the opportunity comes."

"What's the trigger?" asked one of the others.

"Romulus 1954," replied the watcher. "He's been conditioned to obey that trigger for the last two years, there's no way he can ignore it when I say it to him. He'll shoot that leftie Kennedy bastard without any doubt."

"Make sure he does," said the first man. "We don't need that commie scum in America."

"Christ alive!" broke in one of the other, unidentified men. "You're really going to do this again? It was bad enough killing his brother, look at the shit-heap we stirred up and how much effort it took to keep it all under wraps."

"Getting cold feet?" said Cartwright, the contempt obvious in his tone.

"Not cold feet, just concern about what will happen. We got rid of one of these bastards, but these are the Kennedys, not some bunch of nobodies. They may just decide to dig into this if we knock off another one. What do you think would happen if they deliberately reveal who killed these two men?"

"God, you're talking rubbish," said the first man. "This is the CIA, we can cover up anything and everything and there's nothing a bunch of multi-millionaire lefties can do about it."

The other speaker shrugged his shoulders but the doubt in him was obvious in his face.

"All done?" said Cartwright and received nods from the others. All the people in the room rose, except for Sirhan who remained seated, his face staring ahead. Garry could see that the man's face was quite immobile as if heavily sedated.

Declan stopped the images.

"I followed this for much longer," he said. "Cartwright takes Sirhan to a small motel and stays with him all day. At ten that night, he drives him to the Ambassador Hotel, watches the Kennedy speech just after midnight then follows Kennedy down to the kitchens. As Kennedy walks through, Cartwright clearly says "Romulus 1954" into Sirhan's ear and that's when Sirhan takes off and shoots Kennedy."

"Good God!" said Garry. "Any idea what MKUltra is?"

"I had to look it up, but it was easy to find. It was a long-standing experiment the CIA had been running to develop what was known as a "Manchurian Candidate." That's a person who could be given an order under a special trigger and be quite unable to disobey. And once he'd carried out that order, like an assassination, he'd forget all about it. It all came about from a book of that title written in the Fifties during the Korean war. They've made a couple of films of it since. Looks like they were still working on it in 1968. I remember from the tales about all this that Sirhan said he had no recollection of shooting Kennedy."

"Christ alive!" said Garry. "Declan, get those samples, give them to me. Life will be safer if I have them safely stored away and for God's sake, say nothing about this."

Half an hour later, the DNA samples were stored with the others in the bank vault and Garry was left to worry about what sort of monster he'd unleashed on the world.

Chapter 19

Garry's stress levels were climbing. It wasn't because of the difficulties and dangers revealed by the DNA images being discovered, these were business problems that he had always been able to control. But the growing distance from Hannah was wrenching at his gut. Driving home had changed from the delight of growing anticipation about seeing her and spending the evening and night with her to increasing dread at what he might find. While sometimes she was her normal, delightful self, too often he had entered the house to find a sullen, hard-faced, silent woman who talked little and held herself away from him.

This evening, it seemed somewhere in the middle. But when he tried to hold her close for a few moments as had been their standard routine on meeting at home, she pulled away, her face tight.

"All right, so what's the matter?" he asked, sensing his own anger and disappointment at her changes in personality.

"Nothing."

"One thing I've learned from experience is that when a woman says "Nothing" to that question, there's sure as hell something wrong. Now, what is it?"

She shook her head and walked into the kitchen. Feeling his anger rising, he took the steps down to his wine cellar and brought up two bottles of Merlot, took them into the kitchen and opened one, pouring two glasses. He leaned against the counter top with his glass, leaving hers near where she was standing by the stove.

She looked at it as if undecided but finally lifted it and drank half of it in one go.

"You're obviously unhappy with this relationship," he said. "Do you want to leave?"

"You don't tell me anything of what you're doing," she said, her voice hard with tension.

"I tell you what I can. You know there's tight security on it."

She finished her glass and poured a refill. "You mean you don't trust me." It was a flat statement.

"I trust you. But there is always a chance that you could slip something without realising it. Far worse, is that somebody might be so eager to learn about what we're doing that they might apply pressures on you that you couldn't resist."

"What you think somebody might *torture* me?"

"Hannah, what's happening right now is really dangerous. We're learning things that might cause massive social disruption and international stresses."

"You're being ridiculous," she snapped.

Garry refilled their glasses and both of them downed them immediately. He repeated the process and saw that one bottle was almost empty. He opened the second one, aware that he might be overstepping his own rules about secrecy.

"In the last two days, we've discovered that there really was a second gunman in Dallas when Kennedy was shot and that obviously there's been a cover-up. Just as bad, we also saw absolute proof that the man who shot Kennedy's brother, Robert, was set up by the CIA using mind-control techniques that were thought to have been abandoned years earlier. So what do you think would happen if both those facts were revealed? Can you believe that there are some people who might go to any lengths to keep those facts suppressed?"

She was silent, staring into her glass.

"Those were decades ago. You mean you found people who had actually witnessed things about them?"

"That's the other thing." Garry felt a warning signal run through him, somehow telling him he was in the danger zone. But the alcohol was having the usual effect of suppressing inhibition and he ignored the danger signs. "We've also found that our DNA holds the life records of every one of our direct ancestors from birth to the moment of the procreation of the descendant. So what we had was a collection of DNA samples from various regions of the USA and quite accidentally, two of our donors had a parent or grandparent who had witnessed the things we saw."

"And how far back does this go?"

"We've looked back at events of five hundred years ago and it seems that we can go even further."

He could see the growing tension in her body by the way she stood, rigidly staring at her glass, one hand gripping her other wrist as if to stop herself smashing something.

"Hannah, what's the problem? This is amazing historical research and we've got trained specialists looking at history and linguistics experts hearing ancient languages being spoken. One day, we'll be able to release everything and there'll be a massive increase in human knowledge."

"And a lot of it maybe won't be what we want to know," she said hoarsely.

"Yes, I agree and it could cause serious problems, like the facts of the two Kennedy assassinations. But we survived Darwin's discoveries and Galileo's, so I think the human race will survive what we learn here."

"I don't know."

"Hannah, is there something specific that frightens you?"

She shook her head and finished her glass.

"Can you get some more of this?" she asked.

Garry went down the cellar and found another bottle. Dinner passed quietly but without the closeness and warmth that he had grown to love so much. When they went to bed, she curled up on her side and turned her back on him, leaving Garry tense, worried and restless for hours until he finally fell into a light, unsatisfying sleep.

In the morning, the office was abuzz and Garry's attention was soon diverted from the problems at home.

"I think this will amuse you," said Gregory Ball, sitting in the canteen, sipping at a mug of coffee. "I was waiting for you to get here so I could show you."

"Interesting," said Garry. "It must be good! Let me get a coffee and you can show me."

A few moments later, he and Gregory walked through to the new section. As he passed the small office that had been constructed for Helene, she was talking on the phone in a language that Garry didn't recognise.

"Hebrew," said Gregory. "She's talking to Tel Aviv University in Israel. She'd asked for a number of samples to be taken from people around the country."

"Why's that?"

"She's interested in the history and culture of that part of the world." Gregory seemed to cut short the conversation and led Garry to his own desk. "This is something I found late last night. The original donor is a man in his thirties, born in Luton. He had a vague idea that his ancestors came from eastern Europe, but he had nothing specific."

Gregory keyed in the data he needed and the screen came to life. It took a moment for Garry to realise that he was looking at an image in a mirror as the subject stared at himself. It was a man in his forties, Garry estimated, quite handsome, with a large forehead and long curly hair that came over his ears and down below his collar. He was dressed in a highly decorative military uniform. The expression his face was one of smug satisfaction and after a few moments, he grinned happily at his image.

"Who is it?" asked Garry.

"Wait a minute," said Gregory with a smile that matched the image in the mirror for smugness.

The man turned from the self-satisfied look at his image and through his eyes, Garry saw that he was in a luxuriously decorated room with deep red carpets, several silk-covered chairs and one couch, also silk covered. A door opened and a woman appeared. She looked about the same age as the man, her grey hair up-swept above her head above a florid, heavy-set face with a double chin above heavily rouged lips and cheeks. Her expression was one of huge delight.

"Grisha!" she exclaimed and moved to the man and they embraced. Her hair covered some of the man's face so that his vision was partially blocked.

Gregory stopped the recording that he had made earlier that day.

"Grisha! That's when I realised who these two are. That's Catherine the Great! And that's her lover, Gregori Potemkin! Grisha was her pet name for him. I'll have to tell my wife to call me that!"

"Holy cow!" Garry was both astounded and amused. "I'd always heard she had a seriously voracious sexual appetite! And that's the famous Admiral Potemkin!"

"Indeed it is! Grand Admiral Potemkin, later Prince of the Holy Roman Empire and Prince of the Russian Empire, possibly Catherine's husband at some time and certainly her favourite lover! I'd say our man in Luton will be astounded when he hears he's a direct descendent of Grand Admiral Gregori Potemkin."

He restarted the recording and the two moved back through the door from which Catherine had emerged. Clothes began flying, though with difficulty, given the styles of the time, heavily ornate, formal apparel, but somehow both eventually became naked and collapsed onto the enormous canopy bed.

"I don't think I want to watch this!" said Garry, struggling with a mix of horrified fascination and amusement.

Gregory stopped the recording, also laughing. "Well, I did, though of course it was to hear the language! It confirms old reports of the time that Catherine, who was born a Prussian, spoke excellent Russian but with a German accent. I'm going to spend a lot of time with

Potemkin's history, there's so much to learn there! It was a hugely fortunate find!"

"But that's one of the big problems, isn't it?" said Garry. "All these scenes we have found that tell us so much about the past, these are like gold nuggets in a mass of mud. We've got no way of determining the time and the place of what we see and we certainly can't control it. We've got no way of specifying what to look at, so all we can do is take random samples and hope something interesting comes up."

Gregory was nodding all the time Garry was speaking. "That's exactly the problem, and it's made worse by the simple fact of mobility of populations. Who could have forecast that taking a DNA sample from a young man in Luton would give this astonishing scene of Catherine the Great of Russia having wild rompies with one of Russia's greatest military heroes?"

Garry felt overwhelmed and fought to control himself, telling himself he'd faced and conquered far more complex problems than this one.

"I suppose it's much easier if we take samples from groups who haven't experienced that sort of inter-continental mobility? But who would they be?"

"Indigenous people, perhaps like the Aboriginals of Australia or of North America, the ones so wrongly called "Indians." We would certainly have far more coherent life lines and it will be fascinating to follow these back to see their original migrations from Africa in the case of the Australian people or Russia with the Americans."

"But for most of the world's populations, it's almost impossible without some sort of key to the time?"

"That's right," said Gregory. "I found this one by skipping along a generation in turn taking spot checks as I followed each line and trying to see sudden changes in environment. I haven't looked at any of the original donor's other ancestry lines. Who knows? Maybe I'll find Attilla the Hun in one of them?"

"But there's a huge amount of wasted time in that approach, surely?"

"Indeed there is, Garry. But that's the nature of research. Blind alley after blind alley, sometimes whole lines of research abandoned, until one day – BINGO! We've found something earth-shaking! You must have seen that in the pharma industry when compound after compound ends up abandoned with nothing useful found."

"That's a fact," said Garry and stood up. "I'll talk to the team and see if anyone can suggest a line of attack or maybe has seen something that needs to be followed up. Thanks for the entertainment!"

Gregory laughed and waved as Garry walked out of the office.

After an hour of heavy thinking, he made a decision and called his team together in the dining room and waited until everybody had settled down with drinks and snacks. He deliberately kept his manner cheerful, knowing too well that many of the team expected to hear that the department was being closed down in favour of the historians and linguists. While the huge leaving bonus was still on the table, so preventing anxieties of a financial nature, he knew that nobody in the organisation felt that they might get a job that had been so fulfilling as theirs had been.

"Everybody ready?" he asked and received a hum of general assent. "There's a whole new project line we need to be working on," he continued.

The hum returned, but this time it was excited, curious, much like the faces that looked back at him.

"As you've all found in your research into history, there's one massive problem. So far, all of us have just been looking at random and most of what we see is just day-to-day living of very ordinary people. Critical stuff like the Battle of Bosworth or something I just saw, Catherine the Great having wild, energetic and highly imaginative rompies with Grand Admiral Potemkin..."

He was interrupted by an explosion of guffaws and laughter around the room. He grinned and waited for quiet to return.

"Wonderful and valuable as they are, these scenes are very few and far between. As I just said to one of the Cambridge people, they're like gold nuggets in the middle of a sea of mud. What we desperately need is some way of getting to specific times more quickly. I'd like all of you to ponder on this, see if there's anything in what you've already found or think about how such a mechanism could exist."

Unusually, Bill Askins was in the office during the day and he raised a hand.

"Yes, Bill?"

All faces turned to the big man. Everybody in the organisation knew of his genius and they saw him infrequently, so when he spoke, he got everybody's attention.

"I'd say there's some sort of Universal Time recorder," said Bill.

"Why do you think so?" asked Declan from the front row.

"Because none of this is really natural," said Bill. "This whole imaging thing, it doesn't quite stand up to analysis."

The room was dead silent. Clearly Bill had been applying his thoughts to the issue.

"For the life of me, I just can't see what survival mechanism this image recording provides to humans," continued Bill. "It doesn't look like we'll be able to access these visual memories by ourselves, but I could be wrong. Maybe that will develop as our species develops. But there's a reason why all this exists, and I just can't think of one."

"So where does that lead you?" said Garry into the silence.

"I don't know. But I do think that this is somehow given to us. There's something else I need to bring up."

If the silence could get even more concentrated, it did.

"I've been doing the same as all of us, really just playing around, looking at history, seeing very mundane things, though a few more interesting ones here and there and really just checking on that whole backward path through ancestors using the two dots that Penny found earlier on. And I found a problem."

He took several breaths as if working up the courage to continue. "Just once, I worked back through four generations and came to a block," he said. "At the great grandparents of one subject, it stopped. No two dots. Nothing."

He looked around the room. "I don't know what that means," he continued. "I don't know if the genetic code was somehow damaged and the dots were deleted. I read what I could of this person's history and it seemed to begin when he was already a child about eighteen months old, there was nothing before that and there was no reference that I could find to his parents. Has anyone found any other examples like that?"

There was a general murmur of denials. The atmosphere in the room was electric.

"I suppose there could be a reason why the code was missing, damaged like Bill said," Avram said into the silence. "But I don't like the alternative."

"Nor do I," said Bill. "It means that person had no ancestors at all."

"Right," said Avram. "If it's not a genetic fault in the DNA, it means he was somehow created outside of the usual human process."

The silence gave way to noisy conversations as everybody released the shock to the system that this bombshell had produced. Garry finally broke into it.

"Everybody, listen to me. This is a hell of a development and right now we have no idea what it means. If anybody finds another example, go and see Bill and check with him for similarities. But meanwhile, there's work to do. I'd like all of you to focus on this time issue, though you continue to be free to research anything you want, including helping the Cambridge people in their work. It may well be that there's no solution, but we started this company not knowing if there was anything in Karen's theory about DNA and look what we found! But if I can quote one of my favourite characters in fiction, this is getting curiouser and curiouser, just when we thought we'd reached the end of our particular road. It could be that we've just found a whole new road to travel down."

He left the group to their discussions and returned to his office to talk to Karen.

Chapter 20

Several weeks went by. Garry's home life seemed to return to something like normal and Hannah's dark mood was replaced by her normal happy self. It made life so much better for Garry, but at the back of his mind, the worry about what had caused the problems remained and whether it would return never quite went away. He tried to ignore it.

The work continued, but Garry detected some difference in the atmosphere among the Cambridge researchers any time he went into their work space.

"What's going on?" he asked of Gregory Ball one morning as they met over a morning break.

"Not sure what you mean," was the reply.

Garry sensed that something was being held back and Gregory was being evasive.

"We're not seeing many requests for help from most of your people," he said. "Up till now, your guys have all been keen to show us any notable historic scenes, but now you seem to have retreated. And the linguists now have gone very quiet, it looks like you're all concentrating on something. And anyway, I see some new faces but I don't know who they are."

Greg stared at his coffee, lost in thought. "I can't tell you very much, but Helene has been running a major project of her own."

"She's a specialist in Middle-Eastern Studies, right?"

Greg nodded. He seemed to have lost interest in the chocolate donut at his left hand.

"I haven't seen her for a couple of months. Where is she?"

Greg was still looking at anywhere but at Garry. "She's been in Israel for a time."

"Israel? On our project or something else?"

"Definitely our project." Greg's discomfort was showing in the way he moved around in his seat.

"And these new people, they're all linguists in that same field?"

"They are."

"Do you know what that project is?" Garry was feeling disconcerted by the obvious tension Greg was displaying.

"Only a little. But she says she'll be able to announce it in a few days."

"So you've been in touch with her recently?"

"We talked a couple of days ago, but only to keep her up to date with what everybody is doing."

"And you can't tell me what it's about? I remember a promise you two made that you would keep me fully informed of what you were doing."

"Garry, please don't push me. Helene has asked for a complete blackout on this, because it's going to cause problems. But I promise you, when she's ready, you'll all get fully briefed."

Garry sat back. "Okay, I suppose I'll have to settle for that, but I really don't like it. It's breaking the agreement we had."

"I know you'll understand when it gets revealed."

"I hope so." Garry finished his coffee. "How well do you know Helene?"

"Not all that well. I've only been at Cambridge for three years and our paths don't cross all that much. She's very fit, plays squash competitively and I think she's a pretty good glider pilot. But we're very different. I know she's a deeply religious woman, though she's not obvious about it, no lecturing people about sinful behaviour and going to hell if you don't accept Christ or any of that nonsense."

"Interesting." Garry stood up. "Back to the grindstone, I think."

Greg smiled and also stood up, walking away without further comment.

Garry returned to his office and called Karen. Something was disturbing him badly about the situation but he didn't really know why. He suspected that it was because for the first time in the years he had been running Blueprints, something was going on under his nose of which he knew nothing. But he was also worried about the nature of this secret project. It sounded potentially dangerous.

"Good morning, little Welsh person!"

"And a good morning to you, Madam."

"You rarely call me at home, Garry. Something is worrying you?"

"It is. What do you know of a major project that Helene is carrying out? She's been away for a couple of months and she's imposed a blackout of information. I talked to

Gregory Ball this morning and he seemed quite nervous about the whole thing."

There was a moment of silence on the phone.

"Garry, I knew that she wanted to run special project of her own in Israel and I allowed her to take four scanners with her. But I promise you, I don't know details, only that she said it would be fairly earth-shaking."

"They did promise full transparency when we first met, Madam."

"They did. I will call Helene and get back to you when I've spoken to her."

"Thank you, Karen. I hope you find her. It would ease my mind considerably."

He replaced the phone and decided not to think any more about this until Karen called back. He set off on one of his "Management by walking around" stints to talk to each of his staff to determine what they were doing and how they were feeling about the developments of the research, both their own and that of the Cambridge group.

Later that day, he got another in the gold nuggets as he had termed them, though nothing as dramatic or hair-raising as some of those seen so far.

He heard the squeak of astonishment as he was talking to Avram and looked over to the source, Lorrie, one of the original staff from the early days of the company, her doctorate from Oxford in genetics and a violinist with the Reading Festival Orchestra. She was smiling broadly and caught his eye.

"This one's fun!" she said.

"Five minutes!" he said and turned back to Avram. Once caught up with the Israeli's work schedule, he walked over to Lorrie's desk.

"Watcha got?" he said, pulled a seat over and sat down beside her.

She laughed. "Talk about a serendipitous find! You know I play the violin with the local orchestra?"

"I do. I've seen you play a few times."

She pressed a few keys and the monitor lit up. It showed a busy workshop, with several young men working at benches. As Garry looked at the scene, he realised that the objects in their hands and lying on bench tops were parts of violins under construction. He glanced sideways and saw the utter delight in Lorrie's face as she worked. It was clear she wanted to tell this in her own way and he sat back to let her do so.

"I took the sample we'd got from a young American at North Western University near Chicago," she continued. "His name is Massimo Cicuta and I followed his lifeline back a few generations and saw his family arrive in that huge postwar immigration to America from Italy. One branch of my family did the same, so I was interested and kept going back. And then I came up with this. My Italian is still okay and I was able to work out what was being said. I don't know who the observer is, but I sure know who is being watched!"

She paused as the observer focused on a young boy at one of the benches just as an elderly man walked up to him. The clothing was of a time some centuries ago. The older man spoke and Lorrie translated.

"How is that piece coming, Antonio?" he asked.

The boy looked up with a shy smile and Lorrie again translated.

"I think it is well, Signor Nicolo, but I would like to ask you if I can make this small change in the bridge."

Lorrie stopped the recording and spoke, shaking her head in disbelief and delight.

"Those are two of the greatest gods in the music world," she said. "The young boy is Antonio Stradivari. He's about twelve or thirteen here. The old man is Nicolo Amati, the greatest of all the Amati luthiers. He must be about sixty here. His father and his uncle were the sons of Andrea Amati, the real father of the violin and cello. This must be in about 1656 to 1658 in Cremona and it settles one of the debates about whether Stradivari was actually apprenticed to Amati or just worked with him for a time. This looks like an apprenticeship."

She restarted the recording and Garry watched as the older man walked round the apprentices, examining their work and generally talking in friendly terms, judging by the smiles he received from the young boys. With some amusement, he realised that Nicolo Amati was practising the same "Management by walking around" methodology that he used himself.

"This is wonderful," he said. "You're sure of the identities?"

"I really am. I've played through some hours before and after this scene and their full names are used several times."

Her delight was infectious and Garry responded to it.

"Wonderful stuff, Lorrie. You've recorded the path you took to this?"

"Of course, just like you asked us. We all do, and I know that music historians all over the world are going to be ecstatic about all this once it all gets out!"

"The world is going to be a different place, that's for sure," he said. "Brilliant work, Lorrie! Are you quite happy with what's happening these days? It's very different from when you first started here."

Her laugh would have been answer enough, but she added to it. "Garry, just like Kathie said, I could never have dreamed about having so much fun at work and seeing such amazing things. I know that much of the company focus now is on historical and linguistic research and it's wonderful that you allow us to do some of that as well, but I'm also working on just how we control the time lines."

"Any thoughts on that?"

"I think it's telepathy. I've been testing the controls on a lot of different samples. What I've been looking for is any variation on the degree of control we have."

"And what have you found?"

"There are differences, but they're tiny. But I think I've found a trend."

His interest perked up. "A trend?"

"Indeed. There are definite differences between contemporary people, those who are the original DNA sample providers. The degree of control I have on their samples varies quite a lot, so I passed them over to Penny and she did the same tests and found the same variations."

"Meaning?"

"I *think* – and I stress, *think* – that there's a difference in the telepathic strength of the donors."

"How about differences between you and Penny?"

"Thought of that. So I got two others to do the same thing and when we analysed the results, it seems that while there are differences between us, the researchers, the exact same variations still exist in the donors."

"Which means?"

"It means that almost everybody has some sort of telepathic ability, but it varies a lot. But then I did the same with older generations."

"And found?"

"And found a definite but tiny trend there too. It seems to indicate that we are getting better and better at this telepathy thingy with each generation."

He took a deep breath. "You'll give me a report on all this?"

"When I've completed the maths. It's taking some complex trend analysis."

"Okay. Great work, Lorrie. I'll look forward to seeing the report."

"As soon as I can, but I want to check out some more about how Amati worked."

"You know the rules, young lady! There aren't any! Do whatever you want!"

"Thanks boss!" She gave him a glowing smile that seemed to light up the room and he continued his walk around, wondering how many more astounding events and gems of knowledge he would find before the day was over.

As the day drew to a close, Karen called him back.

"It's been interesting day, Garry and you were right to be concerned."

"What have you found, Karen?"

"I finally spoke to Helene. She's been in Tel Aviv for two months."

"Tel Aviv? Yes, she was talking to somebody at Tel Aviv University when I saw her last in her office."

"Garry, she seemed very distressed when we talked earlier, but she won't tell me why."

"Did she say what she's been doing?"

"No, but she did tell me she's had team of four linguists at work. I gave her slush fund for anything she needed, and it looks like she used it."

"Did she tell you anything at all? Say, when is she coming back and will she then tell us what she's been up to?"

"Yes, she did say she's wrapping up her findings and she'll be back in Reading next week to tell us all about her work."

"Well, I suppose that's one good thing."

"I think so, too. But I do fear that what she has to tell us is going to be frightening."

"Karen, being frightened is not something we ever considered when we started all this."

"I agree, but that is scientific research, Garry. We go where it takes us. Meanwhile, what is happening down there by the river?"

"We're seeing wonderful things, Karen and one day the history profession is going to be turned upside down when we can release this technology. But there's one interesting development I need to tell you about."

"Then tell me, funny Welsh person."

"When you get here."

"You think our phones may be tapped?"

"Karen, I'm damned sure of it. It's pretty clear the PM and his off-sider are worried about what we do."

There was a short pause at the other end.

"All right, Garry, I'll see you when Helene comes to present her findings next week."

"Thank you, Madam."

He disconnected the conversation with a nagging worry about what was about to happen.

Chapter 21 – The World Changes

"This is going to be very painful for me, and possible for some of you here," said Helene McCauley, professor of European and Middle East Studies. "The last few weeks have been a series of shocks to my system and I wasn't sure I'd withstand them. I'm still not."

Garry looked carefully at her. The signs of severe stress were evident in the pale face, dark eyes and lines in her cheeks that he could not remember from before. Everybody in the room was silent, seeing the same as Garry. Helene had suffered deeply in recent weeks.

"I need to start by telling you, if you didn't already know, I'm a devout, practicing Christian," she continued. "I have been from an early age, I have always believed firmly in the teachings of Jesus Christ, that he was the son of God, that he was crucified for our sins and that he rose again. These have been truths that have ruled my life and I have tried to live by those teachings."

Garry looked around the room. All the faces were deeply concentrated on Helene. While there might have been some negative reactions from those of the team that Garry knew were atheists or at best, agnostics, Helene's deeply felt pain was so obvious, so genuine, that nobody was untouched by it.

"For those of you that didn't know, I have spent the last few weeks in Israel, at the University of Tel Aviv. Prior to my departure, I had arranged with friends of mine at the Felsenstein Medical Research Centre and the Sackler Faculty of Medicine to collect as many DNA samples from Arab and Jewish people in Israel and where possible, Gaza. We did so, because we were sure that would give us the best chance of continuous ancestries back through the times of the biblical stories of the start of Christianity. I took with me some of the linguists specialising in Aramaic, the language of the time and we borrowed some more from academics at the University. That meant we had to let them into the secret of our technology, but I took that risk."

A small smile appeared in her pale, lined face. "Needless to say, they were thrilled, stunned, excited, every emotion you can think of to learn of this and realise what was now possible. Hearing spoken Aramaic of the time was almost overwhelming to all of them."

The room was still silent. The realisation of what she was telling them was hitting them all hard.

"Our theory was correct," she continued. "It was not difficult to trace ancestors back to the start of what we term the 'Common Era' starting at the presumed birth of Christ. There were a few false leads as people moved to Europe during the Middle Ages and some to the USA in later years, but eventually, with a good number of researchers working flat out, we found a viable number of people living in Palestine in the period between 10BCE, or 'Before Common Era' and 40CE. We documented that period intensively, because we know that in fact, there was a man called Jesus, a preacher and he was born in the time of King Herod who died in 4BCE."

The silence in the room was tangible, as was the tension. Nobody could be un-affected by what she was saying.

"So, using references to external events, spoken words about events, everything we could, we eventually recorded the lives of a number of people who lived in the region during what has always been believed to be the lifetime of Jesus Christ. And then the real work began, going through almost every minute of these lives. It has taken all of us working sixteen hour days for over two months to document these lives as much as we could."

She took a deep breath.

"We found several sightings of a man called Jesus, even conversations with him. We discovered that his father, who was certainly called Joseph, was a stonemason, not a carpenter and this man Jesus was born eight months after his parents had married, and that gave rise to one of the greatest of the myths, something I'll deal with a little later. We heard him preach the teachings we all know about. But then we saw other examples of several other young rabbis preaching the same teachings. They were not disciples, they were just a group of young rabbis with common values who met occasionally. We saw and heard nothing at all about any miracles, such as turning water into wine, healing the sick, walking on water, raising the dead, none of it and had they occurred, they would most certainly have been the topics of conversation. At no point was there ever any mention of virgin birth, divine fatherhood or any other of those beliefs."

She looked around the room, tears in her eyes.

"There was no crucifixion of any of these young men. Sightings of Jesus ended when he was about thirty, it seems he left Palestine and went elsewhere. I expect that one day, as we expand our sampling of DNA and we can make more accurate placements of the time of events, we will learn something of where he went. You may know, there are many stories that indicate that he travelled to India and lived there for the rest of his life, but nobody has ever produced any real evidence for that. Maybe, one day, we'll find such evidence. But the clear indication is that the whole basis of Christianity is nothing but myths and legends that grew as time passed."

The shock in the room was palpable.

"Some of those myths were obviously triggered by ordinary events," Helene continued. "This is normally the way legends start, just simple things that somehow become enlarged and decorated as time passes. We found one of those, the story of turning water into wine. We found the life record of one of the people present at the wedding where this story originated. It wasn't Jesus there, but one of his associates, though we were not able to identify which one. But we saw him arrive at the reception and join in the celebrations. Then it was clear that the wine was running out, so this man simply sent out to a local wine merchant whom he knew and this man sent a wagon with four casks of good-quality wine. That was it, just an event which got blown up into something wildly improbable and over the following decades became recalled as a miracle. And that brings me to the greatest myth of them all, the whole virgin birth thing."

She paused and took a deep breath.

"Jesus and his family were members of a Judaic sect known as the Essenes. That's been established for years. Several historians have mentioned one of the traditions of this sect, that marriages were arranged by the families, not left to chance. The prospective bride and groom were introduced in September, if they didn't already know each other, the engagement was announced and the marriage set for late December, because Essene tradition said that September, nine months later was the most propitious time for a child to be born."

For the first time, a smile appeared on Helene's face and she seemed more relaxed.

"But it seems young people haven't changed over the centuries," she continued. "And young people being young people often managed to get together before the wedding and children appeared some weeks before the official September date. The Essenes even had their standard joke about this common event; they said, *"Lo! A virgin has conceived!"* in a semi-humorous effort to hide the fact of what had happened. It appears that the joke got lost and became a comment later inscribed in some testaments that gradually developed the power of legend."

She stared around the room, the relaxed smile gone from her face.

"We found no other stories that became legends, but of course, we'll keep looking." She took a tissue from her purse, wiped her eyes and then blew her nose. "And that's it for now," she said. "I really don't know what this is going to do when it all gets out."

"I doubt it's going to be good," said Avram. "Most of the world is going to be shattered by the news."

"If they believe it," said Garry. "And it won't be remotely believed until the technology has become widely accepted and in use."

"Can we keep it secret much longer?" asked Avram. "The fact that Helene had to get a number of people involved has weakened the security a hell of a lot. Somebody's bound to start talking soon."

Garry looked around the room and saw mostly white faces, pale with shock. "What do you all think?" he asked. "What's the thinking in this elite group of intellects?"

"Well, I for one find it fascinating, but not earth-shaking," said Kathie. "I've always been an agnostic and honestly, these findings confirm what I've always thought, it's all myths and legends. None of it ever made any real sense to me and all the various offshoots of Christianity just seemed to get dafter and dafter. Look at all those loonies in the States, filled with hate for liberals and their philosophies, which are exactly the philosophies taught by these young rabbis that Helene has seen. If the stories had been true and the Messiah did return, those bastards would kill him again, immediately."

There was a ripple of laughter round the room.

"The critical thing is how the Catholic Church and the Anglican Church will react," said Garry. "They're not fools, many are well educated in the sciences, they'll be confronted by scientific facts that cannot be refuted or ignored."

"Galileo all over again?" said Avram. "I tell you, I think my lot are going to be pleased! They've always said Jesus was just a prophet, exactly as the Muslims have said."

"Which may cause more stress between Jews and Christians, I imagine," said Garry. "Hearing people say, 'I told you so' is not a great aid to friendships."

"Probably," said Avram. "And there's enough stress as it is. I'm a bit scared of what may happen here."

Others in the room nodded and some made sounds of agreement.

"We'll probably have to talk to the government," said Garry. "This has international implications and we're not qualified to deal with it."

"I think the Israelis will hear about it first," said Helene. Her face was blotched by tears and the pain she was feeling was reflected in her expression. "The University is bound to learn about the team's discovery, even if it was a small group working in secrecy."

"No doubt," said Garry. "It's like trying to contain a dynamite explosion in a tin box. Doesn't matter how strong the box, it's going to get out."

"I really wish I hadn't done this," she said.

"Hey, Helene, you're an academic. Learning, research, discovery, it's what you do. This was always going to happen one day. Somebody was bound to discover the DNA facts if we hadn't and the world would learn about it. That's how it has always been."

"I suppose." Helene looked unconvinced.

"I'll talk to Madam," said Garry.

Chapter 22

Even as he drove into his driveway, Garry knew something was wrong. Hannah's car was not there, and although that was not uncommon as she did late duty at the school, this felt different. There was an emptiness surrounding the house. Feeling the sense of wrongness, Garry closed the car and entered through the front door. It was silent. He knew there was no point in calling out to Hannah. He walked into the main bedroom, already expecting what he would find. There were none of her make-up items on the dresser, none of her clothes in the wardrobe. He didn't bother looking in the sideboard drawers.

She had gone.

He moved to the lounge where they had spent so many happy evenings, drinking wine, listening to music and often making love. The place was spotless with the same soul-less perfection of a hotel room. The envelope lying on the coffee table grabbed his attention.

"That's usually left on the mantelpiece," he muttered aloud and picked it up, forcing himself to open it, knowing almost every word of what he would see. But one sentence caught his eye in the brief paragraph she had written.

"My friends in Tel Aviv told me what you found."

Somebody in Helene's research team? He had not foreseen that. He read on.

"I cannot live with a man who has destroyed all my faith and beliefs and will cause so much pain in the world."

It shook him. Religion had never come into their world. She had never expressed any desire to go to church, never commented on religious matters or social matters that had aroused so much dispute, such as gay marriage. The final sentence almost made his legs shake and he sat down on the armchair nearest to him.

"I am sorry I have misled you like this, but my people said we had to know what was going on at Blueprints because it threatened everything we stood for. Being with you allowed me to find out."

He had to read that several times before it sunk in.

"My people?" *"..it threatened everything we stood for?"*

Had she made contact with him, affected a loving relationship, lived with him, shared his bed, all to gain an inside knowledge of what his organisation was doing?

He felt sick. Who were her "people?" He could only assume that it meant a religious body of some sort, possibly an evangelical group and not any regular members of a major church.

He stood up and walked to the drinks cabinet, poured himself a large scotch and sat down again, his head in a whirl of confusion. How could he have been fooled so well and for so long? What will this un-named religious group do with the information? Will they broadcast it? What will the reactions be? Was his team of researchers in any danger?

He sipped at his glass until he'd drunk about half of the contents and then made the obvious decision and called

Karen. To his relief, she was at home in London and not out on one of her many social duties or travelling abroad, which she often did on impulse.

"I have caused us a major problem, Madam," he said.

"Tell me, Garry."

"You never met my live-in lady, Hannah, but she has caused the problem."

"Let me have details."

"She seems to be a member of a religious group, I don't know which. We took a sample from her some years ago and she was one of the first people for whom we were able to see back through her life. She came to the office to confirm what we saw."

"I remember."

"It looks now like she deliberately engineered a later meeting with me, made it seem all romantic and moved in. All this was under the instruction of her sect. They had contacts in Israel, actually in Helene's research team or somehow close to it and they were told about Helene's discovery. Hannah has left."

"I'm very sorry you had to go through this, Garry."

It touched him that Karen would first think about his distress, rather than the problems faced by the company.

"This I'll get over, madam. I don't know about the problems she might cause."

"Word was going to get out before too long, anyway, Garry. So it merely brings forward issue. As I discussed with my executive team, we should probably advise British Government about Helene's discovery because international implications are enormous."

"This is what my team said this morning."

"Your people are quite bright."

Garry could hear the smile in her voice. For a moment, he wondered who her executive team was as she had never mentioned it before.

"So what should do for now?"

"Nothing out of routine, Garry. I will arrange to meet Prime Minister again and I will let you know when that happens. You will of course, come with me."

"Thank you. I'll check all the security access to the building and advise Greg Mullaney on the other side to do the same."

"That seems appropriate. Let me know if anything happens, Garry."

"I will, Madam. Good night."

"Goodnight, nice Welsh person."

Chapter 23

"I definitely prefer your view, Greg."

Mullaney laughed. "I was here first! When I was a kid at school, this was just a cow patch. I still get a real kick every day out of sitting in this office, looking out at this hi-tech, corporate estate and arriving and leaving in my Jaguar. I used to get to the boathouse down there on my tatty old bike."

The two men sat at their ease in armchairs by the coffee table. This meeting was a monthly affair and always enjoyed by both. Their two functions had little in common, but Greg Mullaney, Managing Director of Life Technology was fascinated by what Blueprints did and what they were discovering on a daily basis in recent months. In the early days of Blueprints, Greg had been kept ignorant of Garry's projects for security reasons, but as time wore on and the friendship grew, the ban had fallen away.

"We had an earthquake in the office yesterday," said Garry.

"Can you tell me?"

"I keep nothing from you, Greg. Madam has always known that and approves fully."

Greg nodded his appreciation and leaned forward to refill his coffee cup from the pot on the table. Then he sat back, his coffee cup against his chest.

"All of Christianity is mythology," said Garry.

Greg Mullaney almost froze, staring down at his coffee cup.

"I've heard so many astounding things from you in the last year that I know you aren't joking," he said, a trace of hoarseness in his voice. "Tell me the whole thing."

Garry leaned over the coffee table and refilled his mug, as if needing time to think. He settled back in his seat and stared out of the window.

"Helene took a group of researchers and linguists to Tel Aviv University a few months ago. She found a few more specialists in Aramaic and had already been able to procure a large number of samples from Jews and Palestinians. The teams eventually found vast numbers of scenes from the time of Christ, even direct images of Jesus himself. They've concluded that Jesus was simply one of a number of radical young rabbis wandering around Palestine teaching the lessons that have been attributed to the one man. But there was no evidence of divine inspiration, no virgin birth, no crucifixions of any of these men, no miracles. It's all myths and legends that grew years after the events they were supposed to have taken place."

Greg took a deep breath as Garry took a sip of coffee, obviously having finished the summary.

"I don't want to think about what's going to happen when this gets out," Greg said. "This will change the world."

Despite the stress, Garry laughed. "That's what Karen always promised she would do, but I don't think this is what she meant."

"I'm sure about that. Does she know?"

"I told her last night. She's arranging a meeting with the Prime Minister."

"You'd better keep the whole thing quiet," said Greg. "For as long as you can, anyway."

"That's a problem." Garry described the situation with Hannah and her disappearance. "I don't know when the first signs of public reaction will appear."

Greg nodded towards the window.

"Right now," he said and picked up the phone. "Jenny, immediate lock-down."

Garry stared out at the scene. Large numbers of cars had appeared in the large space outside that served as a common parking area for the offices in the industrial park. As he watched, people climbed out of the cars, apparently four or more people out of each, more in some cases. The mob was huge and as he watched, many of them rolled out signs. Some said, *"Jesus is Lord,"* others said, *"God will punish the wicked,"* yet more read, *"Eternal Hell is for Heretics."*

"They must have been working all night," murmured Greg.

Garry didn't reply. He was staring down at the front of the crowd where he could clearly see Hannah holding a *"Jesus is Lord"* sign, red letters on a white background. He stood up and advanced to the door.

Greg seemed to know what he was planning.

"Garry, you can't go out," he said. "Bullet-proof glass, heavily reinforced doorways, windows and general structure. Karen always anticipated something like this could happen, even when we were just a drug research company. You can't get out, they can't get in."

"Understood," said Garry and walked out of the office. He took the stairs down to the front and to the transparent front door where he stopped and looked out at the mob. Despite the heavy insulation, the noise was obvious. Garry stood still and watched.

The mob had advanced to within a few metres and all the individual faces showed ugly rage as most of them screamed the same slogans that were printed on their signposts.

A brick slammed against the door, just an arm's length from Garry. He flinched but didn't move back. That's when Hannah saw him. She ran right up to the door and glared at him. The rage and hatred in her face were ugly, nothing like the warm, attractive woman with whom he had lived for the last few months.

"God will damn you to hell!" she shrieked at him, picked up the brick that had been thrown and slammed it against the door, right at Garry's head.

"How could I have loved this lunatic?" muttered Garry aloud, a few tears in his eyes and turned his back on her, walking back into the building and across to his own department.

Three police patrol vehicles arrived within minutes. They parked near the building, the officers doing nothing but standing by their vehicles, watching the crowd of protesters. No more bricks were thrown and after an hour, the crowds dispersed quietly.

Watching the evening news, Garry saw the story related, but without pictures and while the fact of the protest was mentioned, no reasons were given.

When the phone rang, Garry was half asleep in a depressed reverie about other, happier evenings spent here with Hannah. He reached out and picked it up.

"GOD WILL KILL YOU!" bellowed a man's voice in his ear. Confused, Garry moved the instrument away from his ear but said nothing.

"YOU HAVE DENIED OUR LORD JESUS CHRIST AND YOU WILL BURN IN HELL FOR ALL ETERNITY!" continued the rage in the telephone. "YOU AND ALL YOUR KIND WILL SUFFER FOR THIS EVIL!"

Mercifully, the phone at the other end was slammed down, leaving Garry shaken, frightened and confused. He could think of little but to call Karen.

"Greg already called me about mob this afternoon," said Karen. "We shouldn't be surprised. This affects people on very deep level."

"Very deep indeed. I've just been threatened with eternal damnation in Hell and death at the hands of God."

Karen was silent for a moment. "Phone call?"

"A phone call. A hysterically angry phone call."

"Then perhaps we should be prepared. Leave it with me, Garry. We will also be meeting with Prime Minister again tomorrow, so please meet me at Downing Street at eleven o'clock."

"Will do, Madam."

"Try not to worry, Garry. This is England. And you have some very fine scotch in your cupboard."

Somehow, her calm had a good effect on him. They said their farewells and Garry did go to his cabinet and pour himself a large helping of very old scotch. He went to bed early, but slept badly.

He rose at five, unable to sleep any further. Feeling low on energy, he followed his morning routines, walked through to the garage and carefully backed out on to the road.

To his surprise, a police patrol car was parked opposite his house. Garry parked behind it and walked up to the driver's side door where an officer was seated.

"You haven't been here all night, surely?" he asked the officer.

"Since midnight, sir! That's when the order came through."

Garry reflected and realised his conversation with Karen had been at about ten last night. She must have set wheels in motion almost immediately.

"I'm most grateful," he said. "I hope this doesn't go on too long." He waved a hand and returned to his car.

That wasn't the last surprise of the morning. Four patrol vehicles were at various locations in the parking lot and Garry saw at least six police officers in heavy gear, each carrying an automatic rifle. He couldn't help a wave of anxiety run through him. Karen was clearly taking this seriously. He made a pot of coffee for his office, busied himself with routine paperwork as the office filled up with his staff, most of them looking nervous at the presence of armed guards, then drove to the station to catch the train to Waterloo, late enough to miss the rush hour to the City but in time to get to Downing Street by eleven.

Chapter 24

The entry into the Prime Minister's office had almost become routine, for Karen and Garry. The brief wait outside the door, the personal assistant tapping gently on that door, opening it just enough to sidle in, the soft voice saying, "Doctor Petrova and Mr Lawson, Prime Minister," and the final stages of entry to be greeted by the two most powerful men in the country, the Prime Minister and the Home Secretary.

This time was a little different. There was a third person in the room. She rose to her feet as the other entered but while the two men shook hands with Karen and Garry with murmurs of "Good morning, Doctor," she resumed her seat as everybody sat down. She was dressed in a severely-cut black suit and a white shirt, open at the neck. Her face was thin, hard, seeming to have no capacity for warmth or humour. Her hair was reddish, shoulder length, tied behind her neck.

The Prime Minister broke the tense silence.

"Doctor Petrova, Mr Lawson, may I introduce Colonel Alana Shimova, the Israeli Ambassador to the Court of Saint James?"

Diplomat-speak for Ambassador to Britain, thought Garry, studying the woman opposite. She looked about forty, he estimated, superbly fit, with a body that had some interesting lines to it. He couldn't help following the curve of her hip to her impressive bosom and the long, graceful legs crossed in front of her. He suddenly realised that she was looking at him with a cold expression.

Damn, she knows everything I'm thinking! he thought in confusion and embarrassment and tried to switch his attention to the Prime Minister.

"Colonel Shimova is here at the request of her government," said the Prime Minister. "They believe that Israel has significant interest in the recent developments with your team, Doctor Petrova. I tend to believe them."

But Karen made no response. She was looking hard at the Israeli with a small smile.

"Alana Shimova?" she said. "Daughter of Yevgeny Shimov, Professor of Genetics at Moscow University and then Tel Aviv? He studied under my father at Cambridge and I have known about you since you were little girl."

"That is correct, Doctor Petrova. We did meet on two occasions in Cambridge." There was no warmth in the Colonel's face.

"I believe you flew fighter jets in Air Force? That is very impressive."

"Thank you Doctor. Yes, I flew F-16 fighters until I retired three years ago."

"And now Ambassador to Britain? You and I, we will get on, Alana."

For the first time, a tiny smile made a brief appearance on the woman's face. It softened her features considerably.

"I hope so, Doctor."

"Ladies and gentlemen, we need to get on," said the Prime Minister who had been watching the exchange with fascination, Garry had noted. "Doctor Petrova, I know you have always said you would change the world. Most of us believed you have already done so with the developments in pharmacology, but this new development is not anything we anticipated and frankly, it terrifies my colleagues and me."

"New ideas usually terrify most people, Prime Minister." Karen's face was without expression.

"Don't try and make me out as some of anti-science creationist or religious fanatic!" snapped the Prime Minister. "But what possessed you to go down this path and why did you release the information before consulting this office?"

"Scientific discovery is not a matter of choice," the Colonel said. "The nature of DNA was there to be found and a great scientist found it. And she did not release the information. Somebody in my country did."

Karen smiled at her. "I was not one who discovered it, Alana," she said. "I just suspected it was there. My colleague here can take more credit."

The Colonel looked coolly at Garry for a second or two but said nothing further.

"Let's not nit-pick," said the Home Secretary. "The problem now is what to do about this. It's going to cause terrible problems. Ambassador, your government is fully aware of this discovery?"

"Yes, Home Secretary."

"And has any other government indicated that they know about it?" asked Karen.

"Not so far," replied the Home Secretary. "But after that riot in Reading, I'd be dead certain they all do."

"There's been no reaction from the Vatican or Canterbury either," added the Prime Minister. "But I'm not really worried about them, they're both highly intelligent men, well educated and I'm more interested than scared about their reactions. It's the average person and their reactions that are scaring me. Ambassador, how much can you tell us of the Israeli reactions and the proposed plan of action?"

"Our concern is that many people are going to see this as some sort of religious "victory" by the Jews," replied the Israeli. "They will believe that we will claim ourselves to be right, that the Messiah never came and that somehow we'll assume some massive moral superiority. They won't like it and they might decide to do something violent as people have done for centuries."

"And what about the Muslims?" The Prime Minister looked tense.

"Impossible to forecast accurately," replied the Ambassador. "They of course have always considered that Jesus was just another prophet, like Moses and Abraham, so this will give them some moral victory. But we imagine that the war between the various sects and their claims as to who is the legitimate successor to Mohammed will continue to dominate their thinking."

"I'm less hopeful," said the Prime Minister. "I believe there is a serious chance that the extremists will take the opportunity to claim the rightness of their views and so justify more violent action against unbelievers."

"Several people in my government share that view," said the Israeli with a nod.

Garry finally decided to join in.

"I believe the riot outside our office is the real indicator of what we are going to see," he said. "It's not the reactions of the Vatican or the Anglican Church, but the hysteria of the masses as they see the discoveries as a massive attack on them personally that frighten me. The hatred I saw in the faces outside our windows was overwhelming."

"Just who was this group?" The Home Secretary looked coldly at Garry. "I believe it included a woman with whom you'd had some relationship?"

Garry refused to react, but it was a shock to realise that he must have been under observation for some time.

"Yes, Home Secretary," he said, meeting the official's glare with his own. "And of course, you will know her name."

"Naturally," said the Home Secretary with a cold smile. "Our security forces are very good at what they do."

"Garry, does your operation need protection?" asked the Prime Minister

"It's a worry," replied Garry. "Karen obviously anticipated problems when she built the place and we have bullet-proof glass in all windows, steel reinforced doors and the best security system money can buy. But our people are vulnerable away from the office."

"Taken care of," said Karen. "All staff now have personal armed guard to escort them any time they leave house and that includes you, Garry."

Garry looked at her. "This is not a nice way for people to work, Karen."

"I believe it will be temporary. We are not insane in England."

"I do hope you are right." Garry's anxiety did not lessen.

"And what about our cousins across the pond?" broke in the Prime Minister. "How will they react?"

"They are my government's greatest concern," said the Israeli. "The so-called "Religious right" display similar philosophies and values to the extreme Muslim jihadists and we believe they will not react with the expected common sense of the major churches. My leaders will talk with the American president and I recommend that you do the same."

"With what objectives, Colonel?"

"Increased border security," replied the Colonel. "Close watch at all points of entry for known terrorists, and Mossad will share with you some data in that field. Be attentive for known religious extremists of any creed, including those from the USA."

"And we will prepare a national campaign of information about the technology and how the information on the Christian story was discovered." The Prime Minister was looking thoughtful. "We should coordinate with the Vatican and the Anglican leaders. And Karen, will you promise me to talk with this office before you unleash any more nuclear devices like this one on the world?"

"Of course, Prime Minister."

"May I suggest that you do not conduct similar searches on Mohammed or Buddha?"

"You can certainly suggest it, Prime Minister, but I am unlikely to follow."

Garry caught a tiny smile on the lips of the Israeli Ambassador, but it vanished immediately and her face resumed its calm, blank appearance.

The Prime Minister looked disturbed. "Karen, this is bad enough as it is! Please, I beg you, do not cause any more potential riots."

"That is trouble with science, Prime Minister," she said. "It is merely facts. International upheavals are not science."

The silence in the room was palpable.

"But I understand your problem," Karen continued. "I will ask Garry to exercise caution in his researchers."

Garry felt all eyes turn on him.

"I'll carry on as I have always done," he said. "We've already seen some episodes that could cause major international difficulties if they were released, but the samples have been locked away off-site."

The Prime Minister leaned forward with a worried expression. "What sort of episodes, Garry?"

"Would you like to know the absolute truth behind the murders of both Kennedys?"

"Good God! You have that?"

Garry stayed silent.

The Prime Minister looked around the room as if seeking advice but received none.

"You'd better keep that on ice for now, Garry," he said. "One day, I hope the world will be able to handle these facts, but for now, it's best to leave it alone."

Nobody else seemed about to speak and the Prime Minister got to his feet to signal the end of the meeting.

As Garry, Karen and the Ambassador moved to the exit, the Israeli spoke quietly.

"The CIA, Garry? And MKUltra was involved?"

Garry was startled and turned to her, but didn't speak.

She smiled. "We have always known," she said. "We know that Sirhan's handler was a man called John Cartwright. Do you know the others?"

Shocked, Garry shook his head.

"But you have seen their faces?" she persisted.

"Yes."

"We need to see them."

"Not yet, Alana," broke in Karen. "Right now, I think it may be too dangerous for Garry to collect those samples."

"I understand," the Ambassador said. "But we can see them when things calm down?"

"We'll arrange it," said Karen.

When they reached the pavement outside Number Ten, a black limousine with the Israeli flag above one headlight was waiting. The uniformed driver was standing outside and he opened the door.

"Can I offer you a lift?" the Ambassador asked.

"Thank you, no," replied Karen as the gates into Downing Street were opened and a white Rolls Royce whispered in and turned round to park behind the limousine. The woman that Garry recognised from his first visit to Karen's apartment got out and opened the rear door.

The Ambassador smiled and for the first time, her face showed some warmth and rather startling for Garry, considerable beauty.

"We will talk again," she said and entered her limousine.

"You can count on it," murmured Karen and waved to Garry to climb into the cool luxury of the Rolls. She followed him in and settled herself as the driver took her place and moved off in near silence. The gate was opened again and they entered London's traffic.

"Tatiana will drop me at home then take you back to Reading," Karen said after a few minutes. "There is something I want to discuss, first."

"I'm sure there is!"

She smiled at his tone. "Not what you think! You are free to handle this situation as you wish, but perhaps you should remind staff that million-pound leaving bonus remains. I imagine some may be frightened of current developments and may wish to leave."

"I'll do that."

"I got telephone call last night from old friend of mine, once student at Cambridge, now Faculty Dean at Northwestern University in Evanston, near Chicago. He wants to buy system for history and linguistics researchers. I think it is time we began to release technology and get it into general academic use. I want you to go over there when they get it and show them how to use it."

"Me, madam? Surely one of the researchers would be better qualified?"

"Yes, they would. But you can also be pioneer in America. We can arrange for some publicity, perhaps television interviews."

"Is that a good idea, Madam? We've already thought that there might be some hostility to this among some sections, particularly the religious extremists."

"So far, very few people know about this latest development," Karen said. "We'll not talk about it and let's hope those lunatics in Reading don't spread it. But it's time our technology became more widely adopted. Academic world has long needed something like this."

"I'll stay concerned," said Garry. "When do you want me to go to Chicago?"

"Not yet. First, we finalise contract. Then we ship system. And then you travel. Perhaps six weeks."

Garry settled down to enjoy the exotic experience of being driven in a Rolls Royce and after dropping Karen at her home, the drive down the M4 to Reading was an utter delight, but the small sense of anxiety remained with him.

Chapter 25

"We're all very excited about this," said Professor Alistair Baker. "We've been hearing about some of the stuff those guys from Cambridge have been finding and we can't wait to look into the past."

"It can be a shattering experience," said Garry. He'd woken in his hotel at 4am after falling into a deep, black sleep at 7pm the previous night, feeling the five-hour time difference between Chicago and London and he was still feeling some jet-lag this morning. But the trip had been a joy, even more than the ride in the Rolls six weeks earlier had been. He'd been thrilled to see that his ticket was first class and he'd revelled in every scrap of luxury he found, from the elegance of the Concorde Lounge at Heathrow to the spacious private suite in the front of the British Boeing 777, from the attentive service of the charming flight attendants, to the quality of the food and drink served and the high-technology entertainment system. Against everything he knew to be sensible, he'd enjoyed several single-malt scotches as he looked out at the view on the right-hand side, seeing the coast of Greenland in the distance at one point and then the landscape of Canada and the USA as they reached Chicago.

By the time he'd made it through Immigration, he was feeling quite unsteady and fell asleep in the cab to his hotel, having to be helped to his room by a large porter after barely managing to complete his registration.

"So what sort of stuff have you seen?" Baker asked. He was a young man, in his early thirties Garry estimated. He had a full head of reddish hair that seemed not to have had a lot of attention from a brush or comb. He was short and stocky, dressed in blue jeans and a white sweater that did nothing to hide a small paunch. His eagerness to hear about Garry's systems was obvious in the way he leaned forward in his chair and the way his eyes sparkled.

Garry grinned. "I saw Richard the Third brought down at the Battle of Bosworth," he said. "That was quite traumatic, so much violence and blood. And I saw Catherine the Great having rompies with Admiral Potemkin."

"Good God!" exclaimed Baker.

"Exactly. I've seen an ancient Norseman burying his wife who had died from the Black Death, speaking to his son in a language that had been dead for centuries."

He thought about telling the Dean about the murders of the two Kennedy brothers and decided against it.

"But we've seen murders committed and directed the police to the killers and as you know, Britain is working on legislation to allow this technology to be used in court cases."

"We'd heard about that," said Baker. "That'll be a massive benefit when you can be a hundred per cent certain about somebody's guilt or innocence."

"We think so. Anyway, the equipment's ready, let's show you how it works."

"Great!"

For the rest of the day, Garry took his client through all the stages of identifying the tracks in the DNA samples, how to track back through previous ancestors and recording the images and sound. The department had prepared a number of DNA samples and Garry carefully and methodically took Baker through the process of identifying the dots at the start of each time line and working back through generations.

By mid-afternoon, Baker was in a state of shock and Garry was feeling seriously jet-lagged again. While most of the scenes they had found had been simple, every-day examples of daily life of ordinary people, some had been shocking. Baker had been forced to run to the washroom when they found a murder, much like Garry's team had found, where a man had bludgeoned a woman into bloody pulp. The killer had been the grandfather of a retired accountant in the city and when recovered, Baker took the details down for passing to the Chicago police, not knowing if the murder was known to them and in the police archives.

"At least we might help them close a cold case," Baker said, his voice still trembling from the shock.

"You might have trouble," said Garry. "We certainly did, the first time we saw something very like this. We had to take a sample from the cop who came to talk to us and show him his childhood before he'd believe a word of it."

"And did he?"

"He did. They finally tracked down the guy and he's in for life."

"We'll probably have to do the same," said Baker.

Garry nodded, beginning to feel the cotton-wool feeling of dulled senses as the jet-lag began to affect him again.

"That's it for me for the day," he said. "I need my bed."

"I think I'll keep going," said Baker. "This is just quite astounding. I'll call a cab for you."

Garry nodded, walked out into the bright sun and waited for the cab to take him back to his hotel. After a quiet meal in the hotel restaurant, he watched the television for a while in his room and was asleep by soon after seven again.

He was awake by five in the morning and he lay and dozed for an hour before dragging himself up and into the bathroom. He was due to return to the University by nine, so he took things slowly, watched the early morning television, somewhat put off by the relentless cheerfulness and bright lights of the studio.

He went down to the restaurant for breakfast, thoroughly enjoyed a huge serving of bacon and eggs and hash browns and took full advantage of the endless servings of coffee.

The phone was ringing when he got into his room. Puzzled as to who could be calling him, he picked up the handset.

"Mr Lawson?" said a female voice.

"It is."

"Good morning, Garry. This is Janelle Wild, I'm the booking officer for the Jim Hanley Show."

"Er... Yes, how can I help you?" Garry had no idea what this call was about.

"We'd love to have you on the show, Garry."

Garry took a deep breath. "Er.. Janelle? You'll have to excuse me, but I have absolutely no idea what this is about."

"Gosh, Garry, I just love your accent! You don't know about the Jim Hanley Show?" The woman's voice echoed the same intense enthusiasm that had put off Garry in the morning television show.

"I'm afraid not. It's been some years since I was last in the States."

"Oh my goodness!" Her squeal of surprise almost hurt Garry's ear. "Well, Garry, the Jimmy Hanley Show is the highest rated talk show in the mid-West. We get the very best people on the show and it's on prime-time television. It's tomorrow night, so we'd just love it if you'd join us and tell us about what you're doing."

Garry thought quickly. He recalled that Karen had suggested she'd arrange for some publicity, so he assumed this was the result and she'd selected a good media outlet.

"How did you hear about me?"

"We knew that the University was buying the equipment and we heard about what it did. It must be so fabulous to look back through somebody's life and see the whole thing like a movie!"

It must be what Karen wanted, thought Garry. It sounded like the woman didn't know about the riot at the office in Reading and he knew he wanted to keep that quiet. But he felt oddly excited about appearing on television and talking a little about what had been accomplished over the last few years.

"Okay," he said. "Tell me where and when."

Garry felt like a complete fool. Sitting in the chair rather like at the barber's, looking at his reflection in the glass while an attractive young woman applied thick make-up to his face, he decided that he could not remember when he last felt so helpless, uncertain and uncomfortable.

"You'd look pale, ill and on your last legs without it!" said the woman, clearly sensing his discomfort.

"So I believe," Garry said, relaxing a bit at the sign of human contact. There had been little of it since arriving at the studios when he'd felt from the start like a farm animal arriving at the slaughter house, being directed from the reception to the make-up rooms by a fey-looking young man who didn't meet his eyes at any time. Once in the room, a brisk, business-like woman had directed him to a seat without any introduction and left him sitting there without a word.

The make-up exponent had introduced herself as Tina and that had been the totality of communications until then. Before either could say another word, a voice spoke from behind him.

"Well, hi, Garry! Welcome to the Jimmy Hanley Show! I'm Jimmy!"

Garry looked up into the mirror and saw a short, slim man with a skull-thin face and a full head of hair that looked horribly false.

"Good evening," he said, struggling to avoid a sense of aversion.

"Oh, you Brits, always so polite!" said Hanley. "I hope you're not nervous about the show? Have you ever been on television before?"

"Yes, I'm a bit nervous and no, I haven't been on television before."

"Well, with that accent, you'll be a hit! Isn't that a lovely accent, Tina?"

"It sure is," the woman said, applying a final spot of powder to Garry's forehead.

"So where in England are you from, London?" asked Hanley.

"I'm Welsh."

Hanley looked uncertain. "Welsh? That's in England, right?"

"No." Garry's irritation was growing.

"Well, whatever. I'm going to ask you about the work your group has been doing, Garry. I'll check with you that you really can see images of a person's life in their DNA and how you think this will affect the world. And we'll talk about just how the University is planning to use the system they've bought from your company. Is that okay?"

"That's fine," said Garry.

"Great! Now, about those nerves. We always have a little prayer session before the show and I hope you'll come along and join us and we'll pray away those nerves. How about that?"

Oh my god, what have I walked into? thought Garry feeling serious anxiety running through him. *Nobody told me this was some sort of religious program.*

"No, I won't join you for that," he said. "I'll sort out my nerves on my own."

Hanley looked shocked. "You don't want Jesus Christ our Lord to help you?"

Garry felt the make-up girl shrink away and step away from the chair.

"I'm sure there are worse problems for him to solve than an attack of nerves in me," he said, struggling to control his anger.

Hanley also took a step away as if Garry had become infectious.

"You'll be the second interview," he said and walked out of the room.

The girl walked back to him and removed the protective sheet from around his shoulders.

"The Green Room is through that door," she said. "If you'll wait there, somebody will come and get you."

Feeling no more need to be polite to anyone here, Garry walked out, his worry growing by the second.

"Many of you may have heard of a British invention in recent years in which British scientists claim to have developed a machine that can read images of a person's life from their DNA," said Jimmy Hanley, reclining cross-legged in an armchair on one side of a coffee table. Garry sat in a similar chair on the other side, feeling uncomfortable in the glare of the studio lights.

"With me in the studio tonight is Garry Lawson, the head of the research team that claims to have developed this science. Good evening, Garry."

"Good evening," replied Garry as he saw the red light come alight on the camera across from him. A slight ripple of applause ran through the studio audience, barely visible in the gloom of the other side of the studio.

"Now, Garry, this is an extraordinary claim to make," said Hanley. "And one might excuse people for not believing it. And what use is just a few images from the whole lifetime of somebody?"

"It's not a few images. It's every second of a person's life from birth to the moment the DNA sample is taken, complete with sound."

"That sounds like completely insane imagination," said Hanley. "How would you prove it to somebody if they said it was not true?"

"The same way we have proved it to many sceptics," said Garry. "We take a sample of their DNA, scan it and show them images on the screen of episodes from their lives. I can do that for you tomorrow, if you care to come along to the University."

Hanley looked frightened.

"That won't be necessary," he said. "But this sounds like the ultimate invasion of privacy. What possible good can come out of it?"

"In the United Kingdom, we are about to use this technology for the criminal justice system. If a person is accused of murder or assault, a sample of the DNA from both perpetrator and victim will provide absolute proof of guilt or innocence. We can see the actual crime being committed. We can even take the DNA from a murder victim and show the murder being committed up the point of actual death. A murder or assault trial can be completed in less than an hour and we have one hundred percent proof of guilt or innocence. That sounds like a pretty good use of technology."

Hanley's anger was showing. "I'm quite certain that God would never have permitted such an appalling thing to be used. How can you justify such an evil thing?"

"Evil? Absolute proof of guilt or innocence is evil?"

"No, not that. Just the mere use of such science, that's what is evil and God would not permit it."

"Well, Jimmy, I'm not as knowledgeable as you are of God's business plan for humanity, but the DNA gives this information and we've been able to find it and use it, so there must be a reason for it being there. Like all data, scientists search for evidence and when proven, use it."

"This sounds as far off the wall as evolution," snapped Hanley. "That's another so-called science that is totally wrong..."

He was interrupted by a burst of cheers and applause from the audience. Hanley turned and grinned at the darkness.

"But this madness is even worse, from what I hear," he continued, turning back to Garry. "Your team of so-called "scientists" have also said that you can track back, not just through a person's life, but through all their ancestors as well."

"This is true. We have found that a person passes on their DNA at the moment of procreation to their child and that DNA also contains the images of their lives from birth to that moment."

"What? Their parents and their grandparents as well?"

"Every direct ancestor, right back through hundreds of years."

"And you have done this?"

"We have."

"And what sort of things have you seen?" For a moment, Hanley's hostility was submerged under his interest.

"We have seen the Empress of Russia, Catherine the Great have an encounter with her lover, Admiral Potemkin. We have seen King Richard III of England killed at the Battle of Bosworth at the end of the Wars of the Roses. We have seen the young Stradivari, the great maker of stringed instruments, working as an apprentice under the Amati family. We have seen an ancient Norseman bury his wife after she had died of the Black Death and heard him speak in a language not heard in centuries. Not all that we see is so historic, most of it is very mundane daily life, but for historians and language specialists, this is very exciting."

Hanley was breathing hard. "But this must mean you could go back and actually see our Lord, Jesus Christ! We could hear him preach, perform the miracles!"

Garry took a deep breath. This was dangerous ground.

"I imagine we could, if we could find the right ancestral paths," he said.

"What does that mean, ancestral paths?" Hanley was looking severely stressed, his eyes wide and his face flushed.

Garry felt great doubts about continuing, but decided to play it moment by moment.

"I imagine it would mean finding people who have a direct ancestry to people who were alive at that time and actually observed some of the episodes in question."

Hanley seemed stunned and the near-invisible audience was dead silent. Garry sat still, sensing the stresses that were obvious in the room.

"And is this what all those leftie academics at the University are doing with your equipment?" the host finally said.

"They are planning on historical and language research," said Garry. "I don't know any more than that."

"Well, we all know that those *intellectuals* are all communists and they hate God and America," said Hanley. A wave of applause ran round the room and a few shouts of "Hallelujah!" were heard.

Garry knew it was time to end the session. He stood up.

"I don't believe there's any more to be gained by this discussion," he said and walked out of the studio, shocked by the roar of abuse that followed him. He unclipped his lapel microphone, unhooked the wireless pack from his belt and put it on a nearby table and headed for the door. There were lots of taxis on the street, he waved one down and rode to his hotel. Receiving some stares because of the heavy layer of make-up on his face, he reached his room and spent a lengthy period under the shower, scrubbing away the greasepaint. He realised his heart was beating fast and he raided the bar fridge for the tiny bottle of cheap scotch that it held and then followed it with a brandy, hoping it would settle his nerves.

It didn't work and he had a bad night, unable to sleep beyond short snatches, images in his mind of the rage in Hanley's face and the bellows of abuse from the audience as he walked out of the studio. Eventually, he managed an hour or two before his alarm came on and his first coherent thought was that he was grateful he had only a short meeting at the University before he would return to O'Hare Field for his flight home. He packed his bag, checked his passport and ticket and went down to the front desk to settle up the bill. He was aware that the staff behind the counter seemed subdued, staring at him and none of them appeared as friendly as they had when he first checked in. He found a taxi at the front entrance and went to the University.

* * *

"Just a wrap-up, guys as we look at the controls."

Garry smiled at the small group of six post-graduate students, half of them from the History Department, the rest from the Languages Department. All of them were thrilled with what they had seen the previous afternoon when they had heard English spoken by the first arrivals to the country, two different Indigenous dialects from the seventeenth century and seen vivid scenes of different times and places, some from America, others in countries from Europe, the homes of different immigrants.

For an hour, Garry showed them the two dots at the start of each timeline which showed the location of the direct ancestor mother and father and they practiced the mental controls that let them move up and down the time lines.

"Several people are going to want to study that mental ability," said Gemma, a History student from St Louis in her second year of a doctoral program.

"Indeed, they..." Garry was interrupted by loud noises from outside, car horns hooting and an incoherent mix of screaming and shouting.

"What the hell...?" Baker muttered, rose from his seat and went to the window, quickly joined by the others.

The scene was chaotic. The road was jammed with cars and crowds of people milling around the sidewalks. It reminded Garry of the mob that had appeared outside his office building in Reading and this group also had signs being held aloft.

"Christ-Killers," said one. "Deny Christ at your peril!" said another.

"What in God's name is all that about?" asked Baker, his face pale under the unruly reddish hair.

"Somehow, they've found about the research one of the groups in Reading had done," said Garry, a sinking feeling of dread in his stomach. "I think that Hanley character already knew about it last night and tried to get me to reveal it, but I walked out."

"You've gone back and looked at the historical Jesus?"

Baker was smart, Garry decided. He nodded, realising the group had gone silent, listening to him. "And we found it was all myths and legends," he continued. "There was nothing at all to confirm the Biblical stories, just a group of young radical rabbis preaching the stories that became attributed to one man. No crucifixion, no resurrection, nothing divine at all."

"There have been a few historians saying much the same, recently," said Baker. "But they have just been theories. It looks like you went and had a proper look."

Outside, the noise was getting louder. Somebody had got a microphone and was bellowing into it, the words clearly coming through the window.

"THOSE WHO DENY CHRIST WILL GO TO HELL!" shouted the voice. "REPENT NOW, ACCEPT OUR LORD JESUS CHRIST AS YOUR SAVIOUR OR YOU WILL BURN IN HELL FOR ALL ETERNITY."

The voice somehow came over the top of the general hooting of cars and screaming of individuals. Some uniforms appeared in the crowd, vastly outnumbered.

"Campus police," said Baker. The worry in his face was extreme. "They'll have called the local cops for backup."

The sirens began as he spoke. The noise got louder and Garry saw three police cars start to force their way through the crowds, sirens howling and lights flashing. Behind them, a black van arrived and disgorged a number of police dressed more as riot police, helmets, face masks and heavy rifles in their hands, plastic shields slung on their backs. They lined up in front of the entrance to the building, facing the crowd. One of the first arrivals also carried a loudspeaker. He began to address the crowd and for a few moments, both giant voices competed with each other's attention before the police officer won out and the voice from the crowd died. There remained a background rumble of anger, but the situation seemed stable.

The door to the office was flung open and a uniformed police officer stood there. He was large, well over six foot tall and his expression was unfriendly, one hand on his gun holster as if ready to draw and fire like any Wild West gunslinger.

"Which of you is Garry Lawson?" he demanded, glaring round the room.

"I am." Garry fought to keep his voice calm.

"You've checked out of your hotel, correct?"

Why have they investigated that? thought Garry. "I have," he said.

"Then I'm taking you to the airport. Come with me, there's a car at the back."

He turned and walked away. Realising he had no choice, Garry waved a general farewell to the students and to Alistair Baker.

"Good luck with the research," he said and followed the police officer, wondering how long the equipment would be permitted to be used and how safe the Dean and his students were.

Garry took a back seat in the police car with the officer sitting in hostile silence next to him as they drove out of the University grounds and through the northern suburbs surrounding Chicago until they reached the expressway and accelerated.

"I saw your program last night," the officer finally spoke. Garry said nothing. The man's hostility was obvious.

"I've taken an oath as a police officer to serve and protect and that's why I'm taking you to the airport and making sure you leave. But believe me, my sympathies are with those people back there."

Garry felt cold and decided he would be safer saying nothing.

At O'Hare, the officer walked with him to the checkout counter, waited until the process was completed and then walked with him to the entrance to the departure areas.

"Don't come back," he said as Garry walked through the doorway.

Garry didn't reply.

Chapter 26

"It was not a comfortable experience," Garry said.

"I'm sorry I caused it," said Karen Petrova. "I'd asked public relations firm to set up more unbiased television interview but they got beaten to punch by that appalling Hanley person's show."

"They certainly caught the story of the riots here."

"They certainly did."

They sat in Garry's office across from each other by the coffee table. Few people remained at this hour of seven in the evening, though three researchers were still at their computer monitors. Garry had brought out the bottle of single-malt scotch that Karen had brought with her and poured two small helpings into the flute glasses. Karen seemed very thoughtful, Garry felt. She was dressed in a dark blue dress, not her usual flowing style, but close-fitting, almost a cocktail dress and looked her normal, immaculate, elegant self.

"News has naturally got out into big wide world," Karen continued and took a gentle sniff of the smoky peat aroma of the scotch. "But there doesn't seem to be reaction that we might have expected. Churches have barely said word."

"I suspect the shock is still rolling around the Vatican and Canterbury."

"Very likely. I'm certain it is proving difficult for them. It may be weeks or months before we see reactions and policies. I was told by people in Government that security forces have been watching carefully and using some informants within various religious bodies, but while there is some chat, nobody is behaving suspiciously."

"That's odd," said Garry. "I would have thought there'd be some hysteria. After all, we've pretty well destroyed the main foundations of the Catholic and Protestant churches and all their various subsidiaries."

"We must just wait and see. But one development you might like. I got call from Home Office this morning. They have approved use of technology in court cases where violence has occurred. Cases of fraud and suchlike they think will be harder to prove but they'll keep testing."

"That is certainly interesting!" Garry raised his glass to her. "That will shake the world up quite a bit! When will they start using it?"

"Some weeks yet. They've established rules, but they need to get some specialists licenced as expert witnesses and to brief legal profession which is unsure about whole thing."

"Not surprising," said Garry. "This will be a real game-changer."

"Pour me another scotch," said Karen.

Silence reigned while Garry reached for the black bottle and poured a trickle of the aromatic liquid into her glass. The smell of peat wafted past his nose and he grinned appreciatively. Karen caught the smile.

"They have kept cask of their oldest scotch just for me," she said and waved her glass under her nose, her eyes closed to get the full effect. "This is twenty-four years old and I flew up to Islay to get bottles last week."

"One of the best perks of this job," he said and took another sip of his own glass.

"What next for your people?" she asked. "We seem to have explored some very wide fields since it all broke. Is it time for more focus?"

Garry sat back, realising that this was not a social call, not that her visits ever were. Karen was checking on her company and the many millions she had spent so far in her mission to change the world.

"Funny you should say that," he said. "I've been working on exactly that question since before we saw the Prime Minister last. These are the issues I believe need more pointed research."

He stood up and went to his desk, picked up a single sheet of paper and handed it to her. She carefully examined it and nodded at him with a smile.

"That seems good," she said. "Exactly my own thoughts. This is why I hired you, Garry, you understand me. Keep me informed."

"I always do, madam," Garry said. "These topics could be even more astonishing than what we have already accomplished."

"We have only started changing world," she said and downed her glass of scotch, took a deep breath and stood up.

Garry followed suit and escorted her down to the front door. None of the work places was occupied at the hour of eight o'clock. "Please drive carefully, Madam," he said.

"I am superlative driver, Garry, as you know."

She walked out and Garry watched, amusement mixed with anxiety at the thought of her driving along the M4 into London. Then he locked up and went home.

Chapter 27

"I think we're all relieved you made it out of Chicago," said Penny from the second row of the conference room. The entire staff of Blueprints was gathered there, some looked apprehensive.

"Me too," replied Garry. "That was scary. I never expected the religious extremists would get organised so quickly. Anyway, one good thing it has caused is that finally the word of what we do has reached the outside world. Karen told me yesterday that the British legal system is about to change dramatically with court cases involving violence to be able to use DNA images as evidence."

A rustle of applause ran through the room.

"So," Garry continued, "Karen has achieved the first stages of her goal, she has, as she put it, *'Changed world.'* And that means a serious review of what we do next."

He looked round the room and smiled. "I see some anxious faces here! Believe me, nobody is being laid off and let me remind you, that million pound leaving bonus is still on offer for anyone who does not want to be part of what is obviously a massive agent of change, with all the excitement and risks that it entails."

The anxious faces changed and instead showed interest.

"Now," said Garry. "We have proved the technology and it's now a commercial proposition. There are a number of universities all over the world who have placed orders and one thing we have to do is train up some trainers who can go to these places and teach the academics how to use it. If any of you want to talk to me about moving to that role, come and talk to me. And we may have to hire a few more people specifically as trainers if this demand keeps growing."

"Any more orders from America?" asked one of the researchers, receiving some laughter.

Garry smiled. "Not as yet. Karen has heard that some congressman in Washington is submitting a bill to ban the use of the system because it represents a Satanic attack on religion. It will be interesting to see if it succeeds and becomes law. Based on what I saw in Chicago, it wouldn't surprise me."

A murmur of disgust ran through the room.

"Anyway, what Karen and I discussed and agreed was a new direction. We've been focused on history and we had our period of language research with the people from Cambridge here, but now all the major universities in Britain have placed orders for the equipment, so there's no need for us to duplicate their work. But you all know that several intriguing questions arose during our work so far and that's where I want us to go. Anyone want to suggest some new research fields?"

A hand went up from the middle of the room.

"Yes, Deborah."

The young woman stood up. She started to speak and then stopped, cleared her throat and started again, obviously nervous.

"The telepathy thingy," she said. "When that came up, it opened up the whole research capability here and I know some more work has been done on it, but I think it could be hugely critical for humans everywhere."

"And you'd like to work on that?"

Deborah nodded enthusiastically. "I really would!"

Garry turned to the white board behind him, picked up a marker and printed, *"Telepathy Thingy."* A murmur of amusement met the words.

"Thanks, Deborah," said Garry. "Any more?"

Avram jumped to his feet. "We've gone back two thousand years, as we all know. I wonder how far back we *can* go? Does this recording thing work right back to Neanderthal man? Maybe earlier? Or is it something that we developed at some stage, somehow?"

Garry nodded and turned back to the board, writing *"How far back?"*

"That leads right into what I'd like to work on," said Bill. He was sitting at the back of the room, away from anyone else. Garry had been worried about the extraordinary genius since the equipment had reached the level of capability that Bill had designed, leaving him at a loose end.

"Yes, Bill?"

"Why is this facility there at all?" asked Bill. "I can't see how it can be a survival factor, seeing as we need all this highfalutin' gear to read it. So, either there is a genuine way of accessing these images ourselves without technology, or..."

There was a moment of silence in the room.

"Or?" prompted Garry.

"Or it's been placed there artificially for somebody to find," said Bill.

This time, a loud murmur erupted in the room. Bill glared at the audience defiantly.

"That's a really scary idea," said Avram. "I can't even *begin* to think of all the implications."

Garry made no comment, but turned back to the white board. *"Why does this exist?"* he wrote.

"Any more?" he asked, turning back to the class.

Penny put up her hand. "Maybe related," she said. "It's also been raised before, when Bill found several people with no history beyond one or two generations. I'd like to follow up on that.

Once more, Garry turned to the white board and wrote, *"Humans without History."*

"Any more?" he asked again, resuming his seat.

Some murmurs buzzed round the room like migrating bees, heads shook, people had silent communications with each other, but no new suggestions were made. Garry reached into his briefcase sitting by his seat, extracted a single sheet of paper and placed it on his knee.

"While I was flying home," he said, "I made some notes on what I thought we needed to research further. These were topics that had been raised during the first stages of the company's research. Let's see what we have. First one was how this telepathy thing worked."

He looked behind him at the white board and then grinned back at the group.

"Check!" he said as a murmur of amusement sounded.

"Number two, how far back does this thing go?" Again, he looked at the white board and back again as the sound of amusement grew louder.

"Check!" he repeated. "Number three, humans without history. Check. And four, what's it all for? Check."

The laughter was now full, joyous and unrestrained. Garry could only sit back and revel in the situation. *How did I ever get so lucky as to have this group of people to work with?* he thought to himself. He waited for the celebration to subside.

"All right, and so to work," he said. "Bill, you take the issue of why this whole thing exists. But I also want you to work on the critical issue of finding some time mechanism that lets us place just when the scenes we look at are taking place. I'm sure there has to be some sort of universal clock. Penny, you're the lead on the parallel issue of those people who seem to have no history beyond a generation or two back. Deborah, the telepathy thingy is yours. Avram, find out how far back this goes. You four can consider yourselves group leaders in that you'll coordinate research by your teams and keep me up to date on what you find. Work out between yourselves who works with you, everybody is free to join whichever group they want, or if you want to become a trainer flying round the world, that's fine, come and see me about it."

He stood up.

"There's one more thing, two actually. Ever since that unpleasant episode when a mob attacked us, the building security has been beefed up. The doors and windows have been strengthened even more. Movement detectors have been installed around the place with security cameras in hidden locations. You will have seen the emergency buttons installed around the building. Pressing one sets off a warning at the police station and also at a private security firm that Karen has set up quite close by. And we have paid for the installation of cameras and similar security systems at each of your homes."

Avram raised a hand. "We've heard nothing from the main religious groups, which surprises me. Any idea of what's going on there?"

"That was the second thing," Garry said. "And it puzzles me, too. No, we've heard nothing, I'm informed by Karen that the spooks have heard nothing either, other than the topic has been raised in various inner sanctums, but nothing concrete has been seen or heard."

"It must be causing serious heartburn," said Avram. "They're going to have to come to terms with this eventually."

"They will, of course. But I'm more concerned about the fanatics behind the last episode."

Avram nodded.

"Okay, everybody," said Garry. "Don't just sit there, wasting my budget! Get to work!"

With more laughter, a cheerful group of researchers left the conference room and found their work places.

Things seem to be returning to normal, Garry thought. For a moment, he contemplated with some amusement one of the many Murphy's Laws that suggested having had such a thought was an indicator of something going wrong, then abandoned the thought as he got back to work.

The following morning, Garry was later than usual reaching the office. A restless night had left him tired and falling asleep again after the radio had come on at its usual hour with the morning news. He drove into the car park about nine, pleased to see that all his staff were already in. But he was annoyed to see that his private parking spot had been taken and he was forced to park some distance from the front door. As he climbed out of the car, sudden movement caught his eye and he turned his head to meet a blunt object that hit him with some force.

Dazed, he fell to the ground, only vaguely seeing three wearing face masks men surround him as heavy boots began thumping into his ribs. Frightened, he tried to cover his head, but suddenly realised the kicking had stopped and the shouting above him reflected more fear than anger. His head clearing, he looked up and saw that more men had appeared and they were efficiently knocking the attackers senseless. The new arrivals were not wearing any form of disguise and looked just like any young men wearing jeans and tee-shirts, and extremely fit. Somebody bent down over him and touched his shoulder.

"It looks like our sources were correct," said a pleasantly female voice. "That attack had been planned for a few days and we've been waiting for it."

Astonished, Garry raised his head and stared into the eyes of Colonel Alana Shimova, Israeli Ambassador to the Court of Saint James.

"What? How on earth...?" Garry stammered, thoroughly confused. His vision rapidly clearing, he looked around and saw that the three attackers were being swiftly bundled into a black van by his rescuers. He slowly got to his feet as the van drove out of the parking area.

"And your ex-girlfriend is over there," said Alana, pointing to the side of the area where Garry recognised Hannah's yellow Honda. One man stood by the driver's door, another one directly in front of the car and Garry could recognise Hannah sitting behind the wheel.

"She brought the men here," said Alana. "She's a moving force in the religious group that caused the riot the last time and there are links with the Americans that organised the affair at Northwestern University the other week."

Garry felt sick, whether from the blow on the head or the news confirming Hannah's actions.

"But what on earth are you doing here?" he asked. "And why?"

"Let's go to your office," she replied and began to lead him to the entrance.

"What's going to happen to Hannah?" he asked as they slowly walked to the office. "You're not going to hurt her?"

"Not a chance," replied the Colonel. "But my men will be interrogating her for a while, together with the three men who attacked you."

Garry looked back at Hannah's car just in time to see it driving away, but with Hannah in the back seat with one of the two men while the other drove.

They walked in silence as Garry absorbed what she had said and tried to make sense of it. When they entered the building, it seemed nobody had seen the attack, as nobody came out to ask about Garry's health. He felt relieved about that, his staff had experienced enough unpleasant drama in recent times. They reached his office and Garry sat in one of the armchairs, feeling a little nauseous from the blow on his head. Alana switched on the coffee maker then took an armchair across from him.

"Why you?" asked Garry. "What happened to the local police?"

She smiled. She was wearing a light fawn trouser suit that fitted her well and even with the nausea and slight headache, Garry was well aware that she was a remarkably beautiful woman.

"Karen Petrova has a lot of influence," she said. "This is all happening with the somewhat reluctant consent of the British Government because my government has expressed very serious concerns about how your work may affect Middle-eastern tensions. We got wind of an attack on you and asked for clearance to conduct this operation. Karen fluttered her eyelashes at the Prime Minister and that sealed it."

Garry tried to imagine Karen flirting with the Prime Minister and failed.

"Got wind? How on earth could you have heard about this?"

She smiled again. "Mossad is the best security agency in the world, Garry. It has to be, our lives depend on it every day. We infiltrated that mob a long time ago, they're an offshoot of one of those particularly insane religious groups in the southern states of the USA and we thought that they might look for help from some jihadist group in damaging you and the company."

"Good God!" exploded Garry. "And Hannah was one of them?"

"A leading light among them," said Alana. "It's going to be interesting interrogating her."

"You said you wouldn't hurt her," said Garry with some worry. Despite the anger he felt about her betrayal, he couldn't stand the idea of any form of physical pain being inflicted.

"Torture doesn't work, Garry, we've known that for decades. The information that we get just cannot be trusted. But we'll certainly scare the pants off her."

"And when you've finished with her?"

"We'll show her the door, give her back her car keys and wave goodbye."

"Seriously?"

"Seriously. Mind you, we'll also pass her details to your government and she'll certainly face charges of incitement to riot."

Garry found that he had no reaction to that information.

"How long is this going on for?" he asked.

"The defence of your operation or Israel's concern for world reaction?"

"Both."

Before answering, Alana got to her feet and poured two mugs of coffee. She carried them back to the table and moved one over to Garry. He sipped at it gratefully.

"Israel's concern over world reaction will last until all the signs are that the Biblical information your system has revealed will no longer cause the crazies to act crazy," Alana continued. "That could be years. It depends on what other upheavals are caused, especially if you discover that Jesus had children and you can trace them to the present. And of course, revelations about Islam, Buddhism or any other major religion could cause eruptions."

Garry groaned. "Sometimes I wonder what monster we have released on the world."

Alana shook her head. "You shouldn't worry. It's always better to know the truth than to labour under delusions and mythology. It will all settle eventually and the world should be a more sane place when it does."

"I do hope so. And what about protecting this company?"

"We proved our point," said Alana. "We told your government that this was going to happen and they were reluctant to believe it. Now they've seen it, they'll take over defence duties again."

"And will I see you again?" Garry suddenly realised just how attractive he found this woman and a wave of need ran through him. After Hannah had left, he had not spoken to any woman outside of his work team.

Alana seemed to read his thought. She smiled, put down her coffee mug and came over to him, kneeling at his feet and taking his hands in hers.

"Garry, you are a very nice man, highly intelligent and very decent and yes, attractive. But I'm the ambassador of the most threatened country on Earth, it's a job that keeps me fully occupied and very much exposed. I can't have a relationship that could be used against me and anyway, I travel too much."

She leaned forward and kissed him lightly on the lips, rose to her feet and moved to the door. She waved back at him and walked out, leaving Garry feeling empty and saddened.

Chapter 28 - 2020

"All rise!" called the court official and the few people in the courtroom stood obediently as the judge took his seat with a small bow to those in front of him and the court settled.

Nobody wore a wig or a gown. These traditions had quietly died as court proceedings had changed radically in the last few weeks. Simple business attire had become the norm.

"Peter Alec Brown," said the court official, reading from the single sheet he held. "You are charged with the murder of Kathleen Rita Hill on September 15th of this year, at Acocks Green, Birmingham. Do you wish to enter a plea?"

The young man in his twenties sitting in the dock between two prison guards didn't move or even acknowledge the question.

"My Lord, the prisoner has declined to enter a plea," said the official and the judge nodded to him.

"Prosecution?" the judge asked.

An elderly woman sitting in a seat a few metres away rose to her feet. "Allyson Bentley for the Crown, My Lord," she stated formally.

"Ms Bentley, as you know, I am required to complete some formalities," the judge said and the woman nodded without speaking.

"Ms Bentley, will you confirm that the Crown Prosecutor Service is registered and licenced to perform prosecutions where the evidence is based entirely on visual DNA records?"

"Yes, My Lord, the certification is valid, up to date and has been submitted to you," the woman replied.

"And your expert witness is similarly licenced by the government as an expert on reading DNA records?"

"Yes, My Lord. Doctor John Read is professor of genetics at London University and has gained all the required accreditations."

"We are familiar with the work of Doctor Read," said the judge. "Please proceed, Ms Bentley."

"Thank you, My Lord," the barrister replied and nodded to her assistant who pressed a button on her computer. A large screen slowly dropped down from the ceiling to the judge's left.

"My Lord, the following images are taken from the DNA sample provided by the accused. They show the events of the day in question. We first saw these images at the laboratories of the Police Forensic Unit. Later, under the supervision of Professor Read, we took our own DNA sample from the accused and found the same images, so there is no doubt that they are images recorded on the accused man's DNA."

The screen flickered into life. The image was of a tunnel under either a road or a railway overhead. From the light evident at the end of the tunnel, it was gathering dusk just as a girl appeared at one end, walking towards the observer.

She was a teenager, dressed in conventional school uniform of a blue dress with a maroon blazer, white socks and conventional shoes and she was carrying a briefcase.

The observer moved rapidly and advanced on the girl who displayed shock and then fear as she tried to turn and run but was gripped firmly by the observer. Her gasps of terror came through clearly on the system loudspeakers and the girl's open-mouthed scream rang out in a shocking underlining of the episode.

The man committing this violence struggled with her and then slammed a violent blow across her face that left a red mark on her left cheek. His arm came into view as he did so and it was obvious that he was wearing a short-sleeved shirt and tattoos were clearly visible along his forearm. He dragged her to the ground and was obviously holding her down with his own weight as he ripped open the front of dress and then the singlet under it. He stared down at the small, slight breasts and then gripped her by the throat and applied pressure.

There was dead silence in the courtroom as the tragedy unfolded, then just a small groan of dismay as the life in the girl appeared to fade and her struggles ended.

The screen went dead and slowly returned to the ceiling, the sound harsh and intrusive in the silence of the courtroom.

The judge cleared his throat, obviously distressed by what he had seen.

"Anything else, Ms Bentley?"

The barrister rose to her feet again, her face pale. "The prosecution has submitted photographs of Mr Brown's arms, My Lord and these photographs confirm that the tattoos are identical to those images we just saw."

The judge nodded. "I have seen those photographs," he said. "Ms Bentley, did you also take DNA from the victim?"

"We did, My Lord, also supervised by Doctor Read."

"And did the images from that correspond to those we have already seen?"

"They did, My Lord. They clearly showed Mister Brown advancing on her, seizing her, ripping open her dress and then placing his hands round her throat. The images stopped a few moments later."

"And does the prosecution wish to show those images?"

The woman appeared to choke a little and carefully wiped a tear from her eye. "My Lord, those images are horrible, but we would ask permission to show them as they make the prosecution's case absolutely solid."

The screen was lowered again and new images flickered into life. The view was clearly the entrance to the tunnel that had been seen before. The observer's gaze seemed focused on the far end, about twenty metres away, but snapped round to the left as something moved. The movement fixed on the image of a young man in jeans and short-sleeved shirt. Even in the gloom of the tunnel, the man's arms were easily seen to be heavily tattooed.

"Stop there," said the prosecutor and the scene became fixed, clearly showing the face of the man.

"We ask the court to look at the face of the accused," said the barrister. "You will see that it is obviously the same face as in the image."

The judge stared for a few seconds and nodded. "Proceed, Ms Bentley," he said.

The man on the screen advanced on the girl, seized her and began to shake her around, the actions causing his face to become fuzzy and unclear, but then he stopped moving as his hands moved underneath the image as they took hold of the girl's throat. His face was ugly as he laughed into the viewer's eyes and then everything faded to black. The girl was dead.

The court was silent as the prosecutor's assistant turned off the computer.

The judge looked at the group on the prisoner's other side. "Defence?" he asked.

A young man got to his feet. "Terence Peterson for the Defence, My Lord."

"I must ask you the same as for the Prosecution, Mr Peterson. Are you legally licenced to conduct such defences?"

"We are, My Lord and the certification is with you. Our expert witness is Doctor Shirley Littleton, head of the Department of Genetics at the University of Reading and she has appeared before you on other occasions."

"Yes, Mr Peterson, that is so. Do you have anything to say to counter the evidence we have seen?"

"My Lord, we conducted the same tests as has the Crown; we took our own samples of Mr Brown's DNA under the supervision of Doctor Littleton and found the same images. We are unable to dispute their validity."

"And do you wish any other images taken from the accused or the victim's DNA to be shown to the court?"

The young man shook his head. "That will not be necessary, My Lord. We have seen those same images in the DNA taken from the victim's body and from the accused and certified as genuine by Doctor Littleton. The defence has no option but to concede Mr Brown's guilt in this matter."

"And the question I must also ask of you, have you checked that Mr Brown does not have an identical twin?"

The barrister nodded. "My Lord, we followed that required procedure as it is well-established that only an identical twin could have similar DNA. The record of Mr Brown's birth showed no twin of any sort. His nearest sibling is a sister, born three years later."

"Then you have nothing to challenge Mr Brown's guilt?"

"Only mitigating circumstances, My Lord."

"We will examine those later," said the judge and turned his face back to look directly at the prisoner in the dock.

"Peter Alec Brown," he said. "There can be no doubt that you committed this horrible crime. Current technology proves it conclusively and the procedures have been designed so that there is no question of having examined some other person's DNA. Not only have we seen you commit the crime but the DNA taken from the victim shows clearly that it was you as the assailant. You are guilty as charged. Is there anything you wish to say?"

The man in the dock didn't seem to have heard the judge. Throughout the entire proceedings, he had kept his face turned to the floor and showed no emotion at all.

"The court will hear and evaluate any mitigating circumstances to be presented by the Defence Counsel over the next two days and sentencing will take place next week."

He nodded at the two guards sitting next to the prisoner. "Take him down," he said. He looked at each of the two barristers in turn. "Counsel in my chambers," he said and rose to his feet.

"All rise!" said the official loudly and the few people in the courtroom stood as the judge left the podium.

* * *

"That could have taken some days under the old system," the judge said, his jacket removed, sipping at a fresh cup of coffee as he sat at ease in an armchair.

"Instead of thirty minutes," said Allyson Bentley. "And with a hundred percent certain result." She leaned over the coffee table and poured herself a cup from the heated jug. She added cream and sugar and sat back with a smile.

"It makes my job a bit of a farce," said the young man in the third armchair. "There's bugger-all I can do to offer any sort of defence."

"That's a fact, Terry," agreed the judge. "But you can try and mitigate it a bit, if you really want to, and at least you have the satisfaction of knowing there's no way we can convict an innocent man."

"Or let a guilty one go free," added Allyson. "It's almost the perfect criminal justice system." She sipped at her cup thoughtfully. "But it's made the process dead boring and far too easy."

"Thank God for whatever geniuses developed this technology," said the judge with a smile. "They'll save the state billions in legal battles."

"I'll drink to that," said the defence counsel.

"Though it's highly disturbing how many convicted criminals have been found not to be guilty and released even in just the last few weeks, as a result of this technology," added Ms Bentley. "God knows how many more will be found as they keep testing. It's going to be hugely disturbing for the justice system and probably embarrassing."

The defence barrister nodded. "It'll probably cut down the number of people studying law for a time until we regain our reputation."

"Will you be offering anything supportive in extenuating circumstances, Terry?" asked the judge.

"I wish I could," replied the counsel. "I can't find anything in his history to justify a plea."

"Well, you've got a couple more days before we hear your case, but failing that I have no option but a life sentence without parole."

"I understand. And that said, I don't think I'm violating any professional ethics in saying the bastard's deserved everything he gets."

The judge looked at his watch. "Okay, children," he said. "Another one for us, an assault charge. You're ready? Good! See you back here in about forty minutes."

There was a small chuckle from all of them as they left the judge's chambers.

Chapter 29

Weeks went by smoothly. The researchers were all thoroughly involved in their work, few of them left the office before seven or eight o'clock in the evening and there was a general air of happiness in the place. Conversations in the restaurant were quiet but intense as the people shared their developments, but during this time, nothing exceptional happened.

Bill continued his regular pattern of working alone at any or all hours, the others fell into natural working groups of shared interests and friendships.

Garry had little to do but keep an eye on things, watching out for signs of stress in the workers, interview two more recent doctoral graduates who had applied for the job of teaching universities how to use the equipment. He enjoyed that, watching the shock and excitement at the applicants' first exposure to seeing their own lives shown on the screen and he took it upon himself to teach them how to use the systems so that they could take the knowledge elsewhere.

At times, he wondered why the churches had shown no reaction to the revelations that had completely wiped away the main foundations of their faith, but no answer came to him.

Until…

"Garry, Home Secretary has just called me." Karen's gentle voice with the slight Russian accent sounded in his ear.

"And what does the second most powerful office-holder in the land have to say?"

"Vatican wishes to send representative to examine your work to establish its credibility."

"Oh my! They've finally responded?"

She chuckled lightly. "They have not been inactive these last months, my strange little Welsh person. As we suspected, issue has exercised some highly educated and trained minds around world."

"So who are they sending?"

"They're not treating this lightly, Garry. Newly-appointed Cardinal is coming, Cardinal Eamon Jackson. He's from Manchester."

"A Cardinal? Good grief, Karen, you're right, they're not mucking about here! When is he coming?"

"In three days. That's Friday, in morning at ten."

"And I have to give him a full demonstration?"

"You do."

"Karen, we both know that the only sure way of convincing him is to show him a scene from his own life."

"Then this is what you must do. You have all equipment?"

"Of course. And we've got the time down to thirty minutes to produce a DNA sample. Will you be here?"

"No, I think not. Let's keep it as low-key as we can. I believe this will be changing point for everything."

"I do believe you're right, Madam. I do hope it's a peaceful change."

He faintly heard a small chuckle as he hung up the phone. He suddenly realised he had no knowledge of the etiquette in dealing with high church personages. He quickly ran a search on his computer, found several Catholic churches in the region, saw that one of them was quite near his home and picked up the phone.

"Good morning," he said when a pleasant tenor voice answered, introducing himself as Father Collins. "I need some help. My company is receiving a visit from Cardinal Jackson this week. I have no idea what the correct mode of address is."

"Ah yes, that will be Blueprints. Am I addressing Mr Garry Lawson?"

Garry was startled. "You know all about this visit?"

"Can you imagine that one of the most eminent people in our church could be in the region without our being briefed about it? And we assumed you would call this church, being the one nearest to your home, though all of us were prepared for it." The tenor voice was amused.

"All right, you're way ahead of me!" Garry began to share the amusement in the other. "So, back to my question. How do I address the Cardinal? And will he be accompanied by others?"

"The standard mode is 'Your Eminence.' And he will have two people with him, acting as secretaries. But Mr Lawson, let me stress, this will be an informal visit. The Cardinal and his escorts will be dressed in normal clothing, not even a dog-collar."

"And what is he expecting to see?"

"He will want to see that there is no way Professor McCauley can be mistaken in her findings."

"That will surely be an unpleasant experience, very hard to take?"

"Mr Lawson, the Catholic Church may have an image of intolerance, ignorance, hatred of science and all that, but let me tell you that Cardinal Jackson has a doctorate in Nuclear Physics from the Massachusetts Institute of Technology in the US. The two men with him, both parish priests, have doctorates also, one in mathematics, one in chemistry. They are trained in the scientific method. Show them what they need to see."

Garry was feeling overwhelmed. "And I suppose you have a doctorate in some science as well, Father Collins?"

The man on the other end finally laughed. "No, nothing so exotic, Garry! I just have the common or garden Master's Degree in Social Work!"

Garry echoed the man's laughter. "Father Collins, I have learned a lot about the Catholic Church from you! Thank you very much, I think I can handle the Cardinal's visit more easily now."

"You're welcome, Garry. Drop in and see us, maybe?"

"You won't try and convert me?"

"No chance! But I'd love to talk about your work."

"Then count on it," said Garry. "That could be an interesting discussion."

Garry watched the blue sedan roll up to the office. Not a luxury car, not even a high class European limousine, just a medium size vehicle that any family might own. Three men climbed out, the older man in the back seat opening the door himself. There was no sign of any VIP visit, just any normal business meeting about to take place.

Garry watched them walk up to the front door. All three looked fit and healthy, the Cardinal no less than the young men. He walked down to the lobby to greet them as they walked through the door.

"Your Eminence, it's a pleasure to have you here," he said and was about to greet the other two when the Cardinal spoke.

"Garry, this is a low-key event, let's not have any ceremony or bowing and scraping. Call me Eamon, this is Andy Prentice and Rob Milford."

He reached out his hand to Garry who shook it. The Cardinal was of average height, the tanned face of a surfer or skier and the face reflected strength of personality. All three of the visitors wore well-cut business suits and looked like business executives the world over.

A little set back, Garry shook hands with the other two men and replied.

"Well... thank you! This is all rather overwhelming. Let's go to my office and talk about how we handle this visit."

"I hope you have a decent coffee pot there," the Cardinal said as they walked up the stairs.

"Always," said Garry and began to relax.

Seated in his office, coffee poured for all of them, the Cardinal began.

"Garry, clearly you've set off a firebomb under every religious body in the world, especially mine and the Protestants. We must be absolutely certain that your facts are correct before we can change to meet them."

"What will prove it to you?" asked Garry.

"Demonstrate the validity."

"That's what I intend, but I must caution you that the only way to do that is to take a sample of your DNA and show you some scenes from your life. We've done it many times and it's a process that invariably causes deep emotional shock to the subject."

The Cardinal nodded. "We'll handle it. You can do that immediately, I understand."

"We can." Garry rose, moved to his desk and reached into a drawer, extracted a box of sterile rubber gloves and put one on each hand. He took out a collection package and walked over to the Cardinal who opened his mouth without being asked. Garry wiped the swab over the inside of the man's cheek, pushed the swab down in the bottle and sealed it. He opened the office door to find Avram who had been briefed for just this and who took the bottle with a wide grin.

Garry returned to the seat and picked up his mug of coffee. "About thirty minutes," he said. He thought for a few moments, wondering about the wisdom of his question.

"Eamon, can I ask you this? Assuming we prove to your satisfaction that this technology does what we say, what will you do?"

"Fair question," said the Cardinal. "The next step will be to review the work of Professor McCauley and test her conclusions."

"And then?"

"And then we must change to meet reality. This is no longer the church that burns heretics at the stake, Garry. You know my background and you know that I and my two colleagues here are scientifically trained people with terminal degrees from world-class universities. But we are priests because we have faith and we are unlikely to lose that. We also have commitments to serving the Creator and we won't lose those, either."

Suddenly, he grinned widely, a sharp contrast with the gravity of his words.

"Mind you," he said, "if you could prove somehow that God doesn't exist, things might be more difficult!"

Garry had to laugh. "I suspect not," he said. "I've never believed that stuff about having to believe in God in order to be a moral, good person. I'm pretty certain, Eamon, that even if we could do that impossible thing, it would not change any of you as the people you are."

"Thank you."

The atmosphere lightened in the room and the two men chatted informally about the work of Blueprints, and the Cardinal's life as an academic before he entered the Church. While the Cardinal gave a small outline of the careers of his two priests, Garry was a little disturbed that neither of them spoke a word.

The knock on the door ended this process and Avram appeared holding the standard plastic envelope that contained the DNA slide for scanning. He ignored the three visitors and handed the envelope to Garry, walking out without a word.

Garry moved to the computer terminal on his desk and inserted the slide in the slot designed for it.

"Look at the big screen," he said. He'd had a large monitor installed in his office the day before for just this purpose. "Eamon, I'm going to show scenes at random. We haven't yet worked out how to find a specific date or time. Do you want your colleagues to remain in the room?"

"It's what they're here for," said the Cardinal, with a casual wave of his hand. Despite the relaxed attitude, Garry was sure he could detect some tension in the priest.

On the screen, the observer was walking along the pavement of a main road. At some point, he turned into a driveway and began approaching a large elegant building. The driveway was populated with many boys apparently in their early and mid teens, wearing school blazers.

Only a small movement betrayed the shock of the man watching.

"Manchester Grammar School," said the Cardinal.

Several boys approached the observer, the Cardinal as a schoolboy. "Hey, Eamon!" said one. He had a wide, cheerful face with profuse freckles. "Did you get the physics homework done last night?"

"Good God, that's Goofy Anderson!" said the Cardinal, hiding whatever response was made. "I'd say we were about thirteen."

"Let's move further," said Garry and made the mental impulse to move the record to a later time. The effect was interesting. A young woman of considerable beauty was removing the last of her clothing and then stood still to receive the admiration she seemed to expect. The two young men shifted nervously in their seats but the Cardinal was undisturbed.

"My word, Mary O'Halloran! Now that does bring back memories! But Garry, move it on, I think you're upsetting my colleagues here!" He managed to control his laughter as he spoke to the young priests. "Do remember, gentlemen, I didn't enter the Church till a lot later! That scene was at Oxford University, I must have been nineteen."

He looked at Garry. "Garry, there's no doubt you have proved that you can see images of a person's life from their DNA. So, now I need to see how you look at the lives of somebody's ancestors."

Garry nodded and reset the scanner to look at the thread, tracking back to the beginning. The Cardinal looked curiously at him.

"Garry, I didn't see you move a mouse or anything else. How did you do that?"

"Telepathy, Eamon."

The Cardinal snorted in derision. "Yeah, right!"

"Stick with it," Garry said. "But let's look at the current issue. See those two tiny dots at the very edge of the thread?"

All three visitors leaned forward and looked at the screen.

"One of those is the life thread of your mother, the other one of your father. Which would you like to see?"

Some tension showed in the Cardinal's posture.

"My father," he said, a little hoarseness in his voice. A moment later a scene appeared. A boy was sitting at a desk, studying a book. He looked about ten or eleven, Garry thought. The observer was shouting at him.

"There's no point in you studying! You're too stupid to pass an exam for a grammar school!"

The boy looked terrified and then cowered as the observer advanced on him and slapped him hard on the head.

"Garry, stop it!" snapped the Cardinal. His face was white and the anger was obvious.

Garry closed the scene. He realised that the boy was the Cardinal being beaten by his father. Silence hung in the room like a winter fog before the Cardinal spoke again, his composure regained.

"That was before the scholarship exams for Manchester Grammar School," he said. "And as you now know, I won a scholarship."

"How did your father react?" asked Garry.

"He never said a word."

"Do you want to see some more?"

"I think so. Can you go back several generations?"

The Cardinal clearly had no doubts that the system worked and could see back in time, Garry thought as he worked back the lifetimes of seven direct male ancestors and began playing a scene at random.

They were in a church. It was a beautifully ornate church and a priest was reciting something while swinging an incense.

"Latin!" said the Cardinal. "It's a high mass! Where and when, I wonder?"

The room occupants listened for a few moments, then the observer turned his head and looked at the woman next to him and spoke. Even from this angle, her swelled stomach was evident.

"It's Polish!" exclaimed the Cardinal. "He said, *'Will you be able to sit to the end, my dear?'* This is incredible! How many generations back is this, Garry?"

"Seven, all through the direct male line. Do you have family records going that far back?"

"I don't think so, though we have always believed that there is Polish ancestry," replied the Cardinal. He fell silent, lost in thought. Finally he stirred.

"Garry, it's obviously impossible to deny that you can look back through time, so you have given my church and others a serious problem. We have to rethink our history, our policies, our entire reason for being. I will next have to meet Professor McCauley and review her research, but I believe I know what I will find and then I must report to His Holiness."

"What do you think will happen?" Garry was feeling great pain, realising he was seeing a man having his whole world turned upside down.

"I believe that we will accept reality. But if perhaps there was no divine Son of God, the words spoken, the teachings delivered, all are still the Words of God, however delivered and we will still teach them. The faithful will continue in the faith, the good works will continue."

"Will there be opposition?"

"Without a doubt. There will be many who deny what you have proved, there will probably be defections from the Church, probably some will set up in opposition."

"An opposition Catholic Church?"

"It's happened before." He thought for another few moments. "You mentioned telepathy earlier. Were you serious?"

"Absolutely, though the more accurate term would be telekinesis."

"The ability to move objects with your mind?"

"Exactly that. Our researchers found that they move along a subject's time line or enter an ancestor's time line simply by thinking it."

"Do all humans have the ability?" The Cardinal was clearly riveted.

"We have only tested our own staff," said Garry. "All of us have it, but some to a greater extent than others. I suspect that the ability will respond to training and practice and all humans have it."

"What is this going to do to the human race, I wonder? Are there any other incredible things to be found?"

Garry shook his head. "No signs of anything else."

"So far," added the Cardinal.

"So far," agreed Garry.

The Cardinal rose and the two others did the same. "We must go."

"I'll see you to the door," said Garry and escorted the visitors out.

"Are we able to buy this equipment?" asked the Cardinal as they reached the lobby.

"Many universities already have. We can train your staff in how to use it."

"I believe we will need several." The Cardinal smiled again. "May God bless you and your work, Garry and may the world stay at peace."

Uncertain of how to reply to that, Garry smiled.

Handshakes all around and the car drove out of the industrial park. Garry realised the two young men had not spoken a word once the demonstration had begun and wondered if they had been carrying recording devices.

* * *

Work proceeded in the office with little happening to break up the quiet concentration. With the linguists and historians returned to Cambridge University, the buzz of new historical discoveries had gone as the teams now concentrated on their particular area of research. Nothing was heard from the main religious organisations and that worried Garry because he felt certain that the discoveries of the mythology of the Christian legends must surely be shaking all the religions to the core.

And then the peaceful concentration was broken.

Chapter 30 – Humanity Changes

Garry looked up from his monitor to see Deborah standing at the doorway. The tension and excitement in her was almost radiating from the slender, pretty woman.

"Come on in," he said, standing up and moving to the open area in his office where the comfortable seats sat around the coffee table. "You look like you've got something," he added as they both sat down.

She nodded and he thought she was almost bursting with pressures inside her. She reached out and placed a tiny white ball on the table. It looked like one of those that made up lightweight packing material.

Garry looked at it curiously and then at Deborah. She was staring with concentration at the tiny ball and Garry followed her gaze. Nothing happened for a few seconds and then... the ball twitched and moved about three centimetres.

Garry shivered. "Did you do that?"

"Yes," said Deborah. "Watch."

The ball moved across the table towards Garry, stopped and turned ninety degrees, moved along the edge, stopped again and then turned back toward the centre of the table.

Deborah sat back in her seat and breathed out. "I did that this morning for the first time, but I only managed a tiny movement, about a centimetre or so. Since then, I've improved it to what you just saw and that's something I only managed about twenty minutes ago."

"Can you make anything heavier than that move?"

"Not yet. I've been trying with matchsticks for the last few minutes before I came in here, but couldn't get a result. That thing was the lightest object I could find and it's what I've been practicing with."

"How do you do it?" Garry was sensing the arrival of a massive change in his life and possibly the whole world.

"It's exactly the same process we use when we move along a DNA life thread or pick one of the dots to move to an ancestor. The more I do it, the more I think it's the same as moving a limb or a finger. We don't think about how we do it. We just do it."

"Any thoughts on why this ability has just developed?" asked Garry.

"I think so. I think it's just grown as we worked on the DNA threads. Our minds got more and more used to being able to do it and it didn't require moving anything physical, so we just got used to the process."

"So it's a matter of once we knew it was possible, we did more and more?"

"Remember back when the athletics world said a four-minute mile was impossible?" said Deborah. "And then that Doctor chap, what was his name, Roger... Bannister? He disagreed and finally ran a mile in just under four minutes. I've seen the films and he collapsed at the end, it took absolutely everything he had. After that, more and more people did the same, just because now they actually *knew* it was possible. And when they did it, they just stopped, caught their breath and then walked around to recover, no collapse, nothing."

"Have any others in your team tried it?"

"They have," she said. "Jack's been able to make that thing twitch a bit, Ruth made it move a centimetre of two. But I reckon all of us could do it now that we know it's possible. I think we've all been working on the life strands this way, so we all know it can be done, we just haven't tried it with physical objects. And there's another thing. I can't prove it, but somehow I suspect the DNA has actually been teaching us how to do it."

"Good grief!" Garry sat back in shock. "You mean our DNA may be actively sending something to our minds as we examine it?"

"Crazy, eh?" said Deborah. "There's no way I can prove that, of course. Anyway, Garry, why don't you try it? Now that you know it can be done."

Garry leaned forward, put his chin on his hands and studied the tiny white ball. He stared at it, tried to enfold it in his mind, thought harder and harder about moving it, concentrated... saw nothing in his mind but the ball, tried to look deep inside the foam... to move it... nothing happened.

He sat back, shaking his head.

"You don't spend as much time as we do moving along time lines and between them," said Deborah. "I'd say your mind just hasn't had enough experience yet."

"That's probably it. What do you want to do next?"

"Keep practicing," she said. "I'm quite certain we'll get better and better. Hang on, let me try something...."

She stared at the ball and utter silence filled the room for twenty seconds. The ball moved gently and then rose into the air and stopped at the watchers' eye level before dropping back on the table silently.

"I knew it. I just knew it. We get better and better the more we practice!" Deborah was breathing hard as if she had just run a great distance.

Garry felt much the same. "Do you want the rest of the staff to know about this?"

She looked thoughtful. "Would it distract them from their own projects?"

"I'm pretty sure it will!" Garry laughed. "They'll all be practicing for a few days and it'll be interesting to see who does it best. So just let people know as you feel appropriate. But we know this crowd – they'll all be back digging into their own fields of research before too much time has gone."

"How about outside the organisation?"

"Best keep it quiet," said Garry. "Nobody will believe it anyway, but we could get them upset. It'll get out there in time."

She smiled and walked out of the office. For a long time, Garry sat and thought about what had just happened and tried to imagine the effects on the world when the news broke and wondered if other people would find they had the ability. At one point, he shivered, thinking that his group might just have released a huge problem rife with unpleasant possibilities on the human race.

"Karen, you sure as hell are changing the world," he muttered and picked up the phone to call her.

* * *

For some two weeks, the deep air of concentration was broken by sheer playfulness as the team learned about Deborah's astonishing discovery and experimented with it. Garry was not sure whether to be surprised or not as all but two of the researchers found that they had somehow developed the telekinetic abilities that Deborah had. For most, the power was limited to moving one of the foam rubber balls around the desk top. But several found that they could lift the balls and even move them across to another location. Avram proved to be the most accomplished and he enjoyed himself occasionally launching a ball to land on another worker's desk and bouncing up and down. Finally, Garry had to tell him to stop, as it was proving irritating to other people. Rather to everybody's astonishment, the acknowledged genius of the group, Bill Hawker could not achieve any such abilities and retreated into a small cone of grumpiness before forgetting all about it as he dug himself deep and deeper into the issues of finding some sort of universal clock to identify the age of the readings in the DNA.

*   *   *

"That's definitely Cro-Magnon man," said Avram.

Garry studied the pictures on the screen by Avram's desk. They showed artists' construction illustrations of Cro-Magnon and Neanderthal people.

"I agree," said Garry. He looked back at the monitor, fascinated by the scene. Several humans wearing assorted skins sat around in the grass. Some were children and they seemed to be playing like children have played throughout history, running around and laughing, burning off excess energy. Occasionally, some sounds were heard, nothing resembling speech that he could identify.

The observer through whose DNA they were seeing this scene moved its gaze around the group, almost as if guarding them.

"I'd say this is the matriarch or patriarch of the tribe," said Avram. "I can't get any sense of what sex it is, but it almost looks as if he or she is regarding the group with some sense of ownership and responsibility. I'll know more as I follow the time line a bit."

"The language boffins are going to go off their brains when they see and hear this," said Garry.

"And the social historians," said Avram.

"How far back?" asked Garry.

"We think fifty thousand years. That's based on taking an average of twenty years per generation and we worked back two thousand, five hundred generations. That was a long, cumbersome process in itself, it took some days, but this is our first research stop, so thought it a good time to call you to have a look."

"I'm glad you did. This is incredible, nobody has ever seen anything like this before. Daily life for a Cro-Magnon family! Who could have anticipated this?"

Avram shook his head. "Not me, for a start!"

"Did you have any difficulties?"

"Mainly concentration. Once we started, we agreed just to take the male line of each ancestor of the original DNA donor and it was very hard to ignore looking at each life in detail, it was so gripping. And then once, just three generations back, we found one of those lives with no ancestor. We passed that one to Penny's team and we started again from a new sample. Of course, we had to note each ancestor as we opened his life stream, if only to get an accurate counting of how far back we were going. So it's been a slow, fascinating project with no signs of reaching the end."

"And this is Cro-Magnon," said Garry. "I wonder if we'll find any links back to Neanderthal man?"

"It will be plain luck if we do," said Avram. "We'll need to do the same long, drawn-out process with samples from around the world and just hope that we find Neanderthals or even better, some hard evidence that the two species interbred as seems to be the case."

Garry continued to stare at the scene on the monitor, his mind churning in fascination, delight and some worry about what he and his team were doing and what might happen.

"It gets to you, doesn't it?" Avram said softly at his side. "These are our ancestors living some fifty thousand years ago. What are we going to find if we can go back a few more thousand years?"

"Pulling back to Southern Africa, I imagine, if current theories about human beginnings are anything to go on."

Avram looked thoughtful. "And what if that's not what we find?"

"That's too much to contemplate," replied Garry with a smile. "We've already turned human history on its head with our recent discoveries. Any more bombshells, we might not survive it."

"That's what worries me," said Avram.

Reluctantly, Garry turned away from the monitor and returned to his office. There were times when he envied his researchers, their excitement at the wonders they were finding almost every day and their youthful ability to ignore potential storms. Other times, he felt overwhelmed by the things that were happening and his role in it and he couldn't help but be frightened by the possibilities for upheaval.

* * *

"Garry! It's Penny. Will you come right way?"

The urgency in Penny's voice was high. Garry had not talked much to her in recent weeks beyond his standard "management by walking around" conversations, but she had made little progress in researching the examples of lives they had found with no ancestors.

He got up and walked round to her desk. She was sitting before her screen, her hands before her mouth in a pose of anxiety.

"Penny?"

"I've got a sample here of a man without ancestors," said Penny.

"We've found a few of those," said Garry. "They've all been from a long way back, at least three generations."

"This one isn't," said Penny, her eyes wide. "He's alive and well and living in Birmingham."

"Holy Shit!" said Garry.

"He may well have," said Penny, a smile finally breaking the look of shock and worry. "But so far, he looks normal in every way."

"Who is he and how did you get the sample?"

"Roland Clarke, aged thirty, a schoolteacher in a High School. He volunteered a sample when we got the University Medical School to ask for a number from patients and staff. He was in for a sinus operation."

"And he wasn't bothered, obviously about giving a sample."

"No, he wasn't."

"Anything odd about his lifeline?"

"There is," said Penny and turned to the screen. She brought up the sample images and moved slowly back to the very beginning. The first image was a shock.

"He's obviously walking," said Garry. "He's probably about eighteen months old. Where's the earlier stuff?"

"That's it," said Penny. "Nothing before that. No dots on the beginning of the strand, nothing. He just appeared out of the blue, it seems."

"What does the rest of his lifeline show?"

"Nothing out of the ordinary. Grew up in Sutton Coldfield, both parents still live there, ordinary schooling, degree in education from Birmingham, this is his first job, still there after six years of teaching history and geography. His major achievement was a very high ability at rugby, he's played for some league teams around the Midlands."

"We need to talk to him. Will you call him? See if he can come down here."

"Garry, it may be better if I go there, then I can talk to his parents as well."

Garry nodded. "Whenever you can set it up."

* * *

Penny stood up and smiled as the young man opened the door to the small office she had hired for the day at a hotel in Birmingham. She had decided not to meet at the school in case anything highly unusual came out of the meeting and caused the young man problems.

"Good morning," she said and held out her hand, intrigued by the dark and quite handsome appearance of the arrival, Roland Clarke. He was tall, solidly built with wide shoulders and narrow hips, the classic athlete's look.

"Hi," he said with a wide grin displaying white teeth.

Careful, Penny, she said to herself. *Mind on the job.*

"So what's all this about?" he asked, sitting down at the circular table in the middle of the room.

"Some months ago, you gave a DNA sample to a research group while you were in the hospital for a sinus operation," she said.

"Right," he said. "I had a deviated septum, nose always blocked, no sense of smell and that fixed it."

Suddenly he looked alarmed. "Is there a problem with my DNA?" he said, his eyes wide.

"No, no, not at all," she said quickly. "Quite the reverse, you seem to be a man in excellent condition."

Roland leaned back and relaxed. "Phew!" he said. "You had me going there!"

He's really quite gorgeous, Penny thought. *Trouble is, what else is he? Possibly not human?*

"I'd better explain," she said. "I work for a privately-owned genetics research lab and we do a lot of work on the human DNA. The hospital team gave us the DNA samples as was indicated in the agreement you signed. Sometimes, we find people who seem unusually fit, strong and full of energy and then we want to follow up to see how that came about and if it's an inherited condition."

The white smile again. "Yeah, I've always been a pretty good athlete," he said, apparently enjoying the chance to show off to a pretty girl.

"And were your parents that way?"

"Hell, no! Dad might have played cricket as a kid, but nothing more than that. I don't think Mum has ever done anything energetic in her life! But I was adopted, so they're not really any sort of indicator."

Oops, thought Penny. *That's interesting.* "Did you bring your birth certificate as I asked?"

Roland reached into his jacket pocket and took out an envelope. "A copy," he said and passed it to her.

Penny opened the envelope and studied the document. "Both parents unknown?"

"The hospital got that done. I was just left at the front door, I was told, no sign of anything to indicate my parents. I was just fourteen months old."

"How very sad," said Penny. "And your adoptive parents took you soon after?'

"Within days of all the standard search procedures and medical checks, yes. And they've been great parents, I must say."

Penny realised that there was little else she could get from this meeting. The key point was his adoption with both parents unknown and that plus the oddity of his lifeline having no record earlier than about fourteen months made him a mystery of much significance.

She took him through the rest of his life, learning nothing new and telling herself she was not prolonging the meeting out of attraction to this young man. After he had left with a slightly longer handshake than normal, she drove up to the northern suburb of Sutton Coldfield and met the parents. Beyond confirming that they had adopted Roland when he was a toddler and that they were very happy with the results, nothing new came up at all. In deep thought, she drove back to Reading to report to Garry.

* * *

"Absolutely human in every way and dead sexy with it!" she said.

Garry laughed. "I hope your overwhelming lust didn't get in the way of your professional research."

"No chance!"

"So did you see any indications at all that he was aware of anything unusual in himself?"

"Nothing, other than a natural pride in his athletic abilities. He's never been ill beyond the sinus issue and that probably came from an accident when he broke his nose playing Rugby. But he's got unusually fast reflexes, perfect eyesight and above average muscular strength."

"Superman, eh? He obviously got to you!"

She blushed. "He could certainly play the part! I reckon he'd look smashing in tights and a cloak!"

Garry chuckled. "But nothing to indicate anything questionable in his origins?"

"Nothing. But it's given me a thought that needs following through."

"Then don't just sit here talking to me, go and follow it through!"

She laughed and went back to her desk.

Three days later, she was back.

"This will fascinate you," she said. Garry waved at the coffee pot and she carefully filled two mugs before sitting down at the coffee table in the middle of his office.

"So far, we've found sixty-three cases of people with no ancestors," she said. "So I looked at every one of them and followed their life lines through from beginning to end. There are two factors common to all of them."

She paused for effect and sipped at her coffee.

"Bloody drama queen," said Garry. "Go on, fascinate me, like you promised."

"Oh, I will. Every single one of those lives apparently began at between twelve and sixteen months. Not one of them has any earlier images and we now know so well, the rest of us mortals start recording from the first moments after birth."

"Okay, you've fascinated me." Garry held his hands round his coffee mug as if seeking reassurance from the warmth. "Anything else?"

"Indeed yes. As you know, we also record right up to the moment of death. For most of us, that's a gradual fading and then blackness. For the unfortunates who met a violent death, the images still show the lead up to that moment and the circumstances, like a soldier seeing a combat zone before he's killed by a shell, or those horrible images we saw of people being murdered."

"These don't?"

"These don't. Not one of them. They just end. The last images are normal, living life images at an advanced age. None of them seemed to have died violently or suddenly, none from disease. It just seems that they vanished from the Earth having turned off the recorder."

Garry stared at his coffee mug and finally took a sip.

"Any thoughts about what it tells us?"

"I've tried to turn my highly trained, doctorate-qualified brilliant mind to this," Penny said. "And all I can come up with is a couple of options. Both are insane."

"Tell me."

"Option One; all of these are mutants, born normally but somehow without the links to their ancestors and the recording mechanism doesn't wake up for a year or so. The same mutation caused the recording mechanism to turn itself off at some late stage in their lives."

"Feasible," agreed Garry. "Option Two?"

"Aliens. They were born or somehow artificially grown somewhere using human DNA and planted among us for some reason and then pulled out when their jobs were done."

"And what were those jobs?"

"Ever seen those natural history programs where naturalists put disguised cameras in the forests or jungles and record films of animals without humans around?"

"That's the way I was thinking," said Garry. "Somebody or some*thing* is studying human life?"

"It seems a strong possibility. And I don't think these people knew that was their task or that they were in any way different from the rest of us. But if that is the case, there must also be some way in which they send the recording of their life to whoever is doing the studying."

"That's a very spooky possibility. What do you want to do now?"

"First, let me tell you how I followed up on this. I went back and checked on all the "zero dot" samples I had. With all of them, the first images were between one and two years of age, as far as I could tell. But all of these were several generations old and I wasn't able to find any evidence of adoption in any case."

"So that rules out one line of research unless we find some more recent samples. Okay, what next?"

"Garry, I think I've done with this line of research. I've gone through every one of the samples we have of this kind, so there's nothing new I'll find. I'd like to move to something else."

"You know the rules, Penny. In my harsh, disciplinarian company, you can do whatever you bloody well like! Take your time, chat to the other teams, see what you'd like to do."

She stood up and came round the table, bent over and kissed his cheek. "You're a lovely man, Garry."

She walked out, leaving him pleased, enjoying the smell of something expensive that she wore and a little sad also, memories of Hannah in front of his mind. Then he returned to the explosive information Penny had uncovered and shivered. Who or what was examining humanity like some naturalist studying animals?

Chapter 31

"Garry, it's Father Collins. We talked when you called me just before Cardinal Jackson came to visit."

Garry woke from the deep reverie in which he was thinking about the possible impact of the recent discoveries when the phone rang on his desk. Swiftly switching gears, he replied.

"Yes, Father Collins! Nice to hear back from you."

But as he spoke, he realised that this could not be a social call. It had been six weeks since the Cardinal's visit to Blueprints and since then, Garry knew that the same three men had visited Professor Helene Macauley in Cambridge and reviewed her findings. Something major was about to happen, he knew.

"Garry, I've been asked to let you know, the Cardinal took all his findings back to Rome and senior personnel, including His Holiness have been discussing the issue intensively. They have finally reached a conclusion and the Church will issue a statement worldwide this week."

"Can you tell me what they have concluded, Father?"

The voice of the priest seemed to reflect sadness.

"As we said, Garry, we no longer burn heretics at the stake and most of our people are highly educated, including, as you know, in the sciences. So we cannot simply ignore what we learned and the Church has no choice but to change. I hope you will watch the statement when it's released. There will be plenty of warning in the media."

"Will this cause stress in the Church, Father?"

"It cannot be avoided, Garry."

"And for you?"

"Oddly enough, no. It may surprise you to know that I'm one of those very liberal priests who has never placed much store on dogma. This job has allowed me to do what I want to do and nothing will change that."

"That relieves my mind, Father. I think you're a very good man."

There was a ghost of a laugh in Garry's ear.

"That's always the objective but I can't say I have always succeeded."

"We'll have to talk again after the announcement."

"I'd like that, Garry. Drop in sometime, I'm sure we'll still be here."

Garry sent an email to all staff, summarising the conversation and suggesting they keep a look-out for the Church's statement.

Two days later, a press release printed in nearly all of the UK's newspapers said that the Vatican would be making a major policy statement the following night. The article said that similar releases had been sent to every newspaper in the world and the websites of nearly every government. The article said that the statement would be made live on television, simultaneously around the world in the major languages and by different personnel. The announcement in English would be made on the BBC by Cardinal Jackson.

Nervously, Garry sat before the television at home, cradling a glass of Karen Petrova's finest scotch and watched as the BBC worked its way up to the broadcast by Cardinal Jackson. For two hours before, an array of pundits had given their forecasts of the contents of the Vatican's announcement, varying from a common suggestion that the Pope was about to abdicate, to ideas that Christmas was to be moved to July in line with commonly accepted historical evidence that Jesus had been born in the summertime and some of the crazier ideas were that aliens had taken over the Vatican and that the Pope would reveal that he was from a far planet and would take over the world.

Nobody came remotely close to the reality.

Finally, at eight o'clock, the news announcer said simply, "And now we cross to the Vatican where England's Cardinal Jackson has an announcement to make on behalf of the Catholic Church."

Immediately, the familiar face of the Cardinal appeared on the screen.

"Good evening," he said. "Several weeks ago, I visited the offices of a scientific research company in England where I was shown an extraordinary technology. Without going into technical details, let me just say that this system allows one to look back through the lives of every one of us and our ancestors to review history, to actually see it as if on film. I have thoroughly examined all the data and I am completely convinced of its validity. You may know that the British Government now uses this technology in the

Criminal Justice System to try cases of violence. We in the Vatican bought several systems and our own people have been testing it. There is simply no doubt that it works.

"One researcher, an eminent professor at one of the world's greatest universities conducted a line of research, working in Israel. She worked through thousands of DNA samples with her team, eventually being able to see day to day life over some years at the start of the Christian era.

"She found that there is no evidence for the life of a divine Jesus Christ. While she certainly looked at the life of a man named Jesus, born in July of 4BC, nothing indicates any more than that he was one of several young radical rabbis preaching around the region. There was no divine birth, no miracles, no crucifixion, no resurrection."

The Cardinal gave a slow, sad smile.

"The Mother of Churches does not burn heretics at the stake. We do not believe in Creationism or an Earth that is six thousand years old, we accept scientific fact where it is provable. We must accept these findings."

He waited a few moments as if allowing time for his explosive words to sink in.

"So how does that affect us? Astonishingly, not that much. What was clear in all the research was that the teachings were given, though by several young Rabbis and they remain valid and appropriate. We will continue to teach them and do the work of the Church according to them. We will also do what history has done, combine all these teachings and attribute them to one source, though now it will be a figurative Christ rather than an actual one. The Mass will change because we cannot any longer conduct a transubstantiation ceremony involving the flesh and blood of Christ. The entire concept of the Holy Trinity must also change. But let me stress, we will continue to teach a message of love, toleration, kindness and forgiveness, for that is what those young people in Palestine taught. We will continue with the good works we have always done, bringing help to the unfortunate and we will continue to hold services of worship to God.

"Over the coming years, things may change more but I cannot forecast those. I pray that these changes will not cause anger, damage and violence and that we all accept the new realities. May God bless you all."

The screen changed to a view of the Vatican for a minute and then the channel returned to the BBC studios. Not wishing to hear what the talking heads would say, Garry switched off and finished his scotch.

Two days later, the Church of England issued a terse statement to all the media and the Archbishop of Canterbury made a short speech on the BBC.

"We echo the fine words spoken by our brothers at the Vatican. We too have examined the scientific evidence and can find no fault in it, so we too must change. We are working on defining just what changes, what doesn't, and how we modify our policies, but like our brothers, there will not be major changes as we continue to do what we can to help our fellow human beings."

The Archbishop let out an astonishing, brilliant and quite unexpected grin.

"I tell you one thing. Those crucifix statues must go. Just as well, I've always thought they were horrible. So I can only ask you to show tolerance and loving kindness in all your deeds and God bless you all."

Two days later, Garry got an unexpected visitor.

"I was in the area and I thought I'd drop by," said Cardinal Eamon Jackson.

"Better come to my office," said Garry and led the way out of the secure reception area.

"Coffee would be good," said the Cardinal as they took their seats at the coffee table by the window.

"No wingmen today?" asked Garry as he poured two mugs from the pot on the side table.

"This is an informal chat," said Jackson. "And they know the topic and don't need any convincing."

"I'm curious," said Garry, placing the coffee mugs on the table and sitting down opposite his visitor. "I saw your broadcast and I heard what Canterbury said. But I've heard no reaction."

"That's why I'm here," the Cardinal said. "Not entirely unexpected, but world reaction has been largely one of acceptance."

"Really? I'm astonished!"

"We're not. Garry, men of the church have not kept out of world changes. Increasingly, research has shown many of the facts that your people revealed. Many historians have produced evidence supporting what you have proved and the Israeli archaeologists have spent years looking for evidence of the Exodus from Egypt and all that was assumed to be history and not finding it. You'd probably be surprised at the number of people in the churches who have never believed the standard dogma. I know at least six of the Vatican Curia who don't believe in the Virgin Birth, the Resurrection, or even in God and there are many at lower levels who share that viewpoint. I talked with Canterbury before he made his announcement and he says the same about his own membership."

"You continue to amaze me," said Garry.

Jackson smiled. "Religions change with the times and ours were due for an update. I'll admit I was surprised by the almost complete lack of reaction, but when you consider the declining memberships of all churches, I should not have been. The world was ready for this change and it has not caused the conflicts we might have assumed."

"So what now?"

"As I said, the Church will continue to follow the teachings once ascribed to Jesus. They're wonderful teachings and must be continued. We will continue to tend to the poor, the sick, the underprivileged. We will continue to hold church services and I strongly suspect that as these become more and more humanitarian, attendance will increase again. You may have done the world a great service, Garry."

"I'm stunned," said Garry. "This was not a result any of us expected from our research."

The Cardinal released a wide, boyish grin. "Research often does this, believe me!"

"But is this acceptance global?" asked Garry.

"Not entirely. There is definite confusion and resentment within the Catholic Church and there are many who will be unable to accept the situation. Personally, I suspect there could even be another schism and a rebel group going its own way with a new Pope. But it won't cause armed conflict. In America, the so-called "religious right" is screaming and bills have already been prepared for Congress to ban the systems and any research using them. But they won't get far, too many people will oppose them and even if they passed out of the lower house up to the Senate, which is almost impossible, the President will veto them."

"So you think it will all settle into general acceptance without too much upheaval?"

The Cardinal shook his head. "Not that quickly. This is really an enormous change that affects the whole world and there are obviously going to be resentments, anger and inability to move with the times. We've heard nothing from the groups like the Russian Orthodox and Greek Orthodox churches or any of the other similar groups who will cling to tradition more than we have. I think there may be trouble there."

"What will the Vatican do in these cases?"

"Diplomacy, I would expect. But it will be a slow process. So keep the security going here, Garry, that mob that attacked before is still hiding somewhere."

"That's a worry, but we do have much enhanced security."

"Good. Garry, it won't be without disturbance, but at least we're not going to have warfare as a result."

"That is very good news indeed," said Garry.

"I thought you'd see it that way," said the Cardinal. "How about another coffee?"

Chapter 32 - 2021

The end came without warning.

Soon after ten o'clock, with the research team concentrating on their work, three vans drove furiously into the parking area. Garry saw them approaching and sensing danger, hit the alarm which locked down the building, sealed the doors and broadcast a warning through the office for all staff to take cover.

One man emerged from the front vehicle and ran at full tilt to the front door. Wondering what he might try, Garry went cold with fear and as the man reached the front door, he reached for his chest. The explosion was dreadful, no building could withstand that and the front doors were blasted into small pieces.

Garry was frozen and simply stood and watched.

From several points of the compass, armed men in uniform erupted into view just as more men came out of the three vans. Gunfire began and several of the uniformed men were cut down but their fire had its effect too. Most of the invaders fell to the ground, dropping their assault rifles but others raced towards the building. One was carrying something more than a rifle and Garry realised it was a grenade launcher such as he had seen on television news programs about Middle-east conflicts. The man aimed and released a grenade which flew through the huge gap where the doors had been. Just then, his head exploded as a heavy calibre bullet hit it but almost immediately, the building shook with the exploding grenade.

His immobility broken, Garry suppressed his terror and ran out of his office, hearing screams of pain and fear from many voices. He just had time to see some of his people hiding under desks, saw that one wall had collapsed then another explosion rumbled through the structure, something hit Garry on the head and he blacked out.

* * *

He had no idea where he was as consciousness slowly returned. He opened his eyes briefly and closed them again as the brightness of the sky hit like a hammer and he realised he was outside. Further exploration with his senses and he decided he was lying on some sort of bed. Apart from a splitting headache, he couldn't detect any injury. Memories flooded into his mind, the horrors of what he had just seen lighting up like a searchlight in his head and he groaned in terrible grief.

"Just stay there," said a man's calm voice. Garry opened his eyes to see a face above him. It was that of a young man and as Garry looked further, he saw that the man was dressed in hospital greens like a nurse.

"You're concussed," said the man. "Otherwise unhurt. You were lucky."

Memories of his last conscious moments returned to Garry with a shock. He tried to sit up but was held down by the medic with a firm hand on his shoulder.

"What happened?" he said. "What about the people in the building?" Panic made his throat dry and he fought for breath.

"We've had eight people taken to hospital," the medic said. "Some of the injuries were severe, some not so."

"Do you know who?" Garry was trembling with the shock now and the terrible need to know who of his team had been hurt.

The medic shook his head and looked around, finally seeming to spot somebody and waved at them. "Somebody's coming to talk to you," he said and stood up. This time, Garry was able to sit up and look around. The scene was appalling. There were three fire engines stationed some fifty yards from the huge gap where the front doors had been and several police cars at random places around the parking lot. There were also three Land Rovers with military plates.

A young army officer walked up to Garry. He was in combat gear and the three stars on his shoulders indicated he was a Captain.

"Mr Lawson, I'm Captain Williams," he said. "We have the situation under control, but I'm so sorry the initial attack was successful. A suicide bombing of this nature was not anything we're used to in this country."

"Who were they?" asked Garry.

"The same mob that was behind the last two episodes here," the officer said.

"Please tell me nobody's dead," said Garry.

The officer shook his head. "I can't yet. I know that there were no fatalities among the people we found here, but several are seriously wounded."

"Oh God!" said Garry, tears blocking his throat. "Do you know who?"

"Not yet. We'll have to wait for the hospital to report. There's a police officer there waiting for results."

"And has anybody told Professor Petrova?"

"Yes, a police officer called her some while ago. She was in London, she's on her way here."

"Okay, now can I get information on the injured?"

The Captain stood up and spoke briefly into his radio, nodded and looked down at Garry. "A nurse is coming over with the details," he said. "I'll leave you and go and check the rest of the situation."

Garry nodded and saw a young woman in hospital greens walking over.

"Hi," she said. "I'm Jess. Here's the situation at the hospital." She consulted her notebook.

"Avram is the worst. He's got a broken arm, some burns to his leg and he's concussed. Penny got hit on the head too, not concussed but she's in deep shock. Deborah has smoke inhalation, but she's recovering. Bill has burns to his left hand, will probably need a skin graft. Nobody else was hurt, but they have shock and they're all under observation."

She looked down, her face full of concern but smiling. "You were all very lucky. No fatalities."

"Thank God!" explained Garry, despite his strong sense of atheism.

"The others weren't so lucky," Jess continued. "Three of the Army men were hit, one is under surgery now for a bullet to the chest, the other two have less critical gunshot wounds. I know that at least five of the attackers are dead and two are also undergoing surgery but the last I heard, they probably won't make it."

"Oh good grief!" said Garry, tears coming back to his eyes. "What a goddammed mess."

"Try and relax," said Jess and walked away.

Garry ignored her and forced himself to stand up, feeling his head spin for a moment until it returned to normal. He had a splitting headache and every limb throbbed with a dull ache. He looked over to the entrance to the parking area and saw Karen's Maserati enter, drive slowly towards the company's area and then stop.

A burst of flame erupted from the underside of the car and then it exploded in a fireball, the heat radiating as far as where Garry was sitting.

For a second or two there was dead silence, then the men by the fire trucks leaped into action, drove rapidly to the inferno and began spraying foam over it.

But Garry knew the worst had happened.

Karen Petrova was dead.

Chapter 33

The next few weeks passed in a miserable haze. Apart from daily visits to his staff at the hospital until all of them had been discharged, Garry sat at home, engulfed in misery.

He read a small number of Obituaries for Karen but stopped after they all were just copies of each other. Somehow, he dragged himself to her funeral at the small church in Hungerford near her farm, sat at the back struggling to control his tears while eminent personages made speeches that he was certain Karen would have regarded with great contempt and again stood with tears rolling down his cheeks as the very small pile of ashes from the remains taken from the burned-out Maserati were scattered over the lawn of the church.

The forensic examination of the car revealed that a bomb had been attached to the underside of the car, probably while Karen was still in London, and it was set off by a radio switch, keyed by somebody watching the scene from a safe distance. Nobody had as yet been identified as the perpetrator but interrogations of Hannah and the surviving members of her team were continuing.

Garry read newspapers from around the world on his computer and watched news broadcasts on television and was cheered to see that Cardinal Jackson's thoughts were being supported around the globe. Instead of the hysteria that he had expected, the world seemed to accept the new facts with equanimity, almost as they were merely getting confirmation of what they had thought for a long time.

Even in the USA, there was little noise, outside of the ranting of some of the televangelists who were rapidly seeing their congregations vanish like morning mist. As Eamon had said several bills were introduced into the American Congress to ban the use of the new technology, but none made it beyond impassioned speeches and all were voted down by significant margins.

The entire complex in the Reading business park had been destroyed, so the whole operation of Life Technology as well as Garry's Blueprints division had nowhere to go. Staff continued to be paid, enough had been left in bank accounts managed by Garry and by Greg Mullaney, the CEO of Life Technology to keep that lifeline going but Garry's misery was mostly that the work had come to a halt and he saw no way of ever recovering.

He knew that everything that had been recorded on the company's computers had been backed up at a remote site and all the DNA samples had also been stored off site, so not all was lost, but he seriously doubted that he could build a team of professionals again, as dedicated as his people had been and he could not imagine any of them would want to continue with Blueprints if there was any chance of rebuilding the company after coming so close to death.

Beyond some sad conversations with the police and the insurance companies, and a call from Captain Williams, he did little but play classical music all day long and drink too much scotch. He slept badly, torn apart by nightmares.

After three weeks, he forced himself to activity, knowing he had a responsibility to his people, emailed them all and arranged a meeting in a conference room at a hotel in Reading.

* * *

"It's good to see you all," he said to the circle of familiar faces around the room. He studied them, one by one, searching for signs of distress.

Bill's left hand was heavily bandaged from the skin graft and he had walked in with some discomfort as the graft had been taken from his inner thigh, but he looked cheerful.

Avram was pale and had walked in with a stick, his left leg heavily bound up in bandages on the burns from ankle to thigh and his right arm in a cast. But he greeted everybody with a wide smile and didn't seem depressed by his condition. Penny looked to have no ill effects from her concussion and Deborah carried a small oxygen pack to help her recovery from smoke inhalation.

There was a murmur of response from everybody in the room. Many of them had greeted each other with tears and hugs, Avram in particular had been welcomed with much emotion.

"Tea, coffee, drinks on the table," said Garry. "Lunch will be brought in at noon."

He waited a few minutes while a few of them went to the table and poured their drinks.

"I'm not a religious man," said Garry, "but I've been thanking every god I could think of these last few weeks that at least we all survived the worst those lunatics could do."

A loud rumble of approval ran round the room.

"And so to updates," continued Garry. "The army told me that the attackers lost six men, including the suicide bomber and the remaining five of them are in police custody, but being heavily interrogated by the spooks. So far, there's nothing to indicate anything but extreme religious fanaticism objecting to our discovery of the origins of Christianity.

"As you may know, the ringleader was my ex-girlfriend, Hannah Ross who has ties to a similar organisation in the USA. The spooks are following up on that connection with their American counterparts. This is something I will never be able to excuse myself for, nor apologise enough to all of you."

"Oh hell, Garry," said Avram. "There was no bloody way you could have seen that one coming. I only met her a couple of times, but she seemed a very sweet, intelligent and thoroughly *normal* woman."

"Thanks, Avram. That helps. Anyway, the spooks have been able to identify a few more of that group and they are all under investigation and that should be the last we'll hear from them. And so to other, more critical matters."

He looked around and saw that he had their full attention.

"The main problem is that the insurance company has denied coverage, claiming that this was an act of terrorism and that's not covered under our policy."

"Typical bloody insurance companies," said Penny. "You're covered until something actually happens."

"Sadly, in today's world, such exceptions are proving the norm," said Garry. "I have checked with Greg Mullaney of the parent company and he's in the same boat. But between us, there is enough in the bank to keep paying everybody for another year and then, that original offer from Karen of a million pound leaving bonus remains applicable, payable any time you choose to go. So at least you are all financially safe."

The relief in the room was palpable and many smiles were evident. But not everybody was happy.

"Garry, is there any chance at all that we'll restart?" asked Deborah. "I know the money is great and all that, but there could never be a place to work that could be so much fun and so satisfying. I used to wake up, feeling happy that I was coming into work, knowing that I'd probably discover something astonishing and at the worst, I'd see incredibly interesting things. And bugger the dangers, we've survived them and they probably won't happen again."

A burst of applause ran round the room. Garry waited for it to die down, feeling warmth at the emotions being displayed so openly.

"I don't know, Deborah," he said. "As I indicated, the insurance doesn't cover rebuilding. I know that Greg Mullaney has already talked to the banks and he'll almost certainly be able to raise the money to restart Life Technology, because it's a money-earning operation. But we're not. I know we've sold a few systems for reading DNA, but they haven't remotely covered all the costs over the last few years of research. There's only one option I can think of and that's asking for government assistance. I'm trying to set up a meeting with the Home Secretary because he's the only person apart from the Prime Minister who knew about us."

"Let me jump in," said Bill from the back of the room. "All our data has been backed up on remote systems elsewhere, so we have the raw material to start again if we can. We can rebuild the equipment and most important, we have the skills here in this room. So if we can somehow raise the money, we can start again."

The room broke into cheers and just then the doors opened and the caterers came in with lunch. Garry sat alone for some minutes, feeling the depression settle on him. There was one piece of information he hadn't given the room. He had already tried to contact the Home Secretary and been rebuffed by a short telephone message that there was no value to the government in maintaining Blueprints.

All doors seemed closed and Blueprints would never recover. Maybe Karen Petrova would not change the world as she had dreamed.

Chapter 34

"Mr Lawson? My name is Scott McKenzie. I'm a partner at the law firm of Graham, McKenzie and James."

"Yes, Scott. What can I do for you?" Garry broke out of a depressed daydream in which Hannah, Blueprints and Alana Shimova all seemed to be mixed up.

"Mr Lawson, we are the firm representing Doctor Karen Petrova and we are the trustees of her estate."

Garry woke up completely. Something interesting was happening here, he sensed it.

"And is there something I need to do for the estate?" he asked.

The voice with a slight Scottish accent seemed amused. "Er.. yes, there is. Our offices are in Reading so could you come and see us?"

"Sure. When?"

"Can you come immediately?"

"Right now? That's short notice, isn't it?"

"It's taken us some time to validate a lot of details. As you can imagine, Doctor Petrova's estates are rather complex and we needed to be certain we had everything tied down. Once we were sure, it seemed obvious that you should come and visit at the earliest possible opportunity."

"Okay, I'll be there in half an hour or so. What's the address?

Armed with that information, Garry dragged himself from his armchair, took a quick shower, decided on casual dress rather than a suit and left for the solicitors' offices in Reading.

On entering the small, pleasantly decorated reception area, he was not surprised to see Greg Mullaney, CEO of Life Technology sitting with a cup of coffee in his hands.

"Hey!" he said with a grin. They had been friends since first meeting. "Any idea what's going on?"

"I'm hoping Karen has left us some money to rebuild," said Greg. "Life Technology was always her baby that made her billions, so I doubt she'd want to see it go. Maybe she's done the same for you, you were the very special project for her and her husband."

"Let's hope," said Garry with a surge of hope and at that moment a young woman came out of a door by the reception desk. She smiled at Garry.

"Mr Lawson? Thank you for coming, Scott is ready for you both."

Greg put his coffee down on the side table by his seat and rose and they followed the receptionist through the door into an open area with several cubicles. Three offices were set along the far wall and in one, a middle-aged man with grey hair was sitting. His sleeves were rolled up and he wore no jacket. Garry felt relieved at the casual, relaxed air and pleased he had dressed in much the same way.

The receptionist led the way, said simply, "This is Scott McKenzie," and walked away. The lawyer rose to his feet.

"Garry, Greg, welcome. Come and sit down."

After the ritual of handshakes, all three were soon seated at the large, walnut desk covered with papers.

"Doctor Petrova revised parts of her will five years ago," said Scott without further introductions. "Let me give you the essential details. I think you may be pleased and surprised."

He looked at Greg as he picked up a single sheet of paper.

"The land on which both Life Technology and Blueprints were built is owned by Doctor Petrova's estate. She bequeaths it to you, Greg. In addition, whatever sums of money are now in the company's bank account are also bequeathed personally to you."

"Good grief," said Greg. "There's over twenty million in there. She's given that to me?"

"She has. But in addition, there is a further sum left to you on the condition that you use it for rebuilding the operation and resuming business."

"That's fabulous! We shouldn't need much more to get things back to where they were."

Scott smiled, an expression of pure mischief on his face. "The additional sum is one billion pounds."

Greg stared at him. "One WHAT?"

"One billion pounds. Karen has put some riders on that. She wants you to offer the same deal to your staff that Garry has, namely a bonus of one million pounds to anyone who leaves, if they have worked for five years or more with you. She has expressed the wish that you will expand your research into some additional areas and these are listed in a document I will give you. She also expects that you will pay salaries well above normal to attract and keep talent."

Greg was having trouble breathing.

"We already do that," he whispered, his voice hoarse. "But we can really expand with that money behind us."

"I know that was Karen's wish," said Scott with a smile. "Now Garry, your turn. As you know very well, Blueprints was a particular passion for Karen, it was her husband's legacy. She once told me that she was frightened that the sort of horror you experienced would happen and she wanted to ensure the work would go on." He put the paper down and smiled.

"Have you ever read Isaac Asimov's sci-fi series, *'The Foundation'*?"

Puzzled, Garry nodded but said nothing.

"Then as you know, The Foundation was a group of scientists with a particular mission to record the history and knowledge of the Galactic Empire for the coming time when the Empire would collapse. But he had also written about a Second Foundation, situated as he put it, 'at the other end of the Galaxy' which would remain secret and hidden.

"Karen had read that series, she was a friend of Asimov and a great fan of his work and she got the idea from that. It's not an exact parallel, because Asimov's Foundation was really a smokescreen and the main scientific developments occurred with the Second Foundation. Your situation is different. Blueprints is the primary mover and shaker."

Garry began to understand.

"There's another Blueprints operation hidden away somewhere?"

"Got it in one!" said the lawyer. "It was established a few years ago and everything you did was copied at the Second Foundation laboratories and their people made sure they could do the same, while also following a couple of additional lines of research. So while all your data was backed up at a remote site, which is in Brighton by the way, it has also been stored and worked on at the other place."

Garry was now in the same state as Greg, feeling breathless and exhilarated to learn that his company and Karen's life's work would continue.

"Where is this place?" he asked, having difficulty framing the words.

"We'll come to that," said Scott. "First, the organisational details. You will take over the managing directorship of the second company as soon as possible. The people there have always known that would be the case and there will be no difficulties, quite the reverse in fact. Your reputation is known and they're looking forward to working with you.

"Second, all your current staff may come with you to the new operation and all relocation costs will be covered. All other conditions of service, including the million pound leaving bonus will apply.

"Third, all the staff at the new operation will continue under similar terms and the work they are doing will continue to be supported."

He smiled. "Okay so far?"

"Good lord, yes!" replied Garry. "How many people are there at this operation?"

"Just six. The head of operations, a manager rather like you and four researchers."

"All geneticists?"

"No, none of them. That field is left to your team. This group has other priorities, more to look at the global impacts of what you're doing. And the head of operations wants to move back to that area of social research, so it should be a smooth transition for you. Her name is Mary Hennessey. Now, the last details."

He picked up the paper again and cleared his throat.

"One billion pounds to be used entirely at your discretion. That will cover new equipment, building expansion, new facilities and lots left over for you to use as you think fit. To both of you..."

He looked each of them in the eye in turn as he spoke.

"Should for any reason that money proves insufficient, you merely have to approach this office as the trustees of her estate. There will be no questions asked. Karen was very firm on that, she trusts you both absolutely."

Garry fought to control his voice. "Insufficient? One billion pounds could be *insufficient?* Karen always did have a quirky view of the world. Okay, just where is this place?"

Scott grinned a wide, cheerful grin.

"Remember how Asimov placed the Second Foundation *"at the other end of the Galaxy?"* That idea tickled Karen, so although that was a bit extreme, she went as far as possible. Your new organisation is in Australia."

Silence reigned for a few moments, broken when both Garry and Greg burst out laughing.

"That tiny genius sure had a sense of the dramatic," said Greg. "I think I envy you! But I'm just so happy that we're not going out of business."

Garry was wiping his eyes. "What an amazing woman. What a loss to the world."

"Indeed," said Scott. "And by the way, there will be no immigration issues. Our PM called their PM and got immediate guarantees. After all, you'll be setting up a multi-million dollar business and you'll be hiring more Australian staff as you consolidate. In addition, the estate is going to invest a few more millions in Australian businesses, something Karen instructed us to do as a further sweetener to the immigration deal. I should add that Karen settled on Australia as being the furthest place away, but also because it's a country with little in the way of religious baggage and unlikely to have too many of the sort of lunatics we have seen recently."

Garry was having trouble holding back his tears, but under the grief was a sense of delight that the crisis was over and he looked forward to telling his staff.

Australia! And then he remembered the other explosive factor. A Billion pounds! Where could Blueprints go with a Billion pounds?"

Scott lifted up a brown envelope and passed it to Garry.

"That's the entire package of information about Blueprints Australia, including all the staff, their backgrounds, the location and everything else. I suggest you call them fairly soon. They have, of course been notified of Karen's death, so they're expecting to hear from you."

Garry took the package, not wanting to open it until he could sit quietly and have the time to review the contents at leisure.

"Both of you need to go to the City branch of the bank," continued Scott. "They already know you, of course from the current banking arrangements, but these new massive sums are in different accounts and you will need to organise your access to them. And that's about it! Good afternoon, gentlemen."

More handshakes and Greg and Garry walked into the Reading streets, both feeling a little dizzy from the events.

That evening, Garry got an unexpected phone call.

"I'm delighted that you will continue the work, Garry."

"Alana! How did you know?"

"Garry, this is Mossad! We know everything!"

He laughed. "That I can believe. So thanks for the support over recent months."

"It was my pleasure, I assure you. As an Israeli, my favourite activity is stopping terrorists of any shape and colour."

"You saved my life and that of others."

"That's our business. You may be interested to know that the mob that attacked you will be tried under some harsh terrorism charges and Hannah has admitted to being the ringleader. She is unlikely to see daylight outside a prison fence again."

For just a moment, Garry felt a twinge of sadness, but it passed.

"Do you know that had this second foundation not existed," Alanna continued, "the Israeli Government was prepared to offer you the facilities and funding to continue here?"

"Good grief! Why would they?"

"We feel it is critical. Already, you have probably helped reduce some massive religious tensions around the world."

"I'm not sure about that. It could just be the world is a bit stunned and not able to do much yet."

"Oh, I'm sure of that," replied the Israeli Ambassador. "And there's no doubt some of the crazies will react some time soon. But a major crisis factor has been removed and in time, things will settle."

"I do hope so, Alana. Will I see you again?"

"Maybe. Perhaps I will be assigned as Israeli Ambassador to Australia."

"That would be great. Then perhaps we can have a small private dinner together somewhere?"

"Just me and my six armed Mossad agents?"

He laughed. "They can hide in the bushes."

"Maybe."

Garry heard the smile in her voice.

"Good night, Excellency," he said.

"Good night, Garry."

Chapter 35

Garry looked around the room at the same faces as had been at the previous meeting.

"Karen was never going to let the company go under," he said. "Let me give you the good news. First, sufficient money has been placed in our account, actually a hell of a lot more than sufficient, enough to let us expand as much as want or do anything we please. So Blueprints survives."

A roar of delight rang round the room and all Garry could see were faces expressing delight and happiness.

"What I learned yesterday was that everything we have done, every scrap of information was copied, not just onto standard backup facilities from which we could have recovered anyway, but rather more remotely, way away from the reach of the religious whackoes who caused our problems. Buildings exist, equipment is installed and there are people keeping it all functioning and keeping themselves aware of what we have done."

He looked around the room and saw that he had their intense interest.

"This may present a problem for some of you," he continued. "Blueprints Two is in the city of Newcastle on the coast of New South Wales, Australia."

He saw the shock run through them, some sitting back in their seats, some worried expressions showing.

"Garry, it's very hard to emigrate to Australia," said Deborah. "What if we can't get approval?"

"Let's clear that one immediately," said Garry. "Every single one of you already has your permanent residency approved. Our Prime Minister talked to their Prime Minister and that was settled without a fuss."

"Wow!" said Avram. "That's doing things at a high level!"

"Karen had a way of getting things done," said Garry with a smile. "This was all arranged a year ago when the first signs of trouble appeared."

"Garry, I've got a house with a brand new mortgage," said a girl in the back row, a new member of the staff that he had hired just a few weeks before. She was red haired and slim and looked very shy and had a doctorate in genetics from Edinburgh University. "I can't just pack up and sell it after just a few weeks."

"Not a problem, Jessica. Remember I said we had rather lots of money? Here's what we'll do if you want to come to Australia. Blueprints will buy your house at ten percent above its valuation and cover any other costs you had, such as legal costs, stamp duty and so on. This applies to any of you that also own your homes. We will commission a management company to rent these homes out and ensure they're kept in good condition, pay all the rates and taxes and any repairs. Then, if you choose to return home at some time, the house will be given back you at no charge."

"Good grief!" said Jessica. "That certainly alleviates that. Thank you, Garry."

"Who else has a mortgage?" asked Garry and saw five hands raised. "Will that arrangement suit you?"

"Oh yes indeed!" said Penny. She looked around at the other four and they all had wide smiles of approval. "I think I just spoke for all of us!"

"The final issue is that I know some of you are married. Does this present difficulties?"

Two hands were raised.

"Gwen? Tell us the problem."

A very thin, dark woman in her thirties stood up. She had been one of the quiet researchers who had never provided any breakthroughs but had always worked methodically, professionally and documented everything immaculately.

"My husband, Errol, he's an accountant with one of those big firms and he thinks he's due for promotion to partnership within a year," said Gwen. "I think it will be very hard for him to leave England."

"Do they have an Australian branch?" asked Garry.

Gwen nodded.

"Would they be interested in transferring an English manager?"

"I don't know," she said. "Trouble is, if he lets it be known he wants to move, it could affect his chances here."

"Tell you what we can do," said Garry, feeling exhilaration at the power and freedom Karen had given him. "First check that he really would want to come to Australia with you. If not, then that offer of a million pound leaving bonus is open. On the other hand, how will this grab him? Blueprints will settle enough on him to start up his own professional office and if he's as good as he must be, he'll do better that way than as a partner with an existing bunch."

Gwen looked stunned and had her hands before her mouth, her eyes wide. "I'll... I'll tell him," she whispered and sat down as if the strings holding her up had been cut.

"Charlie? How about you?"

A short stocky man with a wild growth of red hair looked up.

"Janice is a family person," he said. "She's close to her mother, two sisters and a brother, sees them a lot. She's an aunt to three small kids and loves them to death and she can't wait to start our own family. I don't think there's any way she would leave England for so far away."

Garry nodded. "I understand. The best thing I could suggest if you're interested is that you can have a return flight to England for both of you every six months and two weeks off each time. If one of those is the Christmas break, which is the long summer holiday in Australia, you could have five weeks. See what she thinks."

"Thanks, Garry. I doubt she'll take it, but we'll give it a good try!"

Garry looked around the room, but nobody else seemed to have anything but huge excitement to express.

"As you know, we still have many topics of research in progress. The whole telekinesis matter may be the biggest, but we do have the enormous matter of those samples we have taken that have no ancestors indicated. So far, we have only found one living example of such an individual and it told us nothing. Bill's question of why does this whole recording mechanism exist remains open and is probably linked to the missing ancestor question in some way. We still don't know how far back this whole thing goes. We've seen a Cro-Magnon group, but nothing yet of Neanderthal humans or anything earlier. So we are not short of research to carry out. And I'm sure there are more astounding directions we may find ourselves taking."

He looked around and knew that he had their entire attention.

"I'm going to call the Australian firm tomorrow morning," he said. "I'll see if they can tell me what additional lines of research they have been following, if any. Assuming we can organise ourselves here and at least temporary accommodation there while we find homes for ourselves, I think we should plan on leaving in about a month. That will be November, summer is coming and I understand that the coast around Newcastle is astoundingly beautiful, mile upon mile of beaches."

"Christmas in the summertime!" said Avram. "I wonder if I'll ever get used to the idea."

Garry smiled and sat down as the doors opened for the caterers to bring in lunch. He decided he would not sell his house, but keep it well maintained in the same deal he had offered the others, but not rent it out, so that his extensive wine stocks could be kept safe. And he decided that he would take his beloved MGB sports car to Australia with him.

As he sat quietly, watching his team of extraordinary people getting their lunch, all of them showing such happiness, one thought rose up in his mind.

What had the Australian people been researching?

www.ingramcontent.com/pod-product-compliance
Lightning Source LLC
Chambersburg PA
CBHW071109250626
47159CB00002B/669